*Praise for Debbie Macomber's Bestselling Novels
from Ballantine Books*

CHRISTMAS BOOKS

Starry Night

"Contemporary romance queen Macomber (*Rose Harbor in Bloom*) hits the sweet spot with this tender tale of impractical love. . . . A delicious Christmas miracle well worth waiting for."

—*Publishers Weekly* (starred review)

"[A] holiday confection . . . as much a part of the season for some readers as cookies and candy canes."

—*Kirkus Reviews*

"A sweet contemporary Christmas romance . . . [that] the bestselling author's many fans will enjoy."

—*Library Journal*

"Macomber can be depended on for an excellent story. . . . Readers will remain firmly planted in the beginnings of a beautiful love story between two of the most unlikely characters."

—*RT Book Reviews* (Top Pick, 4½ stars)

"Macomber, the prolific and beloved author of countless bestsellers, has penned a romantic story that will pull at your heartstrings with its holiday theme and emphasis on love and finding that special someone."

—*Bookreporter*

"Magical . . . Macomber has given us another delightful romantic story to cherish. This one will touch your heart just as much as her other Christmas stories. Don't miss it!"

—*Fresh Fiction*

Angels at the Table

"A steaming mug of hot chocolate topped with whipped cream—comforting and familiar. The sparks of magic in this story are thanks to the bumbling angels that bring humor and whimsy. . . . Lovers of all things Macomber will find this tale of heaven and miracles satisfying."

—*RT Book Reviews*

"Debbie Macomber has long been called the 'Official Storyteller of Christmas,' and *Angels at the Table* is further proof of her considerable charms. Not only does she capture the magic and mystery of the season, but she reminds us that family, friendship and faith are the truest of gifts. This delightful mix of romance, humor, hope and happenstance is the perfect recipe for holiday cheer."

—*Examiner*

"Macomber's zillions of fans know that she is a natural storyteller who creates a cast of likable characters in intriguing situations—and *Angels at the Table* demonstrates this talent. The angels' antics are a hugely hilarious and entertaining bonus to a warm love story. For the perfect respite from the holiday frenzy, allow me to prescribe this delightful antidote to be taken cuddled up by a roaring fire while sipping a steaming cup of peppermint tea."

—*Bookreporter*

"Rings in Christmas in tried-and-true Macomber style, with romance and a touch of heavenly magic."

—*Kirkus Reviews*

"[A] sweetly charming holiday romance."

—*Library Journal*

"I absolutely loved this latest tale from Ms. Macomber. She has such a way of telling an entertaining story and sprinkling just enough angst and/or humor throughout the pages to make her readers never want to put one of her books down. . . . Packed with madcap antics, this is a holiday story you'll treasure over and over again throughout the years. I highly recommend it!"

—*Night Owl Romance* (Top Pick)

"In this joyous and whimsical holiday novel, Debbie Macomber rings in the season with the return of Shirley, Goodness, and Mercy, delivering laughs, love, and a charming dose of angelic intervention. . . . An unforgettable Christmas miracle."

—*Fresh Fiction*

"A witty, touching contemporary romance that will have you sighing and leave you with a smile on your face. . . . Macomber has penned a delightful story that is sure to steal your heart."

—*Romance Junkies*

ROSE HARBOR INN

Rose Harbor in Bloom

"[Macomber] draws in threads of her earlier book in this series, *The Inn at Rose Harbor,* in what is likely to be just as comfortable a place for [her] fans as for Jo Marie's guests at the inn."

—*The Seattle Times*

"Macomber's legions of fans will embrace this cozy, heartwarming read."

—*Booklist*

"Readers will find the emotionally impactful storylines and sweet, redemptive character arcs for which the author is famous. Classic Macomber, which will please fans and keep them coming back for more."

—*Kirkus Reviews*

"Macomber is an institution in women's fiction. Her principal talent lies in creating characters with a humble, familiar charm. They possess complex personalities, but it is their kinder qualities that are emphasized in the warm world of her novels—a world much like Rose Harbor Inn, in which one wants to curl up and stay."

—*Shelf Awareness*

"The storybook scenery of lighthouses, cozy bed and breakfast inns dotting the coastline, and seagulls flying above takes readers on personal journeys of first love, lost love and recaptured love ... present[ing] love in its purest and most personal forms."

—*Bookreporter*

"As always, Macomber uses warmth, humor and superb storytelling skills to deliver a tale that charms and entertains."

—*BookPage*

"Just the right blend of emotional turmoil and satisfying resolutions . . . For a feel-good indulgence, this book delivers."

—*RT Book Reviews* (4 stars)

The Inn at Rose Harbor

"Debbie Macomber's Cedar Cove romance novels have a warm, comfy feel to them. Perhaps that's why they've sold millions."

—*USA Today*

"No one tugs at readers' heartstrings quite as effectively as Macomber."

—*Chicago Tribune*

"The characters and their various entanglements are sure to resonate with Macomber fans. . . . The book sets up an appealing milieu of townspeople and visitors that sets the stage for what will doubtless be many further adventures at the Inn at Rose Harbor."

—*The Seattle Times*

"Debbie Macomber is the reigning queen of women's fiction."

—*The Sacramento Bee*

"The prolific Macomber introduces a spin-off of sorts from her popular Cedar Cove series, still set in that fictional small town but centered on Jo Marie Rose, a youngish widow who buys and operates the bed and breakfast of the title. This clever premise allows Macomber to craft stories around the B&B's guests, Abby and Josh in this inaugural effort, while using Jo Marie and her ongoing recovery from the death of her husband Paul in Afghanistan as the series' anchor. . . . With her characteristic optimism, Macomber provides fresh starts for both."

—*Booklist*

"Emotionally charged romance."

—*Kirkus Reviews*

BLOSSOM STREET

Blossom Street Brides

"Fans will happily return to the warm, welcoming sanctuary of Macomber's Blossom Street, catching up with old friends from past Blossom Street books and meeting new ones being welcomed into the fold."

—*Kirkus Reviews*

"Macomber's nondenominational-inspirational women's novel, with its large cast of characters, will resonate with fans of the popular series."

—*Booklist*

"Macomber amply delivers her signature engrossing relationship tales, wrapping her readers in warmth as fuzzy and soft as a hand-knitted creation from everyone's favorite yarn shop. She layers these love stories, making them emotionally rewarding."

—*Bookreporter*

"*Blossom Street Brides* gives Macomber fans sympathetic characters who strive to make the right choices as they cope with issues that face many of today's women. Readers will thoroughly enjoy spending time on Blossom Street once again and watching as Lydia, Bethanne and Lauren struggle to solve their problems, deal with family crises, fall in love and reach their own happy endings."

—*BookPage*

"A master at writing stories that embrace both romance and friendship, Macomber can always be counted on for an enjoyable page-turner, and this Blossom Street installment is no exception. Though this novel can be read as a stand-alone, it's fun to see how new characters fit into the world of Blossom Street. After reading *Blossom Street Brides*, readers will want to go back to previous installments and enjoy them all over again."

—*RT Book Reviews* (4½ stars)

Starting Now

"Macomber has a masterful gift of creating tales that are both mesmerizing and inspiring, and her talent is at its peak with *Starting Now*. Her Blossom Street characters seem as warm and caring as beloved friends, and the new characters ease into the series smoothly. The storyline moves along at a lovely pace, and it is a joy to sit down and savor the world of Blossom Street once again."

—Wichita Falls *Times Record News*

"Macomber understands the often complex nature of a woman's friendships, as well as the emotional language women use with their friends."

—*New York Journal of Books*

"There is a reason that legions of Macomber fans ask for more Blossom Street books. They fully engage her readers as her characters discover happiness, purpose, and meaning in life. . . . Macomber's feel-good novel, emphasizing interpersonal relationships and putting people above status and objects, is truly satisfying."

—*Booklist* (starred review)

"Macomber's writing and storytelling deliver what she's famous for—a smooth, satisfying tale with characters her fans will cheer for and an arc that is cozy, heartwarming and ends with the expected happily-ever-after."

—*Kirkus Reviews*

"Macomber's many fans are going to be over the moon with her latest Blossom Street novel. *Starting Now* combines Macomber's winning elements of romance and friendship, along with a search for one woman's life's meaning—all cozily bundled into a warmly satisfying story that is the very definition of 'comfort reading.'"

—*Bookreporter*

"Macomber's latest Blossom Street novel is a sweet story that tugs on the heartstrings and hits on the joy of family, friends and knitting, as readers have come to expect."

—*RT Book Reviews* (4½ stars)

"The return to Blossom Street is an engaging visit for longtime readers as old friends play secondary roles while newcomers take the lead. . . . Fans will enjoy the mixing of friends and knitting with many kinds of loving relationships."

—*Genre Go Round Reviews*

Christmas 2013

Dear Friends,

As you might have already guessed, I'm one of those Christmas fanatics. Christmas trees, nativity scenes, lights, and a multitude of decorations fill our home and yard from Thanksgiving through New Year's. Because of my love for the season, I've written a Christmas story each year simply because I couldn't allow the holidays to pass without putting my own unique stamp on them.

Many of my readers tell me they started reading my books after picking up one of my Christmas stories. Over the years I've penned tales involving angelic beings—Shirley, Goodness, and Mercy—and I wouldn't dare forget to add Mrs. Miracle, one of your favorites and mine, too. Then there were the romantic comedies, some of which I wrote with tears in my eyes from laughing so hard.

Starry Night is a bit of a departure for me. It's a romance, plain and simple. An absolutely wildly romantic tale involving one of my favorite spots on this green earth—Alaska. I've flown above the Arctic Circle myself with my husband, Wayne, and viewed the northern lights. Some of you might recognize Sawyer O'Halloran, who makes an appearance just for fun, from my Midnight Sons series.

I'm blessed to work with one of the most incredible teams in publishing. Shauna Summers and Jennifer

Hershey edited this story. Theresa Park, my agent, has been my most ardent cheerleader, along with Rachel Bressler. The Random House crew—Libby McGuire, Susan Corcoran, Kim Hovey, and Kristin Fassler—has added its magic touches as well in making sure this story, and all my books, gets the most exposure possible. And that, my friends, is only the tip of the iceberg. My own staff—Renate Roth, Heidi Pollard, Carol Bass, Wanda Roberts, Adele LaCombe, and Katie Rouner—has become both my right and my left hand. To each one I owe a huge note of appreciation.

While I'm eager to fill in details of the story, I refuse to deny you the pleasure of sitting back, turning the pages, and digging in. And when you finish, my hope is that you will close the book, sigh, and claim this is one of my most romantic Christmas stories you've ever read.

Merry Christmas!

Debbie Macomber

P.S. I always enjoy hearing from my readers. You can reach me through Facebook or my website at www.debbiemacomber.com or at P.O. Box 1458, Port Orchard, WA 98366.

DEBBIE MACOMBER

Starry Night

A Christmas Novel

BALLANTINE BOOKS • NEW YORK

Starry Night is a work of fiction. Names, characters, places, and incidents either are the product of the author's imagination or are used fictitiously. Any resemblance to actual persons, living or dead, events, and locales is entirely coincidental.

2014 Ballantine Books Mass Market Edition

Copyright © 2013 by Debbie Macomber
Excerpt from *Mr. Miracle* by Debbie Macomber copyright © 2014 by Debbie Macomber
"Lost and Found in Cedar Cove" by Debbie Macomber © 2013 by Debbie Macomber

Published in the United States by Ballantine Books, an imprint of Random House, a division of Random House LLC, a Penguin Random House Company, New York.

BALLANTINE and the HOUSE colophon are registered trademarks of Random House LLC.

Originally published in hardcover in the United States by Ballantine Books, an imprint of Random House, a division of Random House LLC, in 2013.

"Lost and Found in Cedar Cove" was originally published separately in a digital edition by Ballantine Books, an imprint of Random House, a division of Random House LLC, in 2013.

This book contains an excerpt from the forthcoming book *Mr. Miracle* by Debbie Macomber. This excerpt has been set for this edition only and may not reflect the final content of the forthcoming edition.

ISBN 978-0-345-52890-2
eBook ISBN 978-0-345-54552-7

Cover design: Lynn Andreozzi
Cover illustration: Alan Ayers

Printed in the United States of America

www.ballantinebooks.com

9 8 7 6 5 4 3 2 1

Ballantine Books mass market edition: October 2014

To Conny and Gina Johannesson
in appreciation of your
friendship and talent

Chapter One

Carrie Slayton's feet were killing her. She'd spent the last ninety minutes standing in two-inch heels at a charity art auction in a swanky studio in downtown Chicago. She couldn't understand how shoes that matched her black dress so beautifully could be this painful. Vanity, thy name is fashion.

"My name is spelled with two *l*'s," the middle-aged woman, dripping in diamonds, reminded her. "That's Michelle, with two *l*'s."

"Got it." Carrie underlined the correct spelling. Michelle, spelled with two *l*'s, had just spent thirty thousand dollars for the most ridiculous piece of art Carrie had ever seen. True, it was for a good cause, but now she seemed to feel her name needed to be mentioned in the news article Carrie would write for the next edition of the *Chicago Herald*.

"It would be wonderful to have my husband's and my picture to go along with your article," Michelle added. "Perhaps you should take it in front of the painting."

Carrie looked over her shoulder at Harry, the photographer who'd accompanied her from the newspaper.

"Of course, Lloyd and I would want approval of any photograph you choose to publish."

"Of course," Carrie said, doing her best to keep a smile in place. If she didn't get out of these shoes soon, her feet would be permanently deformed. She wiggled her toes, hoping for relief. Instead they ached even worse.

Harry, bless his heart, dutifully stepped forward, camera in hand, and flashed two or three photos of the couple posing in front of what might have been a red flower or a painting of a squished tomato or possibly the aftermath of a murder scene. Carrie had yet to decide which. The title of the work didn't offer a clue. *Red*. Yes, the painting was in that color, but exactly what it depicted remained a mystery.

"Isn't it stunning?" Michelle asked when she noticed Carrie staring at the canvas.

Carrie tilted her head one way and then another, looking for some clue as to its possible significance. Then, noticing that Michelle, spelled with two *l*'s, was waiting for her response, she said, "Oh, yes, it's amazing."

Harry didn't bother to hide his smile, knowing that all Carrie really wanted was to get out of those ridiculous shoes. And to think she'd gotten her journalism degree for this!

Carrie knew she was fortunate to have a job with such a prestigious newspaper. A professor had pulled a favor and gotten her the interview. Carrie had been stunned when she'd been hired. Surprised and overjoyed.

Two years later, she was less so. Her assignment was the society page. When she was hired, she'd been told that eventually she'd be able to write meatier pieces, do interviews and human-interest stories. To this point, it hadn't happened. Carrie felt trapped, frustrated, and underappreciated. She felt her talent was being wasted.

To make matters worse, her entire family lived in the Pacific Northwest. Carrie had left everything she knew and loved behind, including Steve, her college sweetheart. He'd married less than six months after she took the position in Chicago. It hadn't taken him long, she noted. The worst part was that Carrie was far too busy reporting on social events to have time for much of a social life herself. She dated occasionally, but she hadn't found anyone who made her heart race. Dave Schneider, the man she'd been seeing most recently, was more of a friend than a love interest. She supposed after Steve she was a bit hesitant to get involved again. Maybe once she left the *Herald* and moved home to write for a newspaper in the Seattle area, like she planned, things would be different.

* * *

Back inside her condo, Carrie gingerly removed her shoes and sighed with relief.

This was it. She was done. First thing in the morning she would hand in her two-week notice, sublet her condo, and take her chances in the job market in Seattle. If the managing editor, Nash Jorgen, refused to give her the opportunity to prove she had what it took, then why stay? She refused to be pigeonholed.

That decided, Carrie limped into her bedroom and fell into bed, tired, frustrated, and determined to make a change.

"You can't be serious," argued Sophie Peterson, her closest friend at the newspaper, when Carrie told her of her decision.

"I'm totally serious," she said as she hobbled to her desk.

"What's wrong with your foot?" Sophie asked, tagging behind her.

"Stupidity. This gorgeous pair of shoes was only available in a half-size smaller than what I normally wear. They were so perfect, and they were buy one pair, get the second half off. I couldn't resist, but now I'm paying for it."

"Carrie, don't do it."

"Don't worry, I have no intention of wearing those heels again. I tossed them in a bag for charity."

"Not that," Sophie argued. "Don't hand in your notice! You're needed here."

"Not as a reporter," Carrie assured her, dumping her purse in her bottom drawer and shucking off her thick winter coat. "Sorry, my mind is made up. You and I both know Nash will never give me a decent assignment."

"You're your own worst enemy." Sophie leaned against the wall that separated their two cubicles and crossed her arms and ankles.

"How's that?"

"Well, for one thing, you're the perfect fit for the society page. You're drop-dead gorgeous, tall, and thin. It doesn't hurt that you look fabulous in a slinky black dress and a pair of spike heels. Even if I could get my hair to grow that thick, long, and curly without perming the living daylights out of it, Nash would never consider someone like me. It isn't any wonder he wants you on the job. Give the guy a little credit, will you? He knows what he's doing."

"If looks are the only criterion—"

"There's more," Sophie said, cutting her off. "You're great with people. All you need to do is bat those baby blues at them and strangers open up to you. It's a gift, I tell you, a real gift."

"Okay, I'm friendly, but this isn't the kind of writing I want to do. I've got my heart set on being a reporter, a real reporter, writing about real news and interesting people." In the beginning, Carrie had been flattered by the way people went out of their way to introduce themselves at the events she covered. It didn't take long for her to recognize that they were looking for her to mention their names in print. What shocked her was the extent people were willing to go in order to be noticed. She was quickly becoming jaded, and this bothered her even more than Nash's lack of faith in her abilities.

The holidays were the worst, and while it was only early November, the frenzy had already started. The list of parties Nash assigned her to attend was already mammoth. Halloween decorations were still arranged around her desk, and already there was a Christmas tree in the display window of the department store across the street.

Determined to stick with her plan, Carrie went directly into Nash Jorgen's office.

A veteran newsman, Nash glanced up from his computer screen and glared in her direction. He seemed to sense this wasn't a social visit. His shoulders rose with a weary sigh. "What now?" he growled.

"I'm handing in my two-week notice." If she'd been looking for a response, she would have been disappointed.

He blinked a couple of times, ran his hand down the side of his day-old beard, and asked, "Any particular reason?"

"I hoped to prove I can be a darn good reporter,

but I'll never get the chance writing anything more than copy for society weddings. You said when you hired me that you'd give me a shot at reporting real news."

"I don't remember what I said. What's wrong with what you're writing now? You're good."

"It isn't what I want to write."

"So? You make the best of it, pay your dues, and in time you'll get the break you're looking for."

Carrie was tired of waiting. She straightened her shoulders, her resolve tightening. "I know I'm fortunate to work for the *Herald*. It was a real coup to get this position, but this isn't the career I wanted. You give me no choice." She set her letter of resignation on his desk.

That got Nash's attention. He swiveled his chair around to look at her once more. His frown darkened, and he ran his hand through his thinning hair. "You really are serious, aren't you?"

A chill went down her spine. Nash was actually listening. "Yes, I'm serious."

"Fine, then." He reached across his desk and picked up a hardcover book and handed it to her. "Find Finn Dalton, get an interview, and write me a story I can print."

She grabbed hold of the book, not recognizing the author's name. "And if I do?"

"Well, first, there's a snowball's chance of you even locating him. Every reporter in the universe is dying to interview him. But if you get lucky and he's willing to talk and we print the piece, then I'll take you off the society page."

Carrie wavered. He seemed to be offering her a chance, as impossible as it might seem. Now it was up to her to prove herself. She dared not show him how excited she was. "I'll find him."

He snickered as though he found her confidence amusing, and then sobered. He regarded her with the same dark frown he had earlier before a slow, easy smile slid over his harsh features. "I bet you will. Now, listen up—if you get an interview with Finn Dalton, you can have any assignment you want."

Taking small steps, Carrie backed out of the office. She pointed at Nash. "I'm holding you to your word."

The managing editor was already back to reading his computer screen and didn't appear to have heard her. It didn't matter; she'd heard him, and he'd come across loud and clear.

Once she was out of his office, she examined the book to see the author photo, but couldn't find one, not even on the inside back flap.

Walking back to her cubicle, she paused at Sophie's instead. "You ever heard of Finn Dalton?"

Sophie's eyebrows lifted on her round face. "You mean you haven't?"

"No." The book title wasn't much help. *Alone.* That told her next to nothing. The jacket revealed a snow-covered landscape with a scattering of stubby trees.

Sophie shook her head. "Have you been living under a rock?"

"No. Who is this guy?"

"He's a survivalist who lives alone someplace in the Alaskan wilderness."

"Oh." That was a bit daunting, but Carrie considered herself up to the challenge. She'd been born and raised in Washington State. She'd hoped to join her family for Thanksgiving, but if she needed to use her vacation time to find Finn Dalton, then she was willing to.

"His book has been on the bestseller lists for nearly seven months, mostly at the number-one position."

Carrie was impressed. "What does he write about?"

"He's the kind of guy you can set loose in the wild with a pack of chewing gum, a pocketknife, and a handkerchief, and by the time you find him he's built a shelter and a canoe. From what I've read, his stories about Alaskan life and survival in the tundra would kink your hair. Well, not that yours needs curling."

This was Sophie's idea of a joke. Carrie's wild dark brown curls were the bane of her existence. She tamed them as best she could, but she often found herself the brunt of jokes over her out-of-control hair.

"Nash says he doesn't give interviews."

"Not just doesn't give interviews—this guy is like a ghost. No one has ever met or even talked to him."

"Surely his publisher or his editor—"

"No," Sophie said, cutting her off. "Everything has been done by computer."

"Well, then . . ."

"All anyone knows is that he lives near an Alaskan lake somewhere in the vicinity of the Arctic Circle."

"How is it you know so much about this guy?"

"I don't, and that's just it. No one does. The press has gone wild looking for him. Plenty of reporters have tried to track him down, without success. No one knows how to find him, and Finn Dalton doesn't want to be found. He should have called his book *Leave Me Alone*. Someone could pass him on the street and never know it was him, and from everything I've read, that's exactly how he likes it."

Intrigued, Carrie flipped through the pages of the book. "Nash said I could have any assignment I wanted if I got an interview from Finn Dalton."

"Of course he did. Nash has been around long enough to know he's got you in a no-win situation."

Carrie glanced up. "I don't care. I'm going to try."

"I hate to be a killjoy here, but Carrie, no way

will you find this guy. Better reporters than either of us have tried and failed. Every newspaper, magazine, and media outlet is looking to dig up information about him, without success. Finn Dalton doesn't want to be found."

That might be the case, but Carrie refused to give up without even trying. This was far too important to drop just because it was a long shot. "I'm desperate, Sophie." And really, that said it all. If she was going to have a real career in journalism, she had to find Finn Dalton. Her entire future with the *Chicago Herald* hung in the balance.

"I admire your determination," Sophie murmured, "but I'm afraid you're going to hit one dead end after another."

"That might be the case." Carrie was willing to admit to her friend that finding Finn Dalton wouldn't be easy. "But I refuse to quit without trying." She knew Sophie didn't mean to be negative. "I want this chance, and if it means tracking Finn Dalton into some forsaken tundra, then I will put on my big-girl shoes and go for it." But not the heels she'd worn last night, that was for sure.

The first thing Carrie did in her search for Finn Dalton was read the book. Not once, but three times. She underlined everything that gave her a single hint as to his identity.

For two days she skipped lunch, spending her

time on the computer, seeking any bit of information she could find that would help her locate Finn Dalton. She went from one search engine to another.

"How's it going?" Sophie asked as they met each other on their way out the door a couple of days later.

"Good." Through her fact-finding mission, Carrie was getting a picture of the man who had written this amazing book. After a third read she almost felt as if she knew him. He hadn't always been a recluse. He'd been raised in Alaska and had learned to live off the land from his father, whom he apparently idolized. One thing was certain, he seemed to have no use for women. In the entire book, not once did he mention his mother or any other female influence. It was more of what he didn't say that caught Carrie's attention.

"Any luck?" Sophie asked, breaking into her thoughts.

"Not yet." She hesitated. "Have you read the book?"

Sophie nodded. "Sure. Nearly everyone has."

"Did you notice he has nothing to say about the opposite sex? I have the feeling he distrusts women."

Sophie shrugged as if she hadn't paid much notice, but then she hadn't been reading between the lines the way Carrie had.

"How old do you think he is?" Sophie asked.

"I can't really say." Finn was an excellent writer and storyteller. But the tales he relayed could have happened at nearly any point in the last several decades. Current events were skipped over completely.

Sophie crossed her arms and looked thoughtful. "My guess is that he's fifty or so, to have survived on his own all these years."

Speculation wouldn't do Carrie any good. "Tell you what. When I find out, you'll be the first to know. Deal?"

Sophie smiled and nodded. "Deal."

That night, as Carrie readied for her latest charity event, her cell rang. It was her mother in Seattle. They spoke at least two or three times a week. Carrie was tight with her family and missed them dreadfully.

"Hi, Mom," she answered, pressing her cell to one ear while she attempted to place a pearl earring in her other earlobe.

"Hi, sweetheart. Are you busy?"

"I've got a couple of minutes." She switched ears and stabbed the second pearl into place before tucking her feet into a comfortable pair of high heels. She was scheduled to meet Harry in thirty minutes.

"Dad and I are so excited to see you at Thanksgiving."

"Yes, about that." Carrie grabbed her purse and tucked it under her arm while holding on to her phone. "Mom, I hate to tell you this, but there's a possibility I might not make it home for Thanksgiving."

"What?"

The disappointment in her mother's voice was painful to hear. "Have you ever heard of Finn Dalton?"

"Oh, sure. Your father loved his book so much he bought two additional copies. I read it, too. Now, that's a man."

"I want to interview him."

"Really? From what I understand, he doesn't give interviews."

"Yeah, that's what I heard, too."

"Does he ever come to Chicago?"

"Doubtful," Carrie murmured. If only it could be that easy and he would come to her. Well, that wasn't likely. Then again, something Sophie said had stayed in her mind. She could walk past him on the sidewalk and never know it was him. "I'll need to track Finn Dalton down, but I keep running into dead ends the same as everyone else." She mentioned her online search, the calls to Alaska, and the number of phones slammed in her ear. No one had been willing to talk to her. "I have to look at this from a different angle. Have you got any ideas?"

"From what your father said, Finn Dalton isn't a

man who would enjoy being written up on the society page."

"That's just it, Mom. This would be an investigative piece. My editor told me I could have my pick of assignments if I was able to get this interview. It's important, enough for me to take the vacation days I planned to use for Thanksgiving to find him."

"Oh, Carrie, I hate the thought of you doing that."

"I know, I hate it, too, but it's necessary." Her mother was well aware of Carrie's feelings toward her current work situation.

"Do you really think you can find Finn Dalton?" her mother asked.

"I don't know if I can or not, but if I don't, it won't be for lack of trying."

"I've always admired your tenacious spirit. Can I tell your father you're going to write a piece on the man who wrote *Alone*?"

"Ah . . . not yet. I have to locate Dalton first."

"What have you discovered so far?" Her mother was nothing if not practical. Carrie could visualize her mother pushing up her shirtsleeves, ready to tackle this project with Carrie.

"Do you know where he was born?"

"No. I assumed it must have been Alaska, but there's no record of his birth there. I've started going through the birth records of other states, starting with the northwest, but haven't found his name yet." At this rate, it would be the turn of the next century before she found the right Dalton.

"What about his schooling? Graduation records?"

"I tried that, but he's not listed anywhere. Maybe he was homeschooled."

"You're probably right," her mother said, sounding proud that Carrie had reasoned it out. "One of his stories mentions his father mailing away for books, remember? Those were textbooks, I bet."

Carrie had made the same assumption.

"Finn is a rather unusual name, isn't it?" her mother continued softly, as though she was thinking out loud.

"And of course it could be a pseudonym, but his publisher claims the name is as real as the man." Nothing seemed the norm when it came to Finn Dalton.

"You know, work on the Alaskan pipeline was very big about the time your father and I got married. That was a huge project, and it brought a lot of men to Alaska; many of them stayed. His father might have been one of them."

"Yes." But that was a stab in the dark. She'd already spent hours going over every type of record she could think to research from Alaska, to no avail. Carrie glanced at the time, even though this talk was helping her generate ideas of where to continue looking for the mysterious Mr. Dalton.

"From what I remember, a lot of men left their wives and families for the attraction of big money."

"I could start looking at the employment records for the pipeline from that time period and see what I find," Carrie said.

"That's a terrific idea. And listen, when you find Finn Dalton, make sure your dad gets a chance to chat with him, would you?"

"I can't promise that." First she'd need to convince Finn Dalton to talk to her!

"Just do your best."

"I'll do what I can."

"Bye, sweetie."

"Bye, Mom." Carrie ended the call and dumped her cell in her small bag. After a quick glance in the hallway mirror, she headed out the door to what she hoped would be one of the very last social events she would ever need to cover.

Chapter Two

This had to be Finn Dalton's mother. It simply had to be. From the moment Nash had given Carrie what seemed like the impossible assignment of interviewing Finn, she'd looked for out-of-the-box ways to locate him. Her mother's mention of work on the Alaskan pipeline and that many of those employed came from Washington State had led to a breakthrough. At least she hoped so. The search led Carrie to the birth record for a Finnegan Paul Dalton, not in Alaska but in her own birth state of Washington. That record revealed his mother's name—Joan Finnegan Dalton— which then led to a divorce decree, along with a license for a second marriage several years later. Tax records indicated that Joan, whose married name was now Reese, continued to reside in Washington State. Her hope was that Joan Dalton Reese would be willing to help Carrie find Finn.

The November wind and rain whipped against her as she walked up the short pathway to the single-family house in Kent, a suburb south of Seattle.

Nerves made Carrie tense as she rang the doorbell and waited. After a few moments, she heard footsteps on the other side of the door. The woman who opened it didn't look to be much older than her own mother.

"Joan Finnegan Dalton Reese?" Carrie asked.

The petite, dark-haired woman blinked warily, and her eyes widened as if she wasn't sure what to think. "Yes?"

"By chance are you related to Finnegan Paul Dalton?"

She didn't answer right away, and then her gaze narrowed. "You're another one of those reporters, aren't you?"

"Yes, I—"

Joan started to close the door, but Carrie quickly inserted her foot, stopping her.

The two women stared hard at each other. "Yes, I'm a reporter, but I'm hoping you'll hear me out."

"Why should I?" she demanded, and crossed her arms over her chest.

Carrie frantically searched for something that would convince the other woman to talk to her. "I can't think of a single reason other than the fact that I'm tired of writing for the society page. I gave up spending time with my family over Thanksgiving with the hope that I could get this interview, and I think you have an incredible son, and I'd very much like to meet and interview him."

The delicate woman looked undecided. "What do you mean you write for the society page?"

Carrie explained how she'd taken a few of her precious vacation days and flown to Seattle. It'd been a risk, but one she was willing to take. This would be the first year she'd missed the holiday with her parents, aunts, uncles, and cousins. Although it would be a sacrifice, her parents understood that if she did manage to interview Finn Dalton, then she would have her pick of writing assignments, and not just in Chicago, but perhaps in the Pacific Northwest. "I want to move back to Seattle to be closer to my family, and this is my chance."

Joan eyed her carefully, and then, after what seemed like an eternity, she slowly opened the door, silently inviting Carrie inside.

"Thank you," she whispered. "Thank you so much." Stepping out of the cold, Carrie instantly felt the warm flow of air surround her. She noticed a bronze pumpkin off to the right and a doll-sized set of pilgrims on the dining room table.

Joan motioned toward the living room. "How much do you know about my son?"

Carrie sat on the edge of the sofa cushion, unsure how best to answer. She could attempt to bluff or she could be direct in the hope that Joan Reese would be willing to help her. "Well, only what I've read in his book and what I've learned online, which isn't much."

"Unfortunately, I don't know how much help I'll be. I haven't talked to my Finn in five years, not since his father died . . . he told me he wants nothing more to do with me."

Carrie read the pain in the other woman's eyes, and not knowing how to react, she leaned forward and placed her hand on Joan's forearm.

"I tried to connect with him after his father's death, but Finn made it clear that I had nothing to say that he wanted to hear." She wadded a tissue in her hands and kept her head lowered.

"So you don't have any idea where Finn is living?" Carrie asked, her heart thumping with hope and expectation.

"Alaska, somewhere outside Fairbanks, but then you probably already know that."

Seeing that he'd written extensively about life in the frozen north, this was the one piece of information she did have. And apparently so did every other news agency. His book told of adventures on the tundra, which indicated his cabin was most likely situated near the Arctic Circle. And that meant the only way to reach him would be by air, which would involve hiring a bush pilot.

"I've tried to find someone in Alaska to help me"—Carrie explained her efforts to talk to a number of resources, including bush pilots—"but it's been one dead end after another."

"At least you're honest about being a reporter," Joan said. "You couldn't imagine what some of them have tried, thinking I could give them information that would lead them to my son. You, at least, are willing to admit why you're doing this."

"He probably never suspected this interest in him and his lifestyle would happen. People love his stories, and now they want to know about the man behind them."

"He never forgave me, you see . . ." Joan murmured, her voice trailing away as she methodically tore apart the tissue in her hands.

"Forgave you?"

"I left him and his father when Finn was a boy. Paul loved Alaska, and I was born in Louisiana. I tried to make a life with him up there, but I couldn't bear the cold and the isolation, whereas Paul and Finn seemed to thrive on it. I wanted us to compromise, come back to the lower forty-eight a few months each year, but Paul wasn't willing to consider that. He insisted there was nothing for him outside Alaska. He felt any time away would be a waste. He had a dozen different projects going all the time and refused to leave. I wanted Finn to come with me, but my son chose to stay with his father." She paused and looked away as if she regretted having spoken. "Once I left, Paul cut me completely out of his life, and Finn's, too. Eventually I remarried, but it was more for companionship than love. Finn never forgave me for that, either. I think he must have held on to the dream that his father and I would reunite one day. My second husband died a year ago, so I'm a widow twice over."

"I'm so sorry," Carrie said.

"I wish I knew the man Finn has become," Joan whispered.

"If I find him and have a chance to talk to him, I'll tell him about meeting you. I can give him a message from you, even if it's just to remind him that you love him and want to hear from him."

Joan glanced up and her eyes brightened with what could be described only as ragged hope. "You'd do that?"

"Of course." As close as she was to her own family, Carrie's heart went out to Finn's mother, still looking to connect with her son. Although she didn't know him beyond the pages of his book, she couldn't help wondering about a man who would turn his back on his mother.

"Then perhaps there's a small way I can help," Joan said, her eyes twinkling now.

"There is?" She had Carrie's full attention.

Joan left the room and returned a few moments later with a simple gold ring. "This was Paul's wedding band. When we divorced . . . he was angry and bitter, and he returned the ring to me. I've saved it all these years, and now that Paul is dead I would like Finn to have it."

"You want me to give Finn his father's ring?"

Joan nodded. "Finn has a friend named Sawyer. He's a bush pilot who is often in Fairbanks. I could see Sawyer felt bad for the way Finn spoke to me at his father's funeral, and I think he might be willing to help you find my son if you give him a good enough reason."

Carrie smiled and held the gold band between her index finger and thumb. This ring could very well be her ticket to reaching the elusive Finn Dalton.

"You found him?" Sophie shouted from the other end of the cell phone. "You actually found Finn Dalton?"

Carrie meandered through the Fairbanks airport, dragging her carry-on behind her with one hand and holding the cell phone to her ear with the other. Her high-heeled boots made tapping sounds against the floor as she left the baggage-claim area. "I haven't found him yet," Carrie corrected. "But I'm close."

"Where are you?"

"Fairbanks. I just landed." Carrie had caught the first available flight out of Seattle after meeting with Joan. "So, listen, if I'm not back in Chicago on Monday, make up an excuse, will you?"

"You don't want me to tell Nash you're hot on the trail of Finn Dalton?"

"Not yet. I want to present the article as a done deal."

"I can't believe you were actually able to track him down," Sophie said excitedly.

"Don't get ahead of me; I still don't have that interview. Sorry, I need to go."

"Good luck. I've got my fingers crossed for you."

"Thanks." After ending the call, she stuck her cell phone in the outside pocket of her purse and made her way through the small airport, looking for the hangar where the bush pilots parked. All she had was Sawyer's name, and she wasn't even sure if it was his first or last. It took her awhile to locate the hangar. She asked around until she found someone willing to talk to her.

Clearly she looked enough like a city girl with her full-length double-breasted gray wool coat, fashionable boots, and earmuffs for the pilots and mechanics to recognize she was another pesky reporter in search of the elusive Finn Dalton. She was barely able to get two words out of her mouth before she got the cold shoulder.

"I'm looking for a pilot named Sawyer," she asked a man inside the hangar, doing her best to hide her frustration. He looked like a mechanic, dressed in greasy coveralls. If bush pilots weren't willing to talk to her, then perhaps he would. No one seemed to want to help.

The mechanic's eyes pierced her, slowly taking

her in. "What do you want Sawyer for?" he demanded.

Carrie straightened her shoulders and stood her full five feet ten inches, meeting him almost eye to eye. "I would like to hire him."

"For what?"

"A job."

With his hands braced against his hips, the mechanic regarded her skeptically. "You're another one of them reporters, aren't you?"

Carrie decided to sidestep the question. "I have something to deliver to a friend of Sawyer's, so if you'd kindly point me in his direction, I'd be most appreciative."

"A friend of his named . . ." He left it for her to fill in the blank.

Carrie's shoulders relaxed. "Finn Dalton."

"That's what I thought." Turning his back on her, he walked completely around the outside of his plane, running his hand over the structure as though checking for something, although Carrie couldn't imagine what.

She wasn't giving up. "Can you tell me if Mr. Sawyer is in the area now, or when I can expect to find him?"

"Ah, so it's *Mr. Sawyer* now?"

Carrie ignored his tone and the question.

"I have something to give Finn Dalton."

"Do you, now? And what might that be? A headache?"

Very funny. She ignored that comment, although her patience was wearing thin. "It's something from his mother."

"And his mother's name is?" he asked, whirling around unexpectedly and almost colliding with her.

"Joan," she said quickly. "Joan Finnegan Dalton Reese."

The mechanic regarded her for several moments, studying her, his eyes boring into hers. "I'm Sawyer O'Halloran."

"You're Sawyer?"

"In the flesh."

After a long flight, Carric was tired and hungry and anxious. "I want to hire you to take me to Finn Dalton."

Shaking his head, Sawyer muttered something indecipherable and walked away. "You and every other reporter who has been nosing around here."

Carrie hurried after him. "I'm serious, and I'll pay you anything reasonable if you'll take me to him. You can wait while I talk to Finn. I won't be long, I promise."

"Just as I thought. When will you people give it up? Although I have to admit you're cleverer than most, bringing up his mother."

"I'm telling you the truth. I have something to give him from her."

"Sure you do," Sawyer commented, continuing to walk away from her.

Carrie chased after him, dragging her suitcase. She had to duck her head in order to walk beneath the Cessna's wing. "It's his father's wedding band. Joan asked me to deliver it to Finn." She hated the desperate pleading quality to her voice, but she had to convince Sawyer she was legitimate.

Sawyer hesitated. "Show me the ring."

"Okay." She slid the purse strap off her shoulder and dug inside for the ring, which was wrapped in a tissue inside a plastic bag. Once it was free, she handed it to Sawyer. "His name, Paul Dalton, is engraved on the inside, along with Joan's name and the date of their wedding."

Sawyer carefully examined the gold band, and then Carrie, before returning the ring. "There's a storm due. I'm heading back to Hard Luck in fifteen minutes. I'll land on the lake outside Finn's cabin and return in the morning or whenever, depending on this storm. Is that agreeable?"

"Yes, perfect." At this point, Carrie would have agreed to practically anything.

"Finn isn't going to like this, so I'll radio him you're coming."

"I don't expect he'll have the welcome mat out."

"You've got two things against you."

"Is that all?"

"First, you're a woman, and second, you're a reporter. Make that three things."

"Three?"

"Yes. You're bringing him something from his mother. He doesn't want any reminders of her."

"So she said." Curiosity got the best of her. "Not that I want you to change your mind, but can you tell me why you're helping me?"

The bush pilot shrugged. "I'll probably regret it. Finn's a good friend, but it's time he broadened his horizons some, and you, pretty lady, might be just the ticket."

"Whatever the reason, I'm grateful."

"Finn will probably stop speaking to me, but he'll get over it eventually," Sawyer continued. "I feel I should warn you, though; he's bound to be as inviting as a wolverine."

"Got it. Any other advice?"

Sawyer scratched the side of his head. "I wouldn't start off mentioning the ring and his mother." He gave her the once-over a second time. "You pack anything practical for the weather?"

"I live in Chicago. It freezes there."

He snorted as if to cover a laugh. "You've got fifteen minutes. Make use of them." He pointed in the direction of the airport, and Carrie took off running. She wasn't sure what she'd need, but with the help of the clerk picked up a couple of pieces of gear, including a hat and thick scarf. It seemed extravagant to purchase anything else, seeing that she intended to be in Alaska only a short while.

By the time she returned, Sawyer had moved the

plane out of the hangar and had the engine running. "You ready?" he asked.

Because she was winded and excited, she only nodded.

"Okay, climb inside. We need to get going."

"Right now?" She'd hoped to have a few moments to gather herself.

"Yes, now," he snapped. "There's limited light, and with the coming storm, that window is closing. Ready or not, I'm leaving."

"I'm ready." Carrie had never flown in a private plane, but that one small detail wasn't about to stop her. She eyed the Cessna, sucked in a deep breath, and loaded her suitcase. It wasn't easy climbing inside and locking the passenger door. Carrie was relieved she'd worn her jeans, and thankfully her boots had only a moderate heel.

Within a few minutes they were airborne, circling the airport and heading due north. Carrie clung to her purse as if that would save her from imminent danger and held her breath several times when the plane rocked after encountering moderate turbulence. Sawyer had handed her a pair of headphones, but he wasn't much for conversation, preoccupied as he was with flying the plane. He radioed Finn twice but wasn't able to reach him. Although Sawyer didn't say so, Carrie had the feeling he already regretted agreeing to this. Fearing anything she said might do more harm than good, she remained silent until it was clear that he was preparing to land.

"Where's the airstrip?" she asked, studying the landscape below. In the dim light, all she could see were snow and trees.

"Airstrip?" Sawyer repeated incredulously. "I'm not landing on any strip. Didn't I already mention I'd be landing on a lake?"

Set on convincing him to fly her to Finn, Carrie didn't remember that part of their conversation. A lake? A frozen lake? Peering through the window, she couldn't make out anything but snow. She gasped out loud when the plane's wheels bounced against the ice and skidded sideways out of control.

Sawyer didn't cut the engine but guided the Cessna to the lake's center and turned toward her.

"Under normal conditions, I'd escort you to Finn's cabin. Unfortunately, I'm headed directly into that storm, and I don't have the time to spare. You can see his cabin over there," he said, pointing in the distance.

Carrie squinted in the fading light. "Is it far?"

"You'll happen upon it soon enough. If Finn isn't there, make yourself at home, and have him contact me." He snickered. "Actually, no need, he'll be in touch, I'm sure. You going to be okay?"

Carrie nodded, swallowed hard, and put on a good front. "I was a Girl Scout. I'll be fine." She could see the outline of the cabin through the thick, fat flakes that had already started to fall. Sawyer needed to get back in the air as quickly as possible.

"Good luck," he said, and it sounded as if he meant it.

"We'll square up with what I owe you when you return tomorrow."

"Sure, whatever. But like I said, with the weather, it might be a day or two."

Carrie bit into the soft flesh of her inner lip. "Okay." She was grateful he had brought her this far and would count her blessings.

He hit the throttle, which was her signal to get going. Carrie opened the plane's door and climbed out, but not with a lot of grace. She retrieved her small suitcase and the bag of gear she'd bought and stood back as the plane immediately accelerated across the frozen lake. The wind and snow whipped across Carrie's face with such ferocity that it felt as if she were being stuck with needles.

Other than her brief time in the hangar when she'd first met Sawyer, she hadn't been exposed to the Alaskan elements, and they were as brutal as the bush pilot had warned. Her coat, which had been all the protection she needed in Chicago, felt useless. Already she was so cold she had started to shake. Within moments her toes had lost all feeling. Wrapping her new scarf around her head and face, she started walking in the direction of the cabin.

With the plane airborne now, the thin layer of

snow settled down on the thick ice, and in the distance Carrie saw a twisting tail of smoke. That had to be coming from Finn's cabin.

Carrie hunched her shoulders as close to her head as she could manage, and even through the protection of her gloves, it felt as if her hands were exposed to the raw elements. The ice was uneven, and dragging her suitcase wasn't an easy task. With her hands numb, she twice dropped the suitcase handle and had to stop and pick it back up.

She hadn't even met Finn and already she'd started to feel as if this was a terrible mistake. Everything had happened so quickly, and when she did meet him she wasn't sure what she would say to convince him to give her an interview.

Suddenly it started to snow with such ferocity that she couldn't see more than a few feet in front of her. The wind drove it sideways, and with her head bowed she struggled against the elements until she heard what sounded like a wild beast. Looking up, Carrie squinted, and what she saw caused her heart to shoot up to her throat. It was an animal, a wolf, and he was racing toward her at an alarming pace.

Dropping her suitcase, Carrie did the only thing she could think to do. She started running. The wind made it nearly impossible to make headway as she strained against the force of it.

Then it happened. She stumbled and fell face-first onto the ice.

Before she could right herself, the wolf was nearly on top of her.

Screaming, she twisted around and bunched her fists, determined to do what she could to save her life.

Chapter Three

❄

"Hennessey, sit."

Carrie felt the animal's warm breath against her neck and then didn't. Struggling to sit upright, she turned to see a man walking toward her across the ice. The wind swirled the snow around him, obliterating his features, but his strides were long and powerful. The animal she'd assumed was a wolf appeared now to be a large dog. Hennessey sat on his haunches, awaiting his master.

His master.

This could only be Finn Dalton.

When he reached her, the hulk of a man loomed over her like a beast in his own right. His face was nearly obscured by protective weather gear and a full beard, but his eyes, deep and dark, cut through her the way a diamond slices through rock. As Carrie gazed up at him, in those first few breathless moments, he seemed more intimidating than the wolf/dog had been.

"Who are you?" he shouted, but his voice was

carried away by the wind. Leaning down, he reached for her arm, pulling her to her feet. Upright now, her boots slipped against the freshly fallen snow, and she would have toppled a second time if he hadn't held her in place. Shaking his head in what could be described only as disgust, he grabbed her about the waist and tucked her under his arm as if she were no bigger than a rag doll. Before she could protest, he started walking toward the cabin, eating up the distance with angry strides. Carrie was perpendicular to the ground, so all she could see was the snow on the lake. By now, the hair that had escaped her hat was frozen tendrils that slapped against the tender skin of her cheeks. Hennessey obediently followed. Carrie thought to protest and demand that he put her down, but she knew it would do no good. He probably wouldn't be able to hear her.

"M-y, m-y suitcase," she shouted, or tried. Then she noticed that he had that and her shopping bag in his other hand. His strength astonished her. He carried her with one arm as if she weighed next to nothing. Hennessey trailed behind them, keeping a careful watch on her. Carrie had the impression that if Finn were to mutter one word, Hennessey would happily make a meal out of her.

By the time they reached the cabin, Carrie was shaking from head to foot. Finn kicked the door closed and set her down, but she found it impossible to stand upright. Gripping her by the waist, he promptly placed her in a chair in the kitchen area.

Then he faced her with his feet apart and his hands braced against his hips. "Who the hell are you, and what are you doing here?"

Carrie did her best to answer, but her teeth chattered so hard that speaking coherently was a lost cause. In the cozy warmth of the cabin her frozen hair started to thaw, dripping cold water against her shoulders as tight ringlets formed about her head. Thankfully, the huge wood-burning stove warmed the cabin. The log cabin was a marvel, and she did her best to take in as much of it as she could. From the outside Finn's rustic home didn't look like much, and she was pleasantly surprised by the interior, with plenty of bookshelves, braided rugs, and large furniture.

"What are you doing here?" he demanded a second time.

"A . . . well, my name is . . ."

"I don't care what your name is."

As though he couldn't bear to look at her a moment longer, he filled a pot with water and then placed it atop the old-fashioned cast-iron cookstove. She continued to shiver, bracing her glove-covered hands across her body. In some ways, Carrie felt as if she were actually holding herself together.

Finn studied her as if he'd never seen anyone

more pathetic in his life. "Get out of those wet clothes," he told her gruffly.

He didn't need to remind her that her outfit wasn't suited to the frigid weather. Everything had happened so quickly. Just the day before, she'd met his mother, and then there were the last-minute flight arrangements to Fairbanks. She'd arrived mid-morning, and then there was the roller-coaster ride in the bush plane. Although it was still afternoon, the sun had already gone down.

Still shaking with cold and shock, Carrie removed her wool coat and unwound the newly purchased scarf from her neck. Next she attempted to unzip her boots, but her frozen fingers refused to cooperate. Finn walked over to where she sat, got down on one knee, and undid them for her. Pulling off her boots, he set them by the stove to thaw and then disappeared behind a fabric door, only to return a couple of moments later with a pair of thick wool socks. Still shivering, Carrie managed to pull them on.

Without asking permission, Finn opened her suitcase and sifted through its contents, shook his head, and slammed it shut. She had a couple of thick sweaters, but little else suitable for the harsh Alaskan elements. Once again he disappeared into the other room and returned with a wool shirt, which she slipped on even though it was far too large for her.

Not a word was exchanged between them. She

watched him move, wanting to remember everything she could about him for her article. Right away she noticed that while he was a large man, he moved with a grace and ease that defied his size. His hair was as dark as her own, and shoulder length. Unfortunately, his full beard hid his face. Even without seeing him clean shaven, she doubted that he would be considered traditionally handsome. His nose was a bit too large and his mouth a tad too thin. While he didn't appear to be hunk-calendar material, she found the raw vitality surrounding him strongly appealing.

Although they hadn't spoken, she sensed his irritation and his curiosity. He had probably already guessed she was a reporter, which was why he hadn't pursued his questions. One look told her he was determined not to give her any information she could publish.

When the water was thoroughly heated, Finn brewed coffee and without a word set a mug on the table in front of her. Carrie took it and held on to it with both hands. The first sip scalded her lips, but it was so deliciously hot that she barely minded. Finn remained on the far side of the room, close to the hot stove, as if to keep as much distance between them as possible.

Taking careful note of what she saw, Carrie realized that most everything inside the cabin had been made by hand. The space was compact but utilized beautifully. The kitchen area, complete with sink and countertop, a few open-faced cupboards, the cast-iron stove, and a table with four chairs, flowed naturally into a cozy sitting area. Hennessey lay on an oval-shaped braided rug close to the warmth of the stove. Two rocking chairs rested on either side, with dry wood stacked close by, and a sofa rested against another wall. The windows, of which there were two—one in the kitchen and another in the living area—had coverings that were pulled tightly closed. The cabin had lights, which she assumed were powered by a generator. What she found encouraging were the bookcases built against the walls, which were jam-packed. From what she could see, Finn Dalton was a reader. When possible, she'd check out the titles, which were sure to give her insight into this man.

"My name is Carrie," she offered, hoping that by being open and friendly he'd be willing to chat. "Carrie Slayton."

Finn ignored her and sat down with his back facing her.

Fully capable of moving now, Carrie stood and, taking the coffee with her, claimed the second chair. The heat from the stove felt glorious. "I apologize for arriving unannounced."

"Who brought you?" The question was clipped, angry.

"Sawyer. He tried to reach you, but you didn't pick up and—"

"How much did you pay him?" he asked, cutting her off.

"Well, nothing yet. I told him I'd square up with him in the morning when he returns to pick me up."

Finn snickered.

Carrie wasn't sure what that meant. "We discussed terms, and I found his price reasonable."

"What did he charge? Thirty pieces of silver?"

"No, no, it was nothing like that."

For the first time she noticed a small nook on the other side of the room. He had another table set up there, with a lone chair. On the table was a computer and what she assumed was a radio. If she'd had his email address, she might have been able to convince him to give her the interview. Then again, probably not.

"Your cabin is amazing . . . all the conveniences. You actually have a computer, but then I shouldn't be surprised, right? I know that you worked with your publisher via email."

Nothing. This one-sided conversation wasn't going the least bit well.

"I read your book," she said, trying again. "It was wonderful. The stories are detailed and rich. You make the reader feel part of the story as well. That's a rare gift. My dad read your book, too, long before me. In fact, Mom mentioned that he purchased two additional copies as gifts this Christmas. *Alone* is still on the bestseller lists and has been for months, but then you probably already know that." She realized she was chattering away and stopped.

"I'm grateful you found me when you did," she said, trying again after several tense moments of silence. "Sawyer wanted to stay, but the storm was fast approaching and he needed to get back to Bad Luck." What an unusual name for a town.

"Hard Luck," he corrected.

"Right. Hard Luck." That wasn't much better. It was difficult to maintain this cheerful facade with little to no feedback.

"I bet you'd like to know how I found you." She thought it might work out better if she asked questions.

Nothing. Unfortunately, she'd supposed wrong. Finn Dalton had no interest in speaking to her, no matter how she directed the conversation.

"If you don't want to talk, that's fine, I understand," she said with a labored sigh. "I mean, I've intruded on your life and it's unbelievably rude of me, I know."

They sat in silence for several minutes, but the tension between them was so strong it felt like overactive bass pounding from a speaker. Carrie was quickly losing patience. She hadn't come this far and jumped through all these hoops to be thwarted now.

"You wouldn't believe all the different ways I tried to find you," she said. It felt like a shallow victory now, seeing how uncooperative Finn was. But then, this should have been expected. While she was jubilant, he, on the other hand, was hostile.

Hennessey kept his gaze focused directly on her. "Good boy," she said, and made sure her voice was soft and cajoling. "You're a friendly dog, aren't you?"

Like his master, Hennessey gave no indication that he'd heard. The canine's eyes steadily regarded her, watching her every move. With Finn freezing her out, she looked to his companion for some connection. At this point she was willing to accept whatever Hennessey was willing to give her.

"I hope you know you practically gave me a heart attack, racing up on me like that," she told the dog. She bent forward and stretched out her hand, making sure he understood that all she wanted was to pet him.

"He bites," Finn warned, and from the way he clipped out the words, it seemed he would welcome the sight.

Hennessey's gaze flickered to Finn and then back to Carrie.

"Are you a big, bad wolf?" Carrie asked Hennessey softly.

The dog's eyes met hers, and then Hennessey moved to rest his chin on his paws. Then, to her utter amazement, he wagged his tail. Just one wag, one single shift to indicate that he no longer considered her a threat. It was enough to make Carrie want to shout with delight.

"I'm friendly, Hennessey, really friendly. Can we be friends?" Once again she extended her hand for the dog to see.

Again, Finn warned her. "I wouldn't do that if I were you."

Carrie slowly withdrew her hand.

Hennessey lifted his head and looked up at her and then his tail started to move, this time to a full wag, as if to tell her he was willing to trust Carrie if she was willing to trust him.

"Another traitor," Finn muttered under his breath.

"Sawyer isn't a traitor," Carrie insisted. "And Hennessey isn't, either."

Finn snorted and then sipped his coffee.

"Finn . . . Mr. Dalton," she said, trying again. She didn't mean to sound so familiar, and at the same time, "Mr. Dalton" came off as much too formal. "As you've guessed, I'm a reporter. I write for the *Chicago Herald*. Actually, I cover the society page. It's not my favorite subject, but I was grateful to get the job. I'm a good reporter, and I wanted an opportunity to prove that I was capable of writing something other than who was seen where and with whom. I am sick to death of writing about meaningless parties and who's getting married and who's breaking up. So sick that I was ready to quit, and then my editor, who's been in the business thirty years, said I could have any assignment I wanted if I could manage to interview you. Little did I know how difficult finding you would be."

Once she'd started explaining, she couldn't seem to stop. Her hope was that once Finn heard her story he'd be willing to cooperate.

Eventually he'd have to give an interview to someone, and it might as well be her. She was the one who'd found a way to reach him; that should prove something. He had to know his book was practically a phenomenon and the public was curious to know more about him.

"If I was able to find you, then others will, too . . . eventually."

He glared at her as if to refute her words.

"Your book is amazing, and your readers want to meet the man behind *Alone*. And really, who could blame them? Surely you realized when you submitted the book what it would mean?"

He remained unmoved, so Carrie tried another tactic. Perhaps he would feel sorry for her. "I gave up spending Thanksgiving with my family in order to find you, but it'd be worth every one of my vacation days and a lot more if you were willing to give me an interview." Studying him, she could tell he wasn't the least bit concerned.

"Are you looking for sympathy from me?"

"No, of course not . . . well, maybe, just a little."

He briefly closed his eyes and shook his head.

"I'll tell you what," she said in the same cheerful tone she'd used earlier. "I'll let you preview the piece, give it your stamp of approval. If you don't like it, then it won't get printed."

"Do you honestly expect me to believe that?"

"Well, yes, of course. I'm a woman of my word."

"I've yet to meet one who is." His words dripped with disdain. Snickering softly, he walked over to where the computer and the radio were set up. Pulling out the chair, he sat down, flipped a couple of switches, and put on headphones. It didn't take Carrie long to figure out his call was to Sawyer.

Although Carrie could hear only one side of the conversation, it was enough. She was the main topic of interest.

"If this is a joke, I'm not laughing. Over."

From Finn's reaction, Sawyer was apparently amused.

"You're way off base," Finn shouted into the microphone. "Having a woman here, let alone a woman reporter, isn't my idea of doing me a favor. I don't care who she is or who she knows. Over."

Sawyer replied, but Carrie couldn't make out what he said.

"I don't want her here, and that's putting it mildly. Over."

Silence followed. Finn rubbed his hand over his beard in what she could only assume was frustration.

"You have twenty-four hours to come get her. Over."

He slapped his hand against the top of the table. "No . . . I don't care about any damn storm. You brought this on yourself. Over."

Carrie was worried. She really didn't want to remain with Finn in this isolated cabin any longer than it took to get what she needed for the article. The sooner Sawyer came for her, the better. She needed to be back to work in Chicago. With the holidays coming up, there were any number of social events she'd been assigned to cover. If worse came to worst and she was stuck in Alaska, Nash would forgive her once she handed him the interview with Finn. Even in the short amount of time she'd been with him, she could relay a number of interesting details about the man.

"Twenty-four hours is my limit. Over." Finn ended the conversation with what sounded very much like a threat.

Carrie was left to wonder what he would do if Sawyer didn't return for her in the prescribed amount of time. Surely Finn wouldn't put her out in the cold to deal with the elements alone. Would he?

When he finished, he removed the headphones and turned off the radio.

Carrie remained frozen, hardly knowing what to do or say, so she did nothing.

Finn reached for his mug and drank down the

last dregs of his coffee, and then delivered the empty cup to the kitchen sink. Carrie got out of the chair. Her own coffee was finished, so she followed him, the movement of the wool socks against the cabin floor nearly silent. Unfortunately she was closer behind him than either of them realized, because when he turned, he nearly mowed her down.

With his hands braced against her upper arms, he glared down at her, a deep frown etched into his forehead. "Stay out of my way." Each word was distinctly spoken, leaving her in no doubt as to the strength of his feelings.

"Sorry . . . that was an accident." She stuttered slightly, and while she attempted to figure how best to get his cooperation, Finn grabbed his coat, hat, and gloves, and after getting everything on, promptly walked outside.

Carrie stared at the closed door, too stunned to move. She'd had such high hopes for this interview, but if this "coffee time" was any indication of what was to follow, then she was going down in flames.

Hennessey remained by the stove, seemingly content to stay by the warm fire. Carrie got down on the rug next to him, sitting with her legs folded and her chin braced against her knees.

"He doesn't like me," she told the dog.

Hennessey lifted his head to gaze at her.

"I can't say that I blame him. I barged into his life, and now I'm paying the price."

To her delight, Hennessey lifted his chin and

then rested it on top of her foot. Although Finn had warned her that he might bite, she gently placed her hand on the top of his head. After giving him a moment to adjust to the feel of her touch, she stroked the length of his spine.

"You're nothing like the big, bad wolf Finn makes you out to be," she whispered. "You're a big puffball."

Well, at least Finn's dog liked her, and for now that was enough. She continued stroking his fur, burrowing her fingers into his thick coat. "Maybe I should interview you instead," she suggested quietly. "How does that sound?"

The large wolf/dog didn't indicate his feelings on the matter one way or another.

"Hennessey, tell me, what's it like . . ."

The door opened again, and Finn came in along with a blast of frigid air and an armload of wood. Thankfully, he shut the door and latched it. He set the wood down by the stove, stacking it for the night.

"Can I do anything to help?" Carrie asked.

"Leave."

"I can't," she whispered.

"Don't I know it."

"I'd hoped . . . I'd assumed that Sawyer would fly me in to meet you, and the two of us could briefly chat and then I'd be on my way, mission accomplished."

"And now I'm stuck with you."

"Yes, I know, and I apologize." Seeing that he didn't welcome her help with the evening meal, she felt the least she could do was get her carry-on bag out of the way.

"Is there someplace you'd like me to put my suitcase?" she asked.

"You mean like in a guest bedroom?" he asked with more than a hint of sarcasm.

"Well, yes."

He snickered. "There's only one bedroom, and only one bed, and I'm telling you right now I'm not sleeping on the sofa."

Chapter Four

This was an unwelcome predicament, and Finn wasn't the least bit happy. The biggest shock was that Sawyer had turned on him. Sawyer O'Halloran was a friend, a good friend, and beyond reproach . . . until now. Their brief conversation left more questions than it provided answers. The woman had something for him, Sawyer claimed, but to this point she'd kept it to herself. Finn hadn't questioned his friend, although the temptation had been strong. Whatever it was had convinced Sawyer to fly her in. To his credit, Sawyer had attempted to reach him.

After several hours of tense silence, Finn loaded wood into the stove and brought out the leftover moose-meat stew for his dinner. He glanced at Carrie and grumbled under his breath. She was a pretty thing, with hair dark enough to be called chocolate and startling blue eyes, although he tried not to notice anything about her. Women like Carrie Slayton were sure to leave a string of broken hearts in their wake, and Finn was determined not to be one of them. He noticed that she kept touching her head. It appeared to have something to do with her hair, which had twisted into springy ringlets after it'd gotten wet in the snow. She seemed to be self-conscious about it, waiting for him to tease her. He wouldn't. Truth be known, he found her hair to be one of the most attractive features about her.

Not good. Noticing anything about the woman in his cabin was a sign of weakness, and Finn refused to allow her to take up one iota of consideration.

As much as he hated to admit it, what she said about granting her the interview made sense. If she'd been able to find him, then other reporters would as well, sooner or later. He'd ignored that inevitability longer than he should have. Not that her argument had persuaded him—nothing would. Finn wrote the book to share his love of the wilderness and to fill the long, lonely hours of the winter solitude. Never in his wildest dreams had he expected it to be such an overwhelming success. Thankfully, he'd done all the legal transactions through an attorney, with the stipulation that he maintain his privacy. He hadn't agreed to a single interview, regardless of repeated attempts by his publisher. Despite how it looked, Finn wasn't a recluse but simply a man who enjoyed his solitude.

He wasn't about to disrupt his life and become a media darling.

Finn didn't dislike women; he simply didn't trust a single one of them. Those were lessons he'd learned the hard way. His father was never the same after his mother left. He'd grown bitter and hard, and drummed those lessons into Finn. Later Finn had discovered on his own what his father had tried to tell him. Women were fickle and not worth the trouble they caused in a man's life. He'd fallen for Pamela, but she'd hurt him the same way his mother had hurt his father. Thankfully, Finn had learned early in their relationship that Pamela wasn't trustworthy. It embarrassed him to remember the way she'd played him. Finn made the mistake of believing he was falling in love with her only to learn she was married and bored and looking for a little action on the side while her husband was overseas. Finn was willing to admit he enjoyed being with women, but he knew better than to involve his heart.

He did feel bad about the sleeping situation. But Carrie was the one who'd come uninvited and unannounced. What she'd done was stupid and dangerous, and there were consequences. Finn refused to give her his bed, although the idea of sharing it with her was fairly tempting. He quickly shook his head, casting the image out of his mind.

Despite his best efforts, his gaze wandered back to her and her beautiful hair. Who was he kidding?

It wasn't only her hair that attracted him; she was a knockout. Little wonder Sawyer hadn't been able to refuse her. No doubt she had a string of boyfriends as long as the Alaska shoreline.

Frowning, he realized he wasn't the only one who noticed how attractive she was. Hennessey had cozied right up to her. Finn wouldn't have believed it if he hadn't seen it with his own eyes. Generally, Hennessey didn't take kindly to strangers. It seemed his faithful mutt wasn't immune to her charms, either.

As far as he was concerned, the sooner Carrie Slayton was out of his hair, the better.

Carrie swallowed hard as she surveyed the cozy living room off the kitchen. The couch was old and lumpy, but the only alternative was the floor. "Where would you like me to sleep?" She sat down on the couch, testing it, her hands at her sides. It would do in a pinch, she supposed, and it would be more comfortable than the hard floor.

"Wherever you want. The choice is yours, although I should warn you Hennessey considers the sofa his."

Finn remained in the kitchen, and from what she could see he appeared to be putting dinner together, heating a pot on the stove. Although it was early evening, it seemed much later. The aroma from the stew was heavenly. Carrie's stomach growled, reminding her that it'd been several hours since she'd last eaten, and that had been pretzels the airline handed out during the flight. In her rush to get to the airport, she'd skipped breakfast.

"Getting stuck here for the night wasn't what I planned, either," she reminded him. "I don't appreciate being here any more than you want me," she said, and then felt she should explain further. "I need to be back in Chicago. Sophie will cover for me, but . . ." She stopped when it was clear he had no interest in listening to her concerns.

He paused, glanced up, and said, "You should have considered that earlier."

The wind continued to howl and hiss, reminding her that it could be days before Sawyer would be able to return. This was quickly turning into an unmitigated disaster.

She was deep in her worries, and dinner proved to be a miserable affair. Finn served the stew, which he, thankfully, shared with her. The meat didn't have a familiar taste, and Carrie decided she was better off not knowing what it was. Bear? Walrus? Mountain goat? For his part, Finn seemed to think if he pretended she was invisible he could completely ignore her. He made it clear he wasn't interested in conversation. Carrie took the hint and ate her meal in silence. When she'd finished, she politely complimented his efforts and thanked him.

Almost immediately after dinner, Finn went into the bedroom and returned a few minutes later with two thick blankets and a pillow. Without a word, he handed them to her.

"Thank you," she said, taking them from him and holding them against her chest. He might have the personality of a rattlesnake, but she wasn't about to let his bad mood affect her.

Apologizing to Hennessey, she made her bed on the sofa, scooting it as close to the stove as she dared. As soon as she lay down, Hennessey leaped up and snuggled next to her legs. Stretching out her arm, she welcomed the canine's warmth. This was probably the earliest she'd gone to bed since she was a toddler.

Although she should be exhausted, Carrie found her mind racing. "He's not going to give me the interview," she told the dog, rolling onto her back and staring up at the log beams of the ceiling.

"Maybe I will interview you," she said, and gently petted Hennessey's head.

The dog rested his chin against her knee in a move that both comforted and warmed her.

"Okay, Hennessey, tell me what it's like living with the great Finn Dalton, esteemed author of *Alone*."

She waited, pretending to listen to his answer.

"You can't mean to say you actually like spending countless hours with such a cantankerous owner? I'm wrong, you say, and he really isn't as bad as I assume? Frankly, I find that hard to believe! Oh, I'm sure you're right, Finn Dalton can be civil, but unfortunately he sees me as an evil threat and he wants to boot me out of here as fast as he can. I know, I know, it's a shame we couldn't have reached an understanding. It's only a matter of time, you know, before others track him down."

Again she paused as though taking in the dog's comments.

"Yes, I hear you. To you he's a good guy, but to me he's rude and arrogant and a narcissist. Oh, sorry, *narcissist* is a big word. It means he's completely hung up on himself."

A loud snort came from the other room, which was a sure sign Finn was listening in on their conversation.

"Okay, I realize you have a few questions for me, too. Ask away."

She pretended to be listening before she answered. "Like I explained earlier, America is interested in learning what they can about the man who wrote *Alone*. They see Finn as some sort of hero. Little do they know what he's really like."

She paused and waited for a couple of moments. "Oh, you want to know how I was able to find him when so many others have failed? Sawyer asked me the same question. He told me a handful of reporters have tried to bribe him and a couple of other bush pilots to help locate Finn, but none of Finn's friends would betray him." She yawned as if she were ready to call it a night.

"Answer the dog's question." Finn stood in the

doorway, holding back the fabric partition. "I'm curious to know what you have for me that convinced Sawyer to bring you here. He's a good friend, and I know he wouldn't be easily swayed."

Carrie sat upright and wrapped her arms around her bent knees. So this is what it took to get the mighty Finn to open up. "If you must know, it was what I told him about your mother."

"My mother," Finn repeated slowly. "What does she have to do with any of this?"

"I found her, and—"

"You searched out my mother?" he demanded in what came across as anger mingled with restraint.

"Well, yes. So have others, but I was able to convince her to talk to me. Your mother and I had a good chat, and—"

Finn took two steps into the room and braced his hands against his hips, looking at her as if she were the lowest of the low. "You actually talked to my mother?"

"I just said as much, and she—"

"I don't care what she said. I want nothing to do with her."

Carrie sighed, feeling wretched for Joan when all she wanted was to connect with her son. "She told me that you'd probably react like this the minute I mentioned her to you."

"She walked out on my father and me—"

"Oh, come on, Finn, you have to know it's more

complicated than that. She loves you, and your father didn't give her many options."

"Listen, Ms. Busybody, this is none of your business, so stay out of it." He marched back to the bedroom and pushed aside the curtain with such force she was surprised it didn't rip in half.

Carrie was ready to wash her hands of this obstinate, unfeeling man. He was unreasonable, unforgiving . . . and a dozen more unflattering words that circled her mind. Lying back down, she stared up at the ceiling. Hennessey remained at her side.

"He really has mother issues, doesn't he?" she told the dog, lowering her voice to a whisper.

"I heard that."

Carrie ignored him, seeing how well he'd managed to pretend she didn't exist. "His heart must be as cold as ice not to care about his own mother."

"Stay out of it, Carrie."

She ignored that, too.

"His attitude toward her explains a great deal. It seems to me Finnegan Dalton has distinct abandonment issues, right along with issues regarding all women."

He laughed as though he found her analysis amusing.

"Why else would he choose to live in the Alaska wilderness alone?"

"You think you're clever, don't you?" he muttered.

"But all that is probably just the tip of the ice-berg."

"Would you stop!"

"*Alone* is right." She raised her voice to be sure he heard her loud and clear. "He's probably been running away his entire life. Then he had to go and make the mistake of writing a bestselling book that captured the public's attention. How unfortunate for him."

Silence.

The blizzard howled outside the door, and Carrie was grateful Hennessey had chosen to stay with her. She punched the pillow several times and then lay back down, pulling the thick blanket over her shoulders and forcing her eyes closed. Finn Dalton could thank his lucky stars she wasn't writing the article on him right that minute. She couldn't think of a single flattering comment she could make about this ill-mannered man.

The minutes ticked past, but as hard as she tried, Carrie couldn't fall sleep. The sofa was uncomfortable, and Finn had made her so angry the adrenaline pumped through her, making it impossible to relax.

"He hates all women, doesn't he?" she asked Hennessey, keeping her voice low and soft.

The dog lifted his head, and she almost expected an answer.

"Not true," Finn insisted. He stood in the doorway to the bedroom again, filling it with his bulk.

Ah, so he hadn't been able to fall asleep, either. "Is so," she returned with equal fervor. "How else do you explain yourself? Your mother was given very few options. My goodness, Finn, think about it. She was a southern belle; these harsh elements were too much for her. She wanted to compromise, but your father wouldn't hear of it. She told me it broke her heart to leave you behind, but you and your father were so close she couldn't bear to separate you. When you chose to stay with your father, she could have insisted, could have taken the matter to the courts, but she didn't. She bowed to your wishes even though it broke her heart."

"She told you all this, did she?"

"Yes, and that's not all. She mentioned how rude you were to her when your father died. She attended his funeral to make what amends she could, and you rejected her." Carrie's jaw tightened just thinking about the unkind way Finn had behaved toward his mother.

"She had no right to be there. She remarried."

"She loved your father, and she loves you." It was beyond Carrie's imagination that Finn would continue to shut his mother out, especially after losing his father. "You were a boy when she left. You only heard one side of the story."

"So did you, and frankly, what's between my mother and me is none of your concern."

He was right; Carrie was butting her head into areas that had nothing to do with writing the article. However, now that she'd started, she couldn't seem to stop. "Your mother wants you in her life. You're her only child."

"She should have thought of that twenty-five years ago." As though he was exhausted from their argument, he slowly shook his head and whispered, "Just go to sleep, would you?"

She was about to mention how uncomfortable the sofa was, but he might assume she was looking for an invitation to join him in his bed. Nothing could be further from the truth. "I'm trying, but you make me so angry that I can't think straight."

"Try harder." The curtain between the two rooms swayed as he whirled around and returned to bed.

Carrie didn't know how long it was before she managed to sleep. At some point in the night she woke from the cold and drew the thick blankets more snugly about her shoulders. Later, she was overly warm and kicked them free from her jean-clad legs.

At about midnight, she opened her eyes to find Finn standing by the stove, feeding it the wood he'd brought in earlier.

The next thing she knew, he was gently waking her. "You can have the bed now."

She blinked up at him without understanding. He was fully dressed, and while it surely must be close to morning, the only light that showed came from the fire in the stove.

Finn led her into the bedroom, and once she'd crawled into the ultracomfortable feather bed, he covered her with thick blankets. "I'll be gone for a while."

"Okay," she mumbled, already half asleep. Surrounded by warmth and comfort, she thought sleeping on this soft mattress was heavenly.

When she woke, it was still dark. She quickly put on every bit of clothing that she could fit into until her arms were so thick with two long-sleeved shirts and two sweaters that she could barely bend her elbows.

Although she'd never cooked on a cast-iron stove, it didn't seem that difficult. The coffeepot sat on the stove top, but she was unable to get water from the faucet. Once she got the fire going, she opened the cabin door. She blinked at the cold that seemed to come at her like a giant fist. It stole her breath, but she managed to pack the coffeepot with snow and then quickly came back inside. Searching through Finn's cupboards, she found coffee and quickly assembled a pot. The coffee had just finished brewing when she heard Hennessey bark.

Finn was back.

Carrie couldn't imagine where he'd gone or what he'd been doing, especially in the snow. She automatically reached for a second mug and filled it. Finn came in the door, followed by Hennessey, who instantly went to her side. She bent down and petted her newfound friend. Finn seemed surprised to see her up and about.

"The storm has let up," he murmured. "But not enough for Sawyer to fly."

"Oh." Carrie had been afraid that was the case. She handed him a mug of steaming brew.

"You made coffee," he said, as if this was some gargantuan feat.

"Yes." It was one thing to get into a sparring match with him in the dead of night and quite another to do so when they were standing face-to-face. She'd made several accusations that she wished now had remained unsaid. It embarrassed her that she had delved into his personal life when what he did or didn't do was none of her affair.

Finn, too, seemed uneasy.

"Have you had breakfast?" she asked, although she didn't have a clue what she would cook if he hadn't. It wasn't like she had access to fresh eggs. From what little she'd picked up about life in the frozen north, being this close to the tree line meant that groceries, supplies, or anything else Finn needed would have to be flown in.

"I ate earlier. You?"

"Not yet." This strained politeness was a complete turnaround from the way they'd behaved toward each other previously. Carrie felt responsible for clearing the air, although she wasn't sure what to say or if she should even try. Perhaps it would be best to just pretend their verbal skirmish hadn't happened.

"There's some caribou jerky if you're interested. Made it myself this summer."

His attitude toward her appeared to be a bit more amicable, she noticed. "Thanks, but I'm not much of a breakfast person."

"Suit yourself."

He removed his coat and then sat down at the table with his coffee, his gaze focused on the cup as if he were reading tea leaves.

Carrie sat down across from him and decided to make an effort at conversation. "About last night . . ."

His head shot up, and his gaze narrowed significantly. "What about it?"

"I want to apologize for the things I said about you and your mother."

He bobbed his head as though to assure her all was forgiven. "I don't want to talk about it."

"Okay. But I still think you have issues with women."

"Drop it, would you?" he said between clenched teeth.

Carrie held up her hand. "You're right, sorry."

He relaxed and sipped his coffee.

"I need to do something, and I don't want to make you mad, so I'm telling you in advance."

"Now what?" he asked, as if he'd already grown tired of the conversation.

Carrie slipped the tips of her fingers into her jeans pocket. "Your mother asked me to give you this. I feel honor bound to follow through with my promise to her."

"Give me what?"

"Your father's wedding band."

His face tightened. "Keep it."

"I can't do that; a promise is a promise."

He stared across the short space between them and then smiled. "That's how you convinced Sawyer to fly you in, isn't it? You told him you had something for me, but he didn't say what and I didn't ask."

Carrie didn't feel she could or should lie. "I'm grateful Sawyer was willing to help me, but he didn't do it for me. He did it because he felt he was doing what was best for you. He's a friend, and from what I can see, a good one."

Finn snorted and rubbed his hand down his beard. "I knew it had to be something like that."

She placed the gold band in the center of the table.

"Satisfied now?" he asked.

"Yes."

His chair made a grating noise as he stood and reached for the gold band, which he carried to the front door. He opened it, letting snow and wind into the cabin before he tossed the ring with all his might into the storm.

Chapter Five

❄

Carrie bolted to her feet and raced through the open door, and practically dove face-first into the whirling snow. The wind blinded her but she caught a glimpse of metal and nearly fell on it in her eagerness to retrieve Paul Dalton's wedding band. Clenching the gold band tightly in the palm of her hand, Carrie battled the storm in an effort to hurry back into the house. It took all her strength to close the door against the elements. By the time she was finished she was half frozen and breathless.

"How could you be so uncaring?" Carrie demanded, glaring at Finn. Her lungs hurt from the brief time she'd been in the icy cold. Chicago was known for its brutal winters, but this frigid air was beyond anything she'd ever experienced.

"Why should I care about a wedding ring when the marriage meant nothing to my mother?" he retorted.

Carrie leaned against the door, needing its support to remain upright. Her entire body was rigid with cold and anger. She waited for a moment, letting the warmth of the room revive her enough to think clearly.

"The ring belonged to your father," she reminded him. One would think Finn would hold on to the band as a keepsake, if for no other reason than the fact that his father had once worn and treasured it.

"Dad returned it to my mother at the time of the divorce. If he didn't want it, what makes you think I would?"

"And your mother kept it, which should tell you something." Carrie didn't know why she felt such a strong need to defend his mother. In some way, it felt as though she was sticking up for herself, as well as all the other women of the world.

"As far as I can determine, women are out for what they can get from a man. You don't care who you step on or who you hurt. I made the mistake of thinking I was in love once, but I won't make it again."

"All women?" Carrie challenged. He wasn't making sense. "You see us as selfish and untrustworthy because your mother left you? And you have the nerve to tell me you don't have abandonment issues?" She resisted the urge to laugh. This guy was a real piece of work. "Have you considered counseling?"

"You think this is just about my mother. You don't know anything."

"Then tell me," she urged.

"Pamela," he muttered, "was lesson number two."

"Oh, so that's it. A woman disappointed you and now you're sour on the entire gender. That is such a cliché. What happened? Did Pamela decide she couldn't live in Alaska? Was she too much like your mother?"

"It's none of your business."

"You're right, this has nothing to do with me. I have just one more thing to say and then I promise not to mention it again. *Finn Dalton, get over it.*"

Before she could suck in the next breath, Finn's face was two inches away from her own. They were practically nose-to-nose. If Carrie could have backed away, she would have, but with the door pressed against her backside, she had nowhere to move.

Hennessey was on his feet and stood next to Finn, barking madly. Finn ignored him, and so did Carrie.

"I knew Pamela from the time we were teenagers. Or, better yet, I *thought* I knew her. She moved to Seattle and then came back. I loved her, and then I learned that while she was away, she married a soldier who went off to Afghanistan. She didn't care about me. All she wanted was some entertainment while her husband was out of the country. She was playing me. I don't need a woman in my life—got it? Not one of you is worth the heartache. I saw what losing my mother did to my father, and

I had a small taste of it myself. I don't need another, so back off. Stay out of my life, understand?"

"Loud and clear." His anger seemed to inhale all the oxygen in the room until the small hairs on the back of Carrie's neck bristled. Her hands were flattened against the door, and when he stepped away it took several seconds before Carrie felt like she could breathe normally again.

He stalked over to his desk on the far side of the cabin as if he couldn't get away from her fast enough.

Carrie bent down to pat Hennessey and reassure him that all was well.

The tension left her shoulders, and she realized she was trembling almost uncontrollably in the aftermath of their confrontation. Despite herself, she felt bad for Finn. Not knowing Pamela or the situation that had led to their breakup, she had to believe it must have been traumatic to Finn.

"My college boyfriend dumped me," Carrie said, and was surprised by how low and shaky her voice sounded.

"And you 'got over it,' right? No big deal." He sat with his back to her, his tone cold. The air seemed to vibrate with tension.

"Actually, no . . . I tried to pretend it was a natural parting of the ways. I was in Chicago, working for the newspaper, and he was back in Seattle. But it hurt," she whispered. "He married a friend of mine six months later, and I was a bridesmaid in their wedding, and I had to pretend it didn't matter."

Finn turned around and looked at her for an extra-long moment, frowning as if to gauge whether she was telling the truth. Carrie held his gaze and didn't flinch before moving into the kitchen, feeling the need to sit down. Her bottom lip trembled slightly, and she bit into it, wanting to disguise how upset she was.

Hennessey sat down by Finn's side, and then after a few minutes walked over to where Carrie sat at the table. She petted his thick fur, trying to think of what to say to ease the tension. They were trapped here together, and she had to do something to make it tolerable.

"We've both been hurt, but it isn't the end of the world."

He snorted.

"Can we put this conversation behind us?"

His back was to her again, and he shrugged.

"Do you play chess?" she asked.

"No."

"Scrabble?"

"No."

What do you play?"

"Solitaire."

"Oh." The hand of truce that Carrie had extended had been solidly slapped.

Several tense moments passed before he exhaled harshly and said, "Do you play cribbage?"

"My grandfather taught me," she responded. If they could find common ground, it would help pass the long hours of being cooped up together until Sawyer arrived. "I'm not much good, but I'd be willing to give it a try if you'd like."

He hesitated and then went into his bedroom and returned with a cribbage board and a deck of cards. Sitting down at the kitchen table across from her, he removed the cards from the box and shuffled.

Carrie was grateful they weren't destined to spend the entire storm at each other's throats. "Go ahead and deal. How about coffee?"

He nodded.

Finn had dealt the first hand by the time she returned. Carrie looked at her cards, discarded two into the crib, and then they started. Luck was with her and after several hands, she narrowly pegged to a win. Finn regarded her skeptically. "I thought you said you weren't much good at this?"

"Did I?"

Sipping his coffee, Finn tried to hide his smile, but Carrie saw it and smiled back. "I believe it's my turn to deal."

Keeping his eyes on her, he slid the deck of cards across the table.

Shuffling the cards, Carrie glanced up and smiled ever so sweetly. "Women aren't stupid, you know."

"I never said they were. Heartless, yes, but a few I've happened upon showed meager signs of intelligence."

Carrie suspected he was purposely attempting to bait her. "I'll add *chauvinist* to the long list of words that best describe you, Finn Dalton."

"Better word would be *realist*."

"Oh, puh-leese." She drawled out the word and laughed despite herself.

Finn did, too, and the surprise of hearing his amusement caused her to fumble and lose control of the cards, which scattered across the tabletop.

"You should laugh more often," she said, gathering together the deck.

"Really?"

"Yes, really."

His eyes shone, and despite his grizzled appearance, she found him strongly appealing. If he were clean shaven and his hair groomed, he might even be considered handsome. She must have been staring at him because he frowned and barked, "What?"

"Oh, sorry." Carrie quickly looked away and dealt the cards.

"You're staring at me."

"I know."

"Why?"

This question was harder to answer. She couldn't very well admit she found him intriguing, and so she said the first thing that came to mind. "I want to remember what you look like, and I doubt you'd let me take your photo."

He immediately frowned. "For that article you intend to write?"

Instead of answering, she kept dealing the cards and then waited while he cut the deck.

The second game proved they were well matched. Finn moved his peg around the board and won.

"Tie-breaker?" he asked.

"Of course," she responded. It surprised her how much she enjoyed this mini–battle of the sexes with him.

After shuffling the cards, he dealt.

"Do you do anything special around the cabin for Christmas?" she asked.

Frowning, he glanced at her above his hand. "It isn't even Thanksgiving yet. Why are you asking about Christmas?"

"I guess it's on my mind. A lot of the stores already have their decorations up."

"You've got to be joking."

"I'm not."

He grumbled some. "I suppose you're the sort of woman who goes all out for Christmas."

"Of course," she said, as she counted out her score. "Although I live alone, I put up a tree, hang garlands, and decorate with holly. What about you?"

He finished counting out his hand. "What about me? If you're digging for more information for that article, you can stop right now."

"I wasn't," she said, groaning. It seemed everything she asked was suspect. "You don't have a Christmas tree?"

"No. Why would I?"

Knowing him, he probably didn't like Christmas at all. "Is it just another day for you and Hennessey?"

"For the most part, yes. I'll sometimes join Sawyer and his family or fly to Fairbanks and spend Christmas Day with friends."

It made Carrie feel better to know he wouldn't be alone unless that was what he chose. "Good."

"Good?" he repeated.

"Yes. I would hate the thought of you spending Christmas alone."

He grinned, as if her comment amused him. "Despite what you think, I enjoy my own company, but I have a real life, too. I live a good part of the time here, but I have a condo . . . elsewhere."

"You do? But how do you support yourself? I mean, before the book."

"I have all the work I want with the state, checking on the pipeline." He grimaced, as if he'd said far more than he meant for her to know. "Forget I said that."

She pantomimed zipping her lips closed. There was far more to Finn than she realized. "Listen, this isn't related to anything I might write, so relax."

They broke for lunch. Finn made sandwiches, which they ate in front of the stove, sitting in the rocking chairs. A glance out the window told her the wind had died down and the snow had stopped.

"My mother is probably worried about me," she said, checking her cell phone. Thankfully, her battery wasn't dead, but coverage this far north simply wasn't going to happen. "I told her I'd phone, and I haven't. Is there any way I can get word to her?"

"I have a satellite phone, but it isn't cheap."

"I'll be happy to pay whatever the charges are. I won't talk long."

"Having you out of my hair by tomorrow morning would be payment enough."

Carrie frowned. "Ouch. I thought we were getting along so well, too."

Finn chuckled. "We were almost friends until you whipped me in cribbage."

"Ah, men and their fragile egos."

Finn grumbled something she couldn't hear, and then he showed her how to operate the phone by his desk. It took a moment for the line to connect, and when it did, her father answered.

"Dad, it's me. I don't have a lot of time, but I want you to know I'm still in Alaska. Tell Mom I'm doing great and I'll connect with her once I'm back in Chicago."

"Your mother's been concerned. You said you'd call."

"I know, Dad. I'll explain everything when I'm not paying outrageous satellite charges."

"Satellite charges? Where in heaven's name are you?" Her father was the talker in the family.

"Outside of Fairbanks, Alaska." If she said anything more, her dad would have more questions, and then more after that.

"You found him? You found Finn Dalton?"

"Dad, I can't talk now."

"Okay, okay, but I'm going to want a full report once you're back."

"Will do. Reassure Mom that I'm fine and thank Grandpa for teaching me cribbage."

"What's that?"

"Never mind, I'll explain later."

They said their farewells, and Carrie ended the call. When she turned around, she was surprised to find Finn had put on his parka and heavy boots.

"You're going somewhere?" she asked, surprised.

"The wind has died down and the snow has mostly stopped. I won't be gone long." Hennessey was at the door, eager and ready to be on his way.

At the door, Finn hesitated. "You'll be all right for a while by yourself?"

"Of course." It surprised her that he'd asked. Actually, she welcomed the privacy in order to work on the article. The instant he was out the door, she retrieved her computer. It didn't take her long to organize her thoughts. She'd already gathered more than enough information to write a lengthy piece about him. The rough draft took her the better part of an hour. Feeling good about the piece, which she felt was fair, if not flattering, she tucked her laptop back inside her suitcase, grateful Finn hadn't returned while she'd had it open.

With that out of the way, Carrie soon grew restless and bored, fidgeting, wishing she could talk to Sophie. Had she better planned this trip, she would have brought along her e-reader.

Finding little with which to entertain herself, Carrie took out the paper tablet she had with her, found a pair of scissors, and went about cutting large snowflakes. With the sewing kit at the bottom of her purse, she took thread, stood barefoot on a chair, and suspended the flakes from the ceiling until the entire cabin looked like a magical winter wonderland.

More than likely Finn wouldn't appreciate her effort toward Christmas decorations; however, she wasn't going to let that stop her. Other than keeping her occupied, she hoped this would amuse him.

She was standing on the chair in the middle of the cabin, stretching her arms above her head, when the door unexpectedly opened and Finn and Hennessey stepped inside.

"What the . . ."

Startled, Carrie lost her balance, and with arms flailing at her sides, she started to topple from her perch on the chair. Seeing her predicament, Finn reacted quickly and instinctively, catching her in midair. Carrie issued a small, breathless gasp as her body was pressed hard against his.

For one wild moment all they did was stare at each other. Her pulse raced, and his eyes went directly to her throat as if he could see her reaction. He didn't release her, and she realized she was glad to be in his arms. It wasn't a comfortable feeling.

His gaze traveled from the throbbing pulse in her neck to her lips, and Carrie's mouth went dry as his eyes held hers. When did this happen? Another question quickly followed the first—what were they going to do about it? Carrie knew what she wanted. She closed her eyes, expecting, hoping that Finn would kiss her.

He didn't.

Gradually he released her, setting her feet down on solid ground. Then he stepped back as though having her this close had burned his senses.

"What is this?" he asked, his voice ragged, demanding. He hardly sounded like himself.

"What?" Carrie's own senses became jumbled. Confused. She wasn't sure what he meant. It sounded as if he was asking about this sudden arc of awareness that vibrated between them. "I . . ."

"This!" He pointed at the ceiling.

"Oh, that," she said, feeling foolish, embarrassed, and relieved. "I thought I'd add a bit of holiday spirit to your cabin."

He frowned.

"I can take it down if you want."

His response was a soft snort. "And risk you breaking your fool neck a second time? Leave it."

"I think it looks great."

"You would."

"And you don't?" she pressed.

He didn't bother to answer, but instead announced, "I'll put a roast on for dinner." She stood by while he put together meat, carrots, and onions in a cast-iron pot and placed it in the oven.

"What can I do?" she asked, looking to help.

"You can peel potatoes if you want."

"I want."

They both seemed eager to put that sensual awkwardness behind them. It was important, she supposed, to ignore the awareness that sprang up so unexpectedly. Finn seemed as determined as she was to pretend it had never happened. Carrie was more than eager to do so, seeing that she'd practically begged him to kiss her. Just thinking about it mortified her. She didn't know what she'd been thinking, which explained it, because clearly she hadn't been thinking. Instead, she'd been feeling, and that was dangerous to them both.

Within a couple of hours the scent of the roast filled the cabin. As she set the table for dinner, Finn disappeared for a couple minutes and returned with a bottle of red wine.

"Do you like wine?" he asked.

"Yes, very much."

He set the wine bottle in the middle of the table.

"Are we celebrating?" she asked, teasing him.

"Yes. Sawyer will collect you come morning."

"Of course. How could I have forgotten?" she said. "And you'll be more than ready to see me go."

To her surprise, he didn't immediately respond.

When dinner was ready, they sat down across from each other, the roast and assorted vegetables on a platter between them. Finn opened the wine bottle and poured them each a glass.

"What shall we toast?" she asked, pressing the brim of her glass against his.

"To cribbage," he suggested. "And I demand a rematch after dinner."

"To cribbage," she echoed, and smiled.

Their eyes held for an extra-long moment, and her stomach was filled with butterflies as she realized that this heightened awareness of each other hadn't gone away. If anything, it was stronger, and was growing more so each moment. Although they both tried to ignore what was happening, it was still there, as real and as profound as when he'd caught her and kept her from falling to the floor.

They sipped the wine while their gazes held. Deliberately, Carrie looked away. She needed to remind herself that the sole reason she was in Alaska was for an interview. After spending more than twenty-four hours with Finn, she had what she needed. And as soon as the article was published, Finn Dalton would want nothing more to do with her.

Chapter Six

❄

This wasn't working, Finn realized. When Carrie showed up unexpectedly, he'd been determined to freeze her out. She might have found him, but she wasn't getting one iota of information out of him for that blasted article she intended to write. He would say as little as possible, speak in monosyllables, and be rid of her the instant the weather cleared.

And yet within the span of twenty-four hours she knew more about him than he ever intended. Only a few of his friends knew about his involvement with Pamela. If divulging personal information wasn't bad enough, he'd been keenly tempted to take her in his arms and kiss her. The urge had been so strong that he'd had to leave the cabin. Then, upon his return, he'd found her standing on a chair and she'd fallen directly into his arms. He'd like to think she planned this, but her reactions said otherwise. He'd caught her, and she'd looked up at him with those baby blues of hers, practically begging him to do the very thing he wanted to most. It felt as if he was about to go down for the third time before he gathered the strength to pull away. Not that it was easy. Finn liked to think of himself as disciplined and in control of his emotions. With Carrie, every bit of self-preservation flew out the proverbial window. He didn't like it one bit.

What he needed, Finn decided, was a distraction. He figured if they could play cards, that would keep him sane until he was well rid of her. Then he'd come up with the bright idea of opening a bottle of wine. What *was* he thinking? If he found her beautiful before dinner, she was all the more so during. Stunning, breathtakingly beautiful, and for the life of him he couldn't keep his eyes off her.

He wanted to blame the wine, but she'd intoxicated him with little more than a smile. This was bad, and every minute he spent with her made it worse. Before he knew how it happened, he'd lowered his guard.

"Are you surprised?" she'd asked him. "You know, by how successful the book has been?"

He nodded. It baffled him even now. His editor routinely updated him on sales and his position on the *New York Times* bestseller list. "I've been told it's a publishing sensation."

"It is. Finn, thousands and thousands of people are reading and loving your stories about Alaska. What ever made you think to write it?"

He smiled and leaned back, far more comfortable with her than he should have been. Before he knew it, he was telling her the story. "It was just one of those things. I read an article about the problems with kids having sedentary lives, obsessed with video games and television, and was astonished. While I was growing up, every day was an adventure. I thought if I wrote about some of my own experiences it might inspire kids and adults to step outside their front door and look at nature in an entirely different way."

Carrie's eyes brightened and Finn couldn't have looked away from her if someone had offered him gold ingots.

"Did you know," Carrie said, her smile warm and alive, "there are whole groups that are springing up across the country for organized hikes and other outdoor activities that your book inspired? This would never have happened if it hadn't been for your book. I hope you realize what a strong influence *Alone* has been."

He had heard about such groups, and it pleased him immensely.

The bottom line, Finn realized, was that he needed to keep his trap shut.

The problem was how comfortable he felt with Carrie. Hardly trying, she got him talking. He wasn't sure what it was about her; maybe it was the pain that radiated from her when she spoke of her college sweetheart. At first he assumed she'd made up the story in order to gain his trust. But the hurt he saw in her couldn't be fabricated. No one was that good an actress.

All Finn could hope was that Sawyer didn't get delayed come morning. There was still a chance that Finn might come out of this fiasco unscathed.

Carrie and Finn worked together washing and drying the dinner dishes. Although she pretended not to notice, he kept a careful watch on her. At one point she almost said she had no intention of stealing his silverware.

Dinner had been pleasant enough. The roast had been cooked to perfection, tender and succulent, and the vegetables were a wonderful complement. They'd chatted amicably during the meal, and Carrie was surprised how easy it was to talk to Finn. Without her prompting, he'd started to talk about the book, which shocked her. When he abruptly stopped, she realized he'd said far more than he'd ever intended.

"I like you, Finn," she said as they claimed the chairs by the fire.

"Excuse me?" He arched one thick brow as though questioning her.

"With few exceptions, I've enjoyed spending this time with you."

"Really?" Her announcement appeared to amuse him. He leaned back in his chair and crossed his arms as though he expected her to elaborate.

She rocked a bit before answering. "I'm not going to feed your ego."

"Come on. Why not?"

Carrie had trouble holding back a smile "Okay, fine," she said, "you're so authentic. You are who you are and you aren't willing to apologize for it. I like that."

Actually, she was strongly attracted to the fact that Finn was a man's man, but she wasn't willing to admit it. His strength didn't come from working out in some gym but from living life.

She found he was staring at her, and so she continued, "Covering the society page the way I do, you can't imagine how many men . . . and women I meet who only care about money, appearances, superficial things. Oh, don't get me started, but you . . . you're a refreshing change."

"I'm highly intelligent," he added.

She laughed. "And humble, too, I see."

"Touché." He chuckled and then asked, "What about good-looking?"

"I don't feel qualified to answer that," she said, and cocked her head from one side to the other as though assessing his looks.

"Why not?" he challenged.

She flexed her fingers over her own cheeks. "It's hard to tell with your entire face covered with that beard."

"True, but you should be able to take my word

for it. Besides, beards are a necessity here in Alaska."

"Someone should have told me and I would have grown one," she joked.

He smiled back, and it seemed like their gazes caught and held for an extra-long moment. In order to break the spell, she looked away and added, "You're a good conversationalist."

He frowned at her comment. "Too good."

Their conversation continued for another hour. Carrie discovered that they had a surprising amount in common and agreed on a number of issues; they both loved reading thrillers and were big football fans, especially of the Seattle Seahawks. On others, they were diametrically opposed, the foremost being politics. What struck her, what she found devastatingly attractive about him, was the fact that he could laugh at himself and about Alaska. Finn possessed a wonderful dry wit. When she asked him about the rumor that Alaska was full of bachelors, he replied, "You know what they say about Alaska, don't you? It's where the men are men, and so are the women."

Carrie tried unsuccessfully to hide her laugh, nearly choking with the effort. Once she composed herself she recited something she'd read on a T-shirt. "I heard that if a woman is looking for a husband in Alaska, her odds are good but the goods are odd."

Finn laughed in return, and then it happened

again. Their gazes caught and held for what seemed like an eternity, as neither one of them was keen to break the contact.

Carrie hadn't been joking; she enjoyed Finn's company. The more she got to know him, the stronger her feelings became. Before long, they'd finished off the bottle of wine. Then Finn suggested a rematch of their cribbage game.

"Only this time whoever wins the match gets the bed tonight," he suggested.

Carrie didn't need to think twice about this wager. "You're on." The only decent sleep she'd had the night before had been in Finn's bed, and that had been right before morning. She remembered wrapping herself up in the warm quilts, surrounded by the scent of Finn. The sofa had been lumpy, and half the night she'd shivered with cold. It'd been an uncomfortable experience. The one bonus was having Hennessey with her.

Once again Finn brought out the cribbage board and the cards, and they sat down across from each other as they had before. They cut the cards, and Finn won for the deal. As he shuffled the deck, he made light conversation, almost as if he was looking to distract her.

"You said you work for the *Chicago Herald*?"

"Yeah." She caught the cards as he dealt them to her. "The society page, like I said earlier."

Finn arched his brows.

"I'm fortunate to have a job with such a prestigious newspaper, but quite honestly, Finn, this isn't the type of writing I want to do." The thought of returning to Chicago and immediately being thrust into a series of parties and other social events filled her with dread.

"So that's the reason you went to such desperate lengths to find me."

"Right. An article on you would change everything for me." She glanced up hopefully, but his expression remained blank. He didn't need to tell her his feelings on the matter; they'd already been well stated. But she would write the article. The nearly thirty-six hours she'd spent in his company had proved he was everything he'd claimed in his book and more.

Finn laid down his first card, and she immediately added her own.

Carrie would like to think that it was because she was distracted by their conversation that she handily lost the first game.

"No fair," she muttered.

"Are you suggesting I cheated?" he asked, and seemed to enjoy her loss far too much.

"No, but you distracted me, got me thinking about . . . work."

"That's a convenient excuse, and you know it. The fact is I played a superior game."

"Sure you did," she muttered sarcastically, and reached for the deck. "We're playing for the match, remember."

"Why don't you rest your brain for a few minutes?" Finn suggested, his voice dripping with pretend sympathy. He rose from the table and came to stand behind her, and placed his hands on her shoulders. He rubbed and kneaded the knotted flesh as shivers of awareness shot down her spine. Giving in to his touch, Carrie closed her eyes with a sigh and let her head drop forward. This was divine. It might have been her imagination, but for just an instant she thought she felt his breath against the side of her neck as if he'd bent over to kiss it. His touch was so light, so tender, that it could well have been wishful thinking. From everything Finn had said, he was more than eager to be rid of her.

"What I need," she said, scooting back her chair, anxious to break this trance that had come over her, "is some fresh air." As it was, the room seemed overwhelmingly stuffy. The storm was over, and the night appeared relatively peaceful.

Handing Carrie her coat, Finn walked her to the front door. When she stepped outside, her arms immediately went about her middle as her gaze went to the star-filled heavens. In all her life, Carrie had never seen so many stars. Thousands upon thousands of pinpricks of twinkling light dotted the sky, mesmerizing her.

"Oh, my," she whispered, caught up in the magic of the moment. "This is unbelievable."

Finn came to stand behind her, his hands on her

shoulders. "I never grow tired of this view," he whispered.

"No wonder. It's incredible. Awesome. Breathtaking."

"Now look north." He turned her halfway around so that she faced the arctic.

Carrie gasped. The sky was filled with wave upon wave of color—gold, bronze, and lavender arced across the night sky. "Is that the . . . aurora borealis?"

"You've never seen it before?"

"No. Of course, I've heard about it, but I had no idea it was this beautiful, this dramatic." Just watching the northern lights dance their seductive ballet chased off the chill of the frigid night. Then Carrie realized the source of this toasty feeling was Finn's arms, which surrounded her. He'd tucked his warm body close to hers, warding off the frigid night air.

"Close your eyes," he suggested, his head close to hers.

She did as he requested.

"Do you hear anything?" His breath was warm against her ear.

"Yes," she whispered. "A crackling sound."

"That's the northern lights. Not everyone can hear them."

"Can you?" she asked, barely getting the words out. Having him this close took her breath away.

"Yes." His lips nuzzled her neck, and Carrie sighed audibly.

At the same moment, they both seemed to become aware of the close proximity they shared, knit together, as it were. Without a word, Finn snatched his arms away and returned to the house.

Carrie followed a moment later. Finn was already sitting at the table by the time she closed and latched the door.

"Is your brain working now?" he asked, and cleared his throat, busying himself with shuffling the cards.

"Ah, sure." Her breath trembled slightly, and she hoped that if Finn noticed he wouldn't comment.

"I don't think I've ever seen anything more beautiful," she whispered.

"Me neither," Finn added.

Her mind swirled with the sights and sounds of the innate beauty of Alaska. Inhaling a deep breath, she glanced up to find Finn studying her. She wanted to thank him for sharing his home and his life with her for the past two days. The words were on the tip of her tongue, but she doubted she could murmur a single word without tears leaking from her eyes. These last few minutes had felt almost spiritual, as if she'd been standing in a church and singing hymns of praise.

As best she could, Carrie returned to the game, doing her utmost to pretend nothing out of the ordinary had happened and at the same moment acutely aware that it had.

As luck would have it, she won the second game, but it was no thanks to her skilled card sense. The air between them sizzled and arced much like the northern lights, even as they both chose to ignore it. Perhaps that was for the best, as she would be flying out at first light. An immediate sense of regret filled her. In an amazingly short amount of time, Alaska had won her over, and Finn had, too.

The last cribbage game was close, but in the end Finn won. Little wonder, really, as Carrie's mind was not on the game. She didn't know how she was going to say good-bye when she had the distinct feeling she would be leaving her heart behind.

Finn seemed surprised that he managed to pull out a win. Carrie sighed as she set her cards down and pulled the pegs from the board. She wasn't looking forward to another miserable night on the sofa, but, all things considered, a little discomfort was a small price to pay.

Finn seemed to read her lack of communication as disappointment. "You can have the bed," he told her.

"No. You won," she said much too cheerfully, overcompensating. "I'm the intruder here, remember?" Hennessey would lie at her feet, and he'd keep her company during the night. It wouldn't be so bad, and if she was fortunate enough to catch the flight back to Seattle and then make a quick connection to Chicago, she could sleep on the plane.

Finn reached for the cards and placed them back inside the box.

"I realize having me as your houseguest wasn't what you wanted," she said. "You've been more than gracious, and I want to thank you for putting up with me."

He shrugged, giving the impression it wasn't a big deal. "You aren't so bad."

"Contrary to popular opinion, you aren't, either."

He cracked a smile. "Your opinion?"

"Well," she said, "we didn't exactly start off on the right foot."

"True," he acknowledged.

"Are you still upset with Sawyer?"

He gave the question some consideration before answering. "I'll settle up with him later."

"Don't be too hard on him," Carrie pleaded. "He's a good friend to you."

"He is," Finn agreed.

A short while later Finn announced it was time to call it a night. Despite the fact that it was relatively early, Carrie was tired. He offered her privacy so she could wash up and change clothes. While she was getting ready for bed, Finn contacted Sawyer. She heard the two men talking over the ham radio but was able to make out only half of what was being said.

When she reappeared, Finn said, "Sawyer will arrive early. He'll see you to the terminal and make sure you have a seat on the next available flight out of Fairbanks to Seattle."

"But how . . ." This was the one drawback to her plan. She'd arrived in Alaska, and not knowing when to book her return ticket, she'd left it open. Now she would need to purchase a last-minute ticket back to Chicago at a greatly inflated price. Because of cutbacks with the airlines, almost every plane she'd flown on lately had been packed with passengers like sardines in a can. All she could hope was that there would be a seat available.

"Sawyer works with the airlines. They owe him a favor. Don't worry—it's all being taken care of."

Although the two friends seemed to have reached an understanding, it appeared Finn was still eager to send her on her way. She had to believe he'd experienced the same tenderness and awareness she had. The electricity between them was powerful enough to light up a city block. Surely he felt it, too. Like her, it probably made him uncomfortable, and the best way he could deal with it was to send her packing.

Carrie could find no way of telling him that she wouldn't mind spending a few more days. That was crazy thinking on her part, but she couldn't shake this reluctance to leave. It seemed they were just beginning to come to an understanding, a willingness to explore whatever it was that was happening between them.

"Time for lights out," Finn said, and his voice sounded odd, regretful.

"Right." How she wished she knew what he was thinking.

He brought out the blankets and pillow for her. Carrie held out her arms to take the load, but he hesitated. "You're sure about this? I don't mind taking the sofa tonight."

"That's generous, but a deal is a deal."

"Okay, your choice."

"Right again."

He built up the fire and then returned to the bedroom. Carrie made her bed, sat on the sofa, and wrapped her arms around her bent knees.

To her surprise, Finn hadn't mentioned her article again. She half expected him to argue his case, demand that she honor his privacy. Instead, he'd avoided the subject entirely. He hadn't sought out this notoriety, even if he had written one of the most intriguing and interesting books of the year. Although there was so much more she wanted to know about him, it seemed wrong to press the point. As far as she was concerned, the article was fast becoming secondary to everything else.

Eventually Carrie fell asleep, her mind full of Finn, the man she was just beginning to know and wished to know much better. He wasn't like anyone she'd ever met, which intrigued her all the more. The businessmen and the community leaders she met at social functions were as different as night and day from a man like Finn, and yet she was strongly attracted to him. She found him more appealing than anyone she'd recently dated, that was for sure.

For the last few months she'd gone out with Dave Schneider a number of times. It wasn't anywhere close to serious. She enjoyed his company, but as a salesman, he traveled frequently, and their schedules didn't often mesh. While she had ample opportunities to date, the men she usually met were too slick, too polished, too caught up in themselves and their careers to appeal to her. She couldn't see making a life with anyone in her current social network.

At some point during the night, Carrie stirred awake to find Finn kneeling over her. Leaning up on one elbow, she rubbed the sleep from her eyes. "Is it morning already?" she asked. A sense of dread filled her. She didn't want to leave—not yet. Not so soon.

He shook his head. "Take the bed. I can't sleep."

She wanted to argue but could see it would do her no good. Tossing aside the blanket, she started to get up but instead Finn effortlessly lifted her into his arms and carried her into his bedroom.

He pressed her down on the feather mattress

and, leaning forward, kissed her brow. "Sleep tight," he whispered.

Reaching up, she cupped the side of his face, his beard prickling her palm, and she smiled at him softly, silently wishing that he would kiss her for real. She moistened her lips, inviting him to take what she offered. Surely he could read the longing in her eyes; surely he knew what she wanted. Instead, he reluctantly straightened and left the room.

Carrie tried but found she was unable to fall back to sleep. Apparently, Finn wasn't having much luck, either, because she could hear him moving about the outer room as if he was as restless as she was.

Seeking a comfortable position, Carrie tried sleeping on one side, then the other, and finally lay on her back, staring up at the ceiling. His room had a window, and after what seemed like an eternity, she tossed the thick covers away and climbed out of bed. Her feet made no sound as she walked over to the window and pushed the curtain to one side. Staring into the night, she looked up at the heavens.

Once more she was struck by the brilliant dark sky with countless stars. The moon was full and lit up the frozen lake like stage lighting. No wonder Finn loved Alaska. This was a magical place, beautiful and uncomplicated, so far removed from the craziness of city life.

After a while she returned to the main room to

find Finn sitting at his desk. Right away he heard her and whirled around in his chair. He seemed surprised to find her awake.

"I couldn't sleep, either," she confessed.

He immediately closed the document on his computer, as if he didn't want her to see what he was writing.

"Another book?" she dared to ask.

"If I admit it, will you put that in the article?" The question was more of an accusation.

"I . . . I don't know."

He closed the lid to the laptop.

"If you're writing a sequel, I can tell you your readers will be more than thrilled."

He ignored the comment and glanced at his wrist. "Sawyer should be here within the hour."

"Already?" It seemed far too soon. She wasn't eager to leave. Finn's father's wedding band remained in her jeans pocket, and she thought to simply leave it in the cabin for him to find once she was gone. However, seeing his reaction to it earlier prompted her to keep it for now. She'd return the gold ring to his mother at Christmas.

Sure enough, within the hour the sound of an approaching aircraft filled the house. The noise seemed to multiply, stirring up the atmosphere inside the cabin, building anticipation.

"That must be Sawyer," Finn said.

Carrie nodded. Dragging her carry-on to the

door, she checked the cabin to be sure she hadn't left anything behind.

Finn stood in the kitchen sipping coffee, as if, in these final moments, he wanted to keep as much distance between them as possible.

Hennessey barked, and rushed to the door, wanting out. Finn opened it just as the float plane bounced against the solid ice and skidded for several feet in the surrounding moonlight.

"The trip out here was my first experience in a single-engine plane," she said, more to fill the silence than to make a statement.

Without commenting, Finn reached for her suitcase and carried it outside. Carrie followed, a lump in her throat. That she should get all emotional over this farewell was an embarrassment. She was determined not to let Finn see how discombobulated she felt. It was ridiculous. She barely knew this man. He'd let it be known she was a nuisance and considered himself well rid of her.

By the time she reached the plane, Finn had the passenger door open and her suitcase stored inside. He exchanged a few short sentences with Sawyer, but she couldn't hear what he said over the roar of the engine.

Carrie made sure she had a smile in place when he turned to face her. She hadn't thought what her last words to him would be, and so she said what came instinctively.

"Thank you for everything."

Cupping her shoulders, Finn looked down on her, his dark eyes as intense as she could ever remember seeing them.

She met his gaze, wanting to tell him without words how much the last two days had meant to her, and how impressed she was with the man he was. She longed to thank him for opening her eyes to what it was to be with a man who was passionate about life and who had shared that passion through stories of life in Alaska.

Staring down at her, his hands tightened. He murmured something she didn't understand, and then he pulled her close as if he couldn't help himself and lowered his mouth to hers.

Carrie gave a small cry of welcome and gratitude and clung to him. Finn's hands cupped her face as he tilted her head to receive his kiss, which felt urgent and needy, needs that mirrored her own.

For a moment the sheer wonder of it nearly caused Carrie's knees to collapse from under her. This was exactly what she wanted, what she'd hoped would happen. And his kiss was everything she could have imagined. More. Without fully being aware of what she was doing, Carrie locked her arms around his neck and kissed him back, wanting to return everything that he had given her.

After a long moment, Finn gradually released her from the kiss, but he still hugged her close and tight against him, half lifting her from the frozen lakebed.

"Good-bye, Finn," she whispered close to his ear.

He kissed her neck and then whispered back, "Good-bye."

She started to climb into the airplane but Finn stopped her by gripping hold of her hand. He looked deep into her eyes as if to gauge her reaction, and then leaned forward and said, "Carrie?"

"Yes?" Her heart was in her eyes. Could it be possible that he would ask her to stay? Did it seem as wrong to him as it did to her that they should part now? Surely he felt the very things she did.

Leaning in close, he kissed her one last time and then said, "Don't write the article."

Chapter Seven

❄

The wheels of the Boeing 737 bounced against the O'Hare tarmac as the plane landed safely, jolting Carrie out of a light slumber. She hadn't slept as much on the long flight back to Chicago as she'd hoped, which wasn't surprising. She glanced at her watch and realized she was still on Alaska time.

Finn time.

He'd asked her not to write the article. Surely he understood what that meant. She'd explained to him what this piece could do for her career. It would change everything for her. As she boarded the flight in Seattle, Carrie was forced to ask herself if invading his privacy was worth the cost. Perhaps the answer should seem obvious, but she still wasn't sure what she would do.

The temptation to ignore his request was strong. In every likelihood she might never see or hear from the elusive Finn Dalton again. Surely he understood how unreasonable he was being, how selfish, but then . . . wasn't she being selfish, too?

Monday morning, after sleeping on it, Carrie
had her answer. She wouldn't finish her story about
Finn Dalton. No matter what happened or didn't
happen between them, it wouldn't be worth the
price. Every woman Finn had ever known had be-
trayed him, and she was determined not to be one
of them. If there was a chance he would ever learn
to trust and love again, then the path would start
with her. It meant sacrifice on her end, but all she
could do was hope that someday he would thank
her. Someone else was sure to find him, one day,
and the author of *Alone* would be exposed to the
world, but she wouldn't be the reporter who did it.

Carrie wasn't at her desk two minutes before
Sophie showed up, nearly bouncing with energy
and excitement. "Well?" she asked expectantly.
"How'd it go?"

Glancing up at her friend, Carrie made sure her
face didn't give anything away. "Go?" she repeated,
as though she didn't understand the question.

"Did you find him?"

"You mean Finn Dalton?" Carrie's mind scram-
bled with ways of answering without telling an
outright lie. "It was a needle-in-a-haystack idea. I
must have been out of my mind to think I could jet
off to Alaska and stumble upon the one man half
the world is dying to read about."

"Yeah, but did you find him?"

Leave it to Sophie to press the point. "Honestly,
would I be sitting here so glum if I had?" She was

in a blue funk, but it was due to other reasons. Lack of sleep, for one; missing Finn, for another. Really missing Finn. Thinking back on their final minutes together, there'd been a hundred things she wished she'd said, and she hadn't managed to get out even one coherent thought. Well, other than a generic "thank you for everything." And "goodbye." How lame was that! Nor had she said goodbye to Hennessey.

Sawyer had certainly been curious, drilling her with questions much in the same way Sophie was just now.

"Seems like you two got along just fine," the bush pilot had commented.

"Not at first."

He'd chuckled. "I can well imagine. You won him over, though, I see."

"Did I?" she asked Sawyer. She might never know the answer to that.

"I thought for sure you had a chance," Sophie said, dragging Carrie back into the dreary present. Monday mornings were bad enough, but this Monday was even worse, especially on only a few hours' rest.

Carrie couldn't stop thinking about Finn, couldn't stop dreaming about him. If any two people were dissimilar, it was them, and yet the attraction had been magnetic and powerful. Now that she was gone, she wondered if she remained on his mind the way he did on hers.

"How disappointing for you," Sophie said, her eyes wide with sympathy.

"I really thought I had a line on him, too," Carrie confessed. Only she was the one who'd fallen—hook, line, and sinker.

"You located his mother, though, right?" Sophie leaned against the side of Carrie's desk and crossed her arms.

"Yes, and that got me really excited, but mother and son have been estranged since Finn was ten years old. All she really knew was that he was living in Alaska, and that it was close to Fairbanks. Unfortunately, her directions were too vague to help."

"What happened when you got to Fairbanks?" Sophie hopped up onto the corner of Carrie's desk as though she intended to stay awhile.

"Well, for one thing, I discovered I wasn't the only reporter who'd arrived out of the blue searching for the elusive Finn Dalton."

"Who did you ask?"

"Bush pilots. From what I heard, Finn is a pilot himself." Carrie had learned from Sawyer on their flight back that Finn owned a plane, which was currently in Fairbanks for a routine maintenance check.

"How do you know that?"

"Word of mouth."

"Whose word?"

"Does it matter?" Carrie was growing irritated

with Sophie's questions. In retrospect, she wished she hadn't said anything. At the time, she'd been too excited to keep the information to herself.

"Did any of those pilots give you anything you could use?" Sophie seemed obsessed with this, and Carrie was finding it difficult to give her friend ambiguous answers.

"Don't you have work to do?" Carrie asked instead.

"Yes, but it seems to me the bush pilots must know Finn and would tell you something, anything."

"Wrong. Finn has very loyal friends."

"You could have bribed them; did you think of that?"

"Sophie, please, it's my first day back and I've got a ton of stuff to catch up on."

"All right, all right. I just hope you aren't too disappointed."

She sighed. "I'm not. I gave finding him my best shot and turned up empty. I can't do anything more than that."

"So you're going to give up just like that?" Sophie appeared stunned. "That doesn't sound like you at all. When you left Chicago, you had that bloodhound look in your eyes, your nose to the ground with a determination to go above and beyond to find this guy. Now it seems like you hardly care at all."

"Maybe that's because I'm looking to keep the

job I already have. Now, please leave me alone, would you?" Carrie was fast losing her patience. Sophie made it nearly impossible to continue this charade.

"It's not like you to be so secretive." Sophie leaped off the desk and stood staring at Carrie as though she no longer recognized her friend. Then she sadly shook her head and returned to her own cubicle.

The tension between Carrie's shoulder blades gradually relaxed. She'd passed the first test—at least she hoped she had. Now all she had to do was concentrate on putting her energy into the society page and making the most of her current position. She couldn't help being disappointed. When it came to Finn, she'd made her decision, and right or wrong, she was sticking to it. She cared too much to betray him.

Her morning was completely eaten up by answering emails. She worked straight through lunch and grabbed coffee and a muffin around two. Her phone rang just as she sat back down at her desk. She reached for her extension with one hand and her coffee with the other.

"Carrie Slayton."

"Hi." The lone word sounded as if it had come from the moon.

Carrie nearly came out of her chair. It was Finn. "What are you doing calling me here?" she whispered in a near panic. She leaned halfway over her desk and kept her voice as low as possible.

"I wanted to see if you got back okay."

"I did." Carrie cupped her hand over the phone's mouthpiece. "You shouldn't phone me here; it's dangerous."

"Do you want me to phone you?"

"Yes, oh, yes." She didn't bother to hide her enthusiasm. The sound of his voice washed over her, warming her, filling her with a rush of joy.

"Give me your cell number, then," he suggested.

She rattled it off and had him repeat it to be sure he'd written it down correctly. "Are you on the satellite phone?" she asked, her heart hammering wildly.

"Yes."

"I thought you said it was expensive."

"Very."

She smiled and closed her eyes at the happiness that settled over her. "Does that mean you miss me?"

He grumbled a phrase she didn't understand. "It must," he muttered. "Does that make you happy?"

"Very."

He chuckled. "Can I call you tonight?"

"Yes," she said automatically, then realized she was covering an art gallery opening. "No, sorry. I've got an assignment this evening."

"Will there be lots of men around?"

"Tons."

He grumbled again in the same vague way he had earlier.

"Are you jealous?"

"Should I be?"

Carrie smiled. "That depends. If you're intimidated by clean-shaven, handsome men in slick black suits who hardly know which end of a car has the gas tank, then be my guest."

"Guess I'm in the clear after all."

"I'd say so," she agreed.

"What time will you be home?"

Carrie wished she could give him a definite time. "Can't say. Hopefully before eleven, but I can never predict how long these events will last."

"Which is one reason you dislike this society-page reporting as much as you do."

"You could say that." She clung to the phone, not wanting to end the call, even if the cost was exorbitant. "How did you get my number?"

"Not much of an investigative reporter if you need to ask that. I called the newspaper and asked to be connected to the society-page editor."

"Of course." Plainly, she wasn't thinking clearly. It came to her then the real reason behind his call. As much as she wanted to believe it was because he couldn't live without hearing the sound of her voice, she knew otherwise. "You called because you want to know if I've reached a decision, didn't you?"

He didn't answer right away. "It's more than that, I . . ."

"I know what I'm going to do."

The line went still and silent. "And what did you decide?"

"Rest easy, Dr. Livingston, your secrets are safe with me."

"Doctor who?"

"Livingston. All the world was on a search to find him, too, if you remember."

"Oh, right."

"You could email me."

"What's your email address?"

She gave him her private email address, unwilling to risk someone from the office stumbling upon their communication.

"I should go," he said.

"I know." As much as she wanted to talk to him, someone might overhear and connect the dots. Lowering her voice, she added, "Call me tonight, okay?" It probably wasn't smart to let him know how eager she was to hear from him again, but she couldn't stop herself. She was falling for this guy. And falling hard.

"Okay. Eleven your time, eight mine."

"Perfect." No matter what, she intended to leave the art show in plenty of time to be home for Finn's call.

* * *

Somehow Carrie got through the evening, smiling at all the right times, taking down names, and making the most of the event for the following day's newspaper. Harry, the staff photographer, glanced her way suspiciously a couple of times.

"What's up?" he asked, as they hurriedly walked toward the parking garage. She still had to write the story and get it in before the press deadline.

"What do you mean?" She played innocent, although she was practically trotting in her eagerness to escape.

"I've never seen you in such an all-fired hurry like this. You meeting someone later?"

"No," she said, in complete honesty.

Harry shrugged. "Whatever you say."

Carrie arrived back at her condo fifteen minutes early. She kicked off her shoes, wiggled out of her dress, shimmied out of her pantyhose, and grabbed her warmest pjs. She tossed back the covers to her bed, climbed in, and sat cross-legged with her cell phone clasped in her hand, waiting for Finn's call.

Twice she caught herself falling asleep, so when the phone rang, it surprised her and she nearly dropped it.

"Hi," she said, and knew she sounded breathless. "You're right on time."

"Hi, yourself."

Right away she noticed that the call had a different sound to it. "Where are you?" she asked.

"Fairbanks. I figured it would make talking to you a whole lot more convenient."

"That explains why you sound as if you're in the next room instead of outer space."

"The first call did come from outer space."

She grinned. "Exactly."

"So how did the art show opening go?"

"Harry was suspicious."

"Who's Harry?"

He sounded worried, which thrilled her. "The staff photographer, who's at least fifty and has a half-dozen kids."

"What do you mean he was suspicious?"

This was a bit more difficult to explain. "He could tell I couldn't wait to get out of the show; I kept glancing at my watch."

"Maybe it would be better if we emailed."

She thought about that for a moment. "You're probably right."

"We won't need to worry about the time difference, then."

"Agreed."

"You sound reluctant. Is there a reason?"

To this point, she hadn't done a decent job of hiding her feelings toward him, so now probably wasn't a good time to start. "I like hearing the sound of your voice."

He didn't say anything for a moment. "I like hearing your voice, too. I have something for you."

"What?" Her curiosity was instantly piqued.

"It's a surprise."

"A gift?"

"I wouldn't exactly call it that . . . it's something I'd like you to have. I've already sent it off. I shipped it overnight, so you should have it tomorrow or Wednesday at the latest."

"Oh, Finn, I can't imagine what it could be." Her mind toyed with several possibilities. She'd seen a number of items on the shelves in his cabin that interested her. A beautiful piece of scrimshaw was the first thing that came to mind, and another was a small wood carving. During her short visit she hadn't seen evidence that he carved wood, but it seemed like something that would interest him.

They spoke for a full hour, until Carrie found it impossible to smother her yawns any longer.

"You're exhausted," he whispered. "I need to let you go."

"No, just a few minutes longer," she pleaded, yawning again.

"Carrie, you're practically falling asleep while on the phone. I'll email you so when you wake up there'll be a message waiting for you."

"Promise?"

"Promise."

She smiled sleepily and admitted, "I didn't sleep very well the last couple of nights."

"Me neither."

"I will tonight."

"So will I. Sweet dreams," he whispered.

They would be sweet because they would be filled with Finn.

Six and a half hours later Carrie woke to the sound of her bedside alarm, feeling rested. Stretching her arms above her head, she arched her back and smiled contentedly. Then, remembering Finn's promise, she hurried out of bed and brewed a single cup of coffee while she logged on to her computer. Sure enough, Finn had sent her an email that included the tracking number for the surprise he had mailed her.

Later that same afternoon, a midsize box was delivered to her desk. Carrie knew immediately that it was from Finn.

"What's that?" Sophie asked, coming out of her cubicle.

"I don't know." She lifted the box and carefully shook it. That didn't tell her anything, though.

"Who's it from?"

Carrie pretended to read the return address. "A friend," she said nonchalantly.

"Male or female?"

"Male. Like I said, a friend."

"Well, for heaven's sake, don't keep me in suspense. Open it."

Carrie was more than curious herself. She tore open the box to find it filled with those irritating packing peanuts. She had to dig deep into the box before she found her treasure.

When she pulled it free, Sophie immediately

started to laugh. "Is this someone's idea of a joke?" she asked.

Carrie didn't have an answer. This was quite possibly the very last thing she would even have guessed that Finn could possibly mail her.

Inside the box, carefully packaged and protected with packing peanuts, was an antique toaster.

Chapter Eight

❉

From: girlygirl@chicago.com
Sent: November 13, 2013
To: alaskaman@fairbankscable.com
Subject: A toaster?

Finn,
You spent a fortune to mail me a toaster? My
friend Sophie thinks it's some silly joke, but I
know you, and this isn't a joke. What's the story?
   Carrie

From: alaskaman@fairbankscable.com
Sent: November 13, 2013
To: girlygirl@chicago.com
Subject: Yes, a toaster

Carrie
You are a girly girl, aren't you? The picture of
you wearing your high-heeled boots slipping and

sliding across the ice on my lake, tugging your suitcase behind you, plays in my mind.

Yes, a toaster, and it isn't a joke. I want you to have it. I'll call you later tonight. Eleven your time. Work for you?

Finn

From: girlygirl@chicago.com
Sent: November 13, 2013
To: alaskaman@fairbankscable.com
Subject: Waiting for you

Yes, Finn, I'll be here. Call anytime. I'm planning on listening to Christmas music, getting in the mood for the holidays, and sipping hot chocolate. Wish you were here.

Carrie

Finn leaned back in his chair and slowly exhaled. The picture of Carrie sipping hot chocolate and listening to Christmas music while waiting for his call filled his mind. That shouldn't surprise him. Carrie Slayton had dominated his thoughts from the moment she'd left Alaska. And if he was honest, even before that, too.

It wasn't supposed to be like this. He'd assumed that once she was out of sight he'd be able to forget her. That hadn't happened. If anything, it was ten times worse—thoughts of Carrie hounded him. He went to sleep thinking about her, and when he woke, she was right there, filling his mind and his heart.

Even Hennessey missed her. She'd won over his dog in record time, and now that she was gone, Hennessey moped around, his tail between his legs. His eighty-pound dog acted like a lost and lonely puppy. That shouldn't be any surprise, seeing that Finn had reacted much the same since she'd left.

Whatever was happening to him didn't sit well. This was a dead-end relationship, and the sooner he accepted that, the better off they both would be.

And yet . . . Finn couldn't forget Carrie. It was bad enough that she was in the forefront of his thoughts during the day, but it was getting worse, as she had invaded his dreams as well. The kiss they shared was what had started it all. He'd managed to restrain himself from taking her in his arms until the very last minute. Once she was gone, life would right itself again. He even managed to convince himself this attraction was a simple matter of proximity. Naturally, they were attracted to each other, he'd reasoned. They were both young and single, and they'd been cooped up together for nearly forty-eight hours. As soon as she was gone, life would return to normal.

Carrie had been back in Chicago nearly a week now, and it hadn't happened. It was as if Carrie had indelibly stamped his heart with her own brand and he was marked for life.

What Finn feared most was repeating the mistake his father had made and falling in love with the wrong woman. After his mother left, Finn's father was never the same again. When they learned Joan had remarried, it had about killed the man. In his entire life, his father had only loved one woman. Now, just like his father, Finn was irresistibly drawn to a woman who was his opposite in far too many ways. It was enough to send warning bells ringing so loud they threatened to activate an avalanche.

He glanced at his watch, calculating the time difference between Fairbanks and Chicago. Carrie would be home by now, unless she was meeting a friend for dinner. Instantly, Finn's gut tightened and his blood pressure spiked. He couldn't bear the thought of Carrie with another man. It drove him to madness. Never having experienced jealousy this strong, he found the emotion distressing and worrisome.

This was the end of it. He was finished walking around like a wounded moose. He made the decision right then and there not to contact her again. But an immediate sense of emptiness and loss settled over him. After talking to her nearly every day and sharing an almost constant flow of emails, cutting off their relationship abruptly wouldn't be good. He'd ease himself out of it, he reasoned, and instantly he felt better. Baby steps. That decided, he made a second decision—no further contact with her for the rest of the day.

Restless now, he stalked the condo and then decided to get out and do something. He headed to a local hangout, had a beer with one of his friends, and before he knew it, he was back in his condo.

Immediately his gaze flew to the telephone. He tilted back his head and stared at the ceiling. Unable to stop himself, he reached for his cell. He wouldn't contact her tomorrow. But for now she was impossible to resist. He dialed Carrie's number, as eager to hear the sound of her voice as a starved man is for nourishment. Oh, yes, he had it bad.

The phone rang, and Carrie nearly stumbled over her own feet in her eagerness to get to it.

"Hello." She nearly blurted out Finn's name but stopped herself in the nick of time. They'd spoken every day, sometimes two and three times. Finn had upgraded his cell phone so they could now text when he was in Fairbanks. He seemed to commute between the cabin and his condo on a regular basis.

"Carrie, it's Mom. What's up with you, honey? We've hardly spoken to you since you got back to Chicago. The only time we've talked is when Dad and I called you about your Christmas gift."

"Oh, Mom." Carrie tried to hide the disappointment in her voice. "I'm sorry. I've been meaning to call." Which was true.

"I have to tell you, honey, Thanksgiving just won't be the same without you."

"I know. I wish I could be there, too." Carrie was upset about it herself. This was the choice she'd made before flying to Alaska. The thought of spending the holiday alone filled her with dismay. She would miss the huge family gathering for the first time in her life.

"It isn't like you not to call."

This was a bit more difficult to explain. "Well, for one thing, being away from my desk for so long means I'm swamped at the office."

"But, honey, you know your father and I are dying to hear what happened in Fairbanks; we've only heard snippets. Tell us more about Finn Dalton. Everyone here wants to know what he's like and if the things he wrote about in his book could really be true."

Carrie's stomach twisted in a huge knot. "Mom, who have you told about me meeting Finn?"

Her mother must have heard the panic in Carrie's voice, because she asked, "Are you keeping it a secret?"

"Yes," she nearly shouted. "This is important. Please don't mention my meeting Finn to anyone, okay?"

"If that's what you want, but surely once the article—"

"There isn't going to be an article."

"But I thought—"

"I know, but I've come to know Finn and want to respect his privacy." Her voice softened as her mind traveled back to the moment when he'd passionately kissed her and held her in his arms before she boarded the flight with Sawyer.

"Carrie?" her mother said. "You better tell me what happened between you and this wilderness man. And don't try to hide it from me. Clearly there's something going on here; I can hear it in your voice."

Carrie swore her mother had special radar where she was concerned. It seemed she was unable to keep anything from her mother, and perhaps that was a good thing. Besides, Carrie felt like she would burst if she couldn't talk about her feelings for Finn. The way she'd been lately with her head in a cloud was causing all kinds of speculation among her friends, especially Sophie.

"I'm falling in love with Finn Dalton." It felt good to admit it, good to say out loud what was already in her heart.

Her announcement was followed by a short, stunned silence. "After only two days?"

"Does it sound crazy?" Then, before she could stop herself, Carrie blurted out nearly the entire story right to the point when he'd kissed her and asked Carrie not to write the article.

"Love is a strong emotion after such a short acquaintance," her mother warned softly.

"I agree, I do, but I can't help how I feel. It was all sorts of crazy and wonderful. Finn and I were playing cribbage, and I looked up at him and something happened. Something physical. All at once my pulse started racing and I looked at this burly, unshaven man and I thought Finn Dalton was the most attractive, appealing man I'd ever met. At first I tried to ignore it, tried to rationalize this attraction away with an entire list of excuses why a relationship between us simply wouldn't work. It hasn't done me any good. And since I've left Fairbanks, that feeling has grown stronger and stronger. He's on my mind nearly every minute of the day. It's like I'm only half alive since I returned."

"Oh, dear, you do have it bad," her mother said with a sympathetic sigh.

Carrie didn't need her mother to tell her the obvious.

"But surely there's a way for you to write the article and maintain the relationship," her mother suggested. "You could write it and give it to him to read and approve. That way he would have control over what information was released to the public."

"I thought of that, too." Her mind had worked its way around several scenarios, but in the end she feared even approaching Finn with the idea would be a breach of trust.

"Doesn't he realize what that article would do for you and your career?"

"He knows. Finn didn't ask for this notoriety when he wrote his book. He doesn't want the focus to be on him but on the beauty of the land and the adventures that await those willing to explore the great outdoors."

"Well, he should have thought of that before he wrote the book."

In theory, Carrie agreed, but Finn had had no idea how popular his tales of life in Alaska would be. "Do you know why he decided to write *Alone*?" she said, thinking back over a recent conversation. "He said he saw what was happening to men and boys in America, addicted to computer games. People are not getting outside and enjoying the outdoors and the wilderness nearly enough. He wanted to awaken a sense of adventure in people to get excited about what's outside their front doors."

"It worked," her mother said. "I wonder if he knows all the outdoor groups his book has inspired."

"I told him about that, but I don't believe he truly grasps the extent of it. I think he finds it all rather humbling. Finn never sought the national spotlight. In hindsight, I wonder if he'd have written the book if he'd known what a sensation it would cause." His motives were good. If Carrie had learned anything in the time they'd been together, it was that he deeply loved Alaska and that he had respect for nature.

"Sweetheart, just where do you think this relationship is headed?" her mother asked, clearly concerned for Carrie.

She appreciated her mother's question. "I don't know, and I don't think Finn does, either. For right now, we're taking it one day at a time. And, Mom, you won't believe what he sent me. He actually mailed me a toaster. It looks like an antique."

"A what?"

"You heard me right. A toaster. I realize it probably has some special significance to him that he wanted to share with me. But if that's the case, he hasn't explained it yet. I have it in my kitchen."

Her mother chuckled. "Oh, dear, Carrie. Listen, honey. I don't want to burst your bubble. You're new into this relationship, and this is a honeymoon period, but soon enough reality is going to settle in. I don't want you to set yourself up for heartache. Just be careful, okay?"

"I will, Mom." And while she agreed, Carrie couldn't help thinking that love would see her and Finn through any obstacle. She was crazy for this guy, toaster and all.

Once they'd finished chatting, Carrie returned to her computer. Finn was scheduled to phone, but he hadn't, which concerned her. Just then her cell phone chirped, letting her know she had a text message.

Carrie grabbed her phone.

What are you doing?

Listening to "Mary, Did You Know," which was playing softly in the background. It was one of her favorite Christmas songs.

A little early for Christmas music, isn't it?

Reading Finn's text, she punched in her answer. Not for me. Besides, you have your Christmas decorations in your cabin. How are they holding up?

He responded within seconds. Snowflakes dangling from my ceiling. Utterly ridiculous.

But they are still up?

Yes. Remind me of you.

Very sweet, thank you.

I look at them and think of the stars we saw that night.

That incredible starry night. Makes me miss being with you all the more.

G-r-r-r. Hennessey misses you.

Hennessey? What about you?

Finn texted back a smiley face.

Carrie laughed. She had just tucked her cell phone in her jeans pocket when it rang. A sweet joy went through her when she saw it was Finn. So she was going to get her phone call after all.

"Hi," she said.

"Hi. It seemed ridiculous to be texting you when we could be talking."

"I agree. You must be in Fairbanks. I had no idea you spent that much time in town."

"Generally, I don't. Fact is, until these last few days, it's been weeks since I was at the condo."

In other words, he'd come into town in order to be able to communicate more easily with her. Finn wasn't a romantic man. The fact that he would mail her a toaster told her it was highly unlikely that he would look to win her heart with flowers or jewels.

"I had bread from my toaster for breakfast this morning." She mentioned this so he'd know that she'd put his gift to good use.

"That isn't much of a breakfast."

"I was in a hurry to get to church. I'm in the choir, and we had an early practice for the Christmas pageant."

"You sing, too?"

"I'm an alto. I harmonize well. Come to think of it, I play well with others, too."

"Clearly you're a woman of many talents."

She ran her fingers through a tousle of dark curls. "I'd like to think so."

They spoke for an hour until her cell phone battery was nearly depleted. Before they ended their conversation, Finn told her he would be out of reach for a couple of days, checking the pipeline outside of Fairbanks.

"I'll survive," she assured him. Although she made it sound as if it wouldn't trouble her, she was already dreading not hearing from him.

"Maybe you'll survive, but I'm not sure about me."

"Finn." She laughed, her heart warmed by his words. "That's the most romantic thing you've ever said to me."

He snickered softly. "I'm not a romantic kind of guy."

"I sort of guessed that, which makes these little comments precious. I'll miss hearing from you, too."

He grumbled as if he didn't quite know how to respond.

"Oh, before you go, I wanted to tell you that I'll be in Chicago for Thanksgiving—it'll be my first alone, but I'll be in Seattle for Christmas." She mentioned this with the hope that he would take the hint and fly down for a visit. Seattle was relatively close to him, much closer than Chicago. When he didn't immediately pick up on her hint, she added, "My parents feel bad that I won't be with everyone on Thanksgiving, so for Christmas they're giving me a ticket to fly home."

"Good idea."

He hesitated and then asked with what seemed like reluctance, "Have you talked to my mother since your return?"

"No. I haven't had a chance to get in touch with her. I know she's anxious to hear what happened with the ring." Truth was, Carrie felt terrible having to tell Joan that her plan had backfired. Given the turn in her relationship with Finn, maybe she'd hang on to the ring a bit longer, rather than returning it at Christmas, as she'd planned.

"Does my mother need anything?" he asked. His voice was low, concerned, and different from the teasing banter they had exchanged earlier.

"She's well physically, if that's what you're asking. As for her other needs, there was only one thing I picked up on."

"And that is?"

Carrie knew she was wading into deep waters, but she felt she had to try. Finn's mother had entrusted her with something precious, and she wanted to repay the favor. "She needs her son."

His response was a dismissive snort.

"That's what I thought you'd say."

"I'll be in touch in a couple of days."

"Okay." Not being able to talk to him for even a short amount of time would feel like an eternity. "I have a busy week with the holidays close and all."

"You going to be with Harry?" he asked, mentioning the staff photographer.

Now it was Carrie's turn to hesitate. "For a couple of events, and then I'll be out the Tuesday before Thanksgiving with a . . . friend."

"A male friend?"

She didn't want to mislead Finn. "Dave and I set this up a while ago, Finn. Trust me, you don't have anything to worry about."

He grumbled something unintelligible.

This was another romantic jewel he offered her without even realizing what he was doing. Carrie's smile took up her entire face. "I love it that you're jealous."

"I'm not jealous," he insisted. "Just concerned. No guy likes the idea of his girl spending time with some other guy."

Oh, boy, he walked right into that. "Am I your girl, Finn?"

"Would a guy send you a toaster if you weren't?" he asked.

"You have me there," she said, smiling. Her phone beeped, reminding her that her battery was almost dead. "I really need to recharge my phone. Fly safely, Finn."

"I always fly safely."

"And hug Hennessey for me."

"What about me?"

"Do you want a hug, too?"

"I'll take that as a bare minimum, but I'd like a whole lot more."

"So would I," she whispered, before she ended the call.

Chapter Nine

"What's with you lately?" Sophie asked Wednesday afternoon as they waited in line to order lunch.

"What do you mean?" Carrie pretended to be reading the menu posted on the wall above the cashier. She almost always ordered the same thing. Egg-salad sandwich on wheat with a small garden salad, ranch dressing on the side.

"Ever since you were away you've been . . . I don't know, different, I guess. Happier."

Carrie smiled. Oh, yes, she was happier.

"You've met someone, haven't you?"

How could she deny it and keep a straight face? "Could be."

"Carrie, it isn't like you to keep secrets. It's the guy who sent you that joke gift, isn't it?"

"The toaster isn't a joke, but yes, and if you must know, his name is Paul." *Middle name,* she added silently.

"Paul is from Seattle?"

Technically, that was where Finn was born. "Yes."

"What's his story? Is he married? Is that the reason you're keeping this to yourself?"

"Married? Of course not." It irritated Carrie that Sophie would believe she'd even consider dating a married man. "You know, I'm thinking I'll order the curried chicken-salad sandwich instead of my usual egg salad. I'm in the mood to live on the edge."

"You're changing the subject."

"Yes. Get the hint, Sophie. I'll tell you more when there's more to tell. For now, I'm not talking."

"Fine, then, have it your way," Sophie pouted.

Carrie's cell phone beeped.

I'm back. It was Finn.

"It's him, isn't it?" Sophie demanded, attempting to look over Carrie's shoulder.

Carrie ignored her and stepped up to the counter to place her lunch order. When it was Sophie's turn, she grabbed her phone and texted back. Can't talk now.

Have you missed me?

Oh, yes. Am having lunch with snoopy friend.

Got ya. In an hour?

OK.

She dropped her phone back inside her purse just before Sophie rejoined her. They found a vacant spot, set their order numbers on the table, and then went for their drinks. Carrie was antsy to talk to

Finn. Two days had never seemed so long. She was dying to know if he'd missed talking to her nearly half as much as she'd missed chatting with him.

Carrie had her coffee and Sophie her soft drink when they reclaimed their table.

"We should talk about the party," Sophie said. Their orders arrived, and she thanked the waiter with a smile.

Party? What party? Then Carrie remembered that just before she left for Alaska they'd decided to host a small party in Carrie's condo after Thanksgiving. Her place was bigger and could accommodate more guests.

"I was thinking the first week of December. Friday or Saturday."

"Sounds good." Carrie mentally reviewed her calendar. As far as she could remember, both days were clear.

"If we don't get the word out soon, it won't happen. Besides, everyone gets so busy this time of year."

Sophie was a party girl, and Carrie had agreed, looking to make the most of the holiday season.

"I thought we'd throw together a few appetizers and bring out the eggnog. Four or five couples should keep it manageable. We don't need to make a huge thing out of it—just a few friends getting together to celebrate the holidays."

"Ah, sure."

Sophie reached for the pepper shaker and doused

her Oriental chicken salad. "You going to ask Dave?"

He was Carrie's Tuesday-night theater date. "Probably not."

"Because of this other guy?"

Sophie was digging for information, but Carrie wasn't going to let anything out. In response, she shrugged.

"David's a prize, you know."

"For someone else, maybe."

"From what I've seen, he'd like to be more than a friend."

Carrie had sensed as much. But even before she met Finn she knew it wasn't happening for her. She felt vastly different when it came to Finn. He was a man's man. Dave was personable and fun, but he wouldn't be able to last a day on his own in an Alaskan winter. He wouldn't even know where to start in order to survive. Oh, he could dress like a male model and flatter a woman with compliments and sweet talk. In simple terms, he wasn't, and would never be, another Finn.

As they munched through their meal they quickly pared down the guest list. Sophie promised to send out email invites that afternoon. A little more than two weeks wasn't much notice, but it should be adequate.

Eager to hear from Finn, Carrie rushed back to the office and straight to her cubicle. She still had one sleeve in her coat when she grabbed her cell phone and texted Finn.

I'm back in the office.

It didn't take long for him to reply. Snoopy friend?

Need to be careful; suspicions running rampant. Told her you were from Seattle, which you are, right?

Born there.

Close enough.

Sophie?

Yes. Talk tonight?

OK.

Carrie had her phone tucked back inside her purse and her coat off when her desk phone rang. She answered the way she always did. "Carrie Slayton."

"Carrie?"

The voice on the other end of the line was vaguely familiar.

"It's Joan Reese, Finn Dalton's mother. I hope you don't mind me contacting you, but I hadn't heard from you and I've been anxious for news of my son."

Carrie felt dreadful that she'd delayed getting in touch with Finn's mother. "Joan, I am so sorry. I've been meaning to call." She started to make a convenient excuse, the way she had with her own family, then stopped herself.

"Were you able to talk to Finn?" Joan asked.

"Yes." Carrie couldn't find the words to tell this gentle woman that Finn wanted nothing to do with her or the wedding band Joan had asked her to deliver.

"Did you give him the ring?"

"I tried." That should tell her what had happened without Carrie going into a long explanation.

"Oh." In a single word, her disappointment rang like a cathedral bell.

Carrie lowered her voice for fear someone might be listening in on the conversation. "I spent two days alone with him at his cabin outside of Fairbanks. Well, his dog was with us, too."

"How is he?" Joan asked, with such longing that it nearly brought tears to Carrie's eyes.

Carrie hardly knew how to answer, knowing she meant more than Finn's physical well-being. Joan hungered for information, and Carrie didn't have those kinds of answers. "He's doing well," she started off. "He looks good. He has a big dog named Hennessey."

"Hennessey?"

"Yes. When I first saw him I thought he was a wolf, interested in dinner and that meal was me." She hoped the story would bring levity to their conversation.

Joan laughed softly. "Paul must have named him. Hennessey was his mother's maiden name."

Carrie remembered how the large dog had spent the night warming her and longed to see him again.

Joan hesitated. "Finn wouldn't take the ring, would he?"

"No, but he did ask after you."

"He did?" How quickly joy flooded her words. "That gives me hope."

"It's a positive sign. Given time, I think Finn will come around, I really do." Carrie couldn't leave the older woman without some positive news. Perhaps in time Carrie would be able to influence Finn to give his mother another chance.

Joan softly sighed. "I hope you're right. I really appreciate your efforts."

"He might not realize it yet, but one day Finn will figure out that he needs you, too."

"Thank you, Carrie," Joan said, and she seemed to struggle to sound encouraged. "I won't keep you any longer. I apologize for contacting you at your work."

"Joan, before I let you go I need to ask you something . . ."

"Of course, anything."

"Finn mailed me a gift. It's a toaster, a really old one. I asked him about it, but his answers have been vague. Is there some significance to it?"

His mother started to laugh. "He gave you the toaster?"

"Yes. I have it in my kitchen . . . I've been using it."

Joan exhaled and seemed to be gathering her thoughts. "Paul bought that toaster for me when we were first dating. My goodness, I had no idea he'd kept it. That toaster is nearly forty years old.

It was the first sign I had that Paul had any feelings for me."

"Why do you think Finn would want me to have it?"

"My dear, isn't it obvious?" she asked, and appeared to get real enjoyment out of the telling. "My son is crazy about you. He's repeating what his father did when he first fell in love with me. Finn is telling you the only way he knows how that you're important to him."

"He's important to me, too."

The line went silent for a moment. "Oh, dear. Are you in love with my son?"

"I think so," Carrie said, lowering her voice. She wasn't sure why she hesitated. "Yes," she said, plainly, distinctly. They'd known each other less than a month and yet her heart knew. No man had ever made her feel the way she did about Finn.

"Proceed carefully, my dear," Joan warned. "If Finn is anything like his father, and I suspect he is, then he doesn't give his heart lightly; he loves deeply, completely, and when he's hurt he'll react like a wounded grizzly bear."

Carrie mulled over Finn's mother's words the rest of the afternoon. The conversation with her own mother lingered in her mind, as well. She and Finn were very different people, living in entirely different worlds. She was a girly girl, just as her email address claimed, and he lived and worked in the

Alaskan wilderness. The practical side of Carrie reminded her that they had little in common, but her heart was unwilling to listen.

Carrie's mother had referred to this as the honeymoon part of the relationship, when they were so caught up in the intensity of their feelings that they willingly ignored their differences. It was easy to do, which was exactly what her mother was trying to tell her.

Finn's mother, too, had issued her own dire warning. It seemed everyone she told about her and Finn was filled with doubts about the two of them. One reason Carrie hadn't told Sophie about Finn was because she knew her best friend would become a naysayer as well, and Carrie didn't want to hear it.

That evening Carrie was anxious to talk to Finn. She sat on the sofa with her legs tucked under her and the phone clenched tightly in her hand, ready to answer the instant he rang. Her thick, wild hair was tied at the base of her neck with a scrunchie.

By the time he phoned, Carrie felt ready to weep. "I'm so glad you called," she blurted out the minute she heard his voice.

"What's wrong?" He was immediately concerned.

"Your mother. My mother."

"What's going on? You talked to my mother?" He didn't sound happy about it, either.

"Oh, sure, get upset with me, too, that's all I need."

"Carrie, take a deep breath and start at the beginning."

She inhaled deeply and then exhaled. "My mom and I spoke recently, and she warned me about falling for you . . . she said right now nothing seems impossible, but eventually we're going to have to face our differences."

The line went silent as he seemed to take in her mother's words of wisdom. "And my mother said the same thing," he said gruffly, sounding annoyed.

"More or less."

"And that worries you?"

"Yes. I don't want it to, but it does. It's been nearly three weeks since I last saw you and it feels like an eternity. Is it really possible to feel this strongly about someone I've known only a short while?"

"Do you want to call it quits now and save us both a lot of hassle and heartache?" he asked starkly.

"No." Her response was vehement and instant. "Are you saying that's what you want?"

"No way. I found myself whistling the other day. I haven't whistled since I was a kid. I climbed into bed at the cabin the other night and I felt your presence from just that small amount of time you slept in my bed. I rested better than I have in years."

"Oh, Finn, you make me want to cry." Carrie didn't know why she'd thought this man couldn't be romantic.

"Sawyer just looks at me and shakes his head, as if he no longer recognizes me. I'm not alone, either. Hennessey mopes around the cabin, looking lost and miserable."

"It's the same with me. What's happened to us? I think about you and then my insides get all mushy and I feel like I want to cry because I have no idea when I'll see you again," she whispered.

She heard the sound of him exhaling. "We don't have to make any decisions tonight, do we?"

"No," she agreed.

"I can't give you up yet, Carrie."

"Do you have to give me up at all?" she asked. "Do I have to give you up?"

"Not now, and hopefully not for a very long time."

"Good," she whispered, "because I don't think I could bear it."

"Great," he said with some enthusiasm. "Now that we have that settled, let's talk about something else. Tell me about this hot date of yours."

"Oh, Finn, honestly, you have nothing to fear from Dave."

"Ah, so his name is Dave."

"He's a nice guy, but he would never think to give a woman a toaster. He doesn't have a heart nearly as big as yours."

"You realize I'm going to be worrying about you with this guy the entire time you're out with him."

His words cheered her considerably. "I'm glad to hear it."

"You are?"

"Well, sure. It will keep you on your toes. If this kind of competition continues, I could end up with a can opener that matches that toaster."

Chapter Ten

❄

The night of her dinner date with Dave, Carrie hurried home from the office in order to change clothes. Cool, suave, sophisticated Dave. Finn had been suspiciously quiet all day. She hadn't received a single text from him in nearly twenty-four hours, which was unusual. She knew he was concerned about her going to the theater, even with a friend, and seemed to view any man she saw as a potential threat. It was clear he didn't have a clue how head-over-heels nuts she was over him.

Perhaps she was living in a fool's garden, not thinking about the future. Frankly, she didn't care what chances anyone gave their relationship. Finn felt as much a part of her now as her arms and legs.

She changed clothes but kept her cell phone handy, hoping to hear the ding that would tell her she had a text message. The earlier one she'd sent him remained unanswered. Perhaps he'd returned to the lake cabin, but it seemed he would have mentioned it, if that was the case.

Once she refreshed her makeup, she glanced out the window and saw that the snow, which had been threatening most of the afternoon, had started to fall in thick flakes. With the holidays so close, everyone seemed preoccupied. Carrie had gotten three invitations to parties and other social events from friends. Sophie had invited Carrie to join her family for Thanksgiving. Knowing she would be alone, even Harry had extended an invite. Carrie had declined both invitations, feeling she would be an add-on. She would have her own Thanksgiving, she decided, and make the best of it by herself.

The last time she'd seen snow she'd been with Finn and Hennessey. The reminder made her miss them both dreadfully.

Unable to bear this silence any longer, she reached for her cell and typed out with practiced ease. Miss you.

Almost right away she got a response. Good.

Where have you been all day? Finn had to know she'd been anxiously waiting to hear from him.

In the air. Still have your hot date tonight?

In the air? That didn't make sense—a flight to Fairbanks from his cabin was less than thirty minutes. Are you jealous?

You bet.

Carrie grinned, and a warm sensation came over her. It's snowing here; makes me miss you all the more.

I know it's snowing in Chicago.

You know it's snowing?????

Big, fat flakes.

Carrie gasped, and her fingers moved with urgency across the tiny alphabet on her cell phone. Finn, where are you?

Chicago.

She hardly had time to take in the fact that Finn was in town before her phone rang. She hit the answer button so hard the cell nearly dropped out of her hands.

"Surprise," he whispered.

Carrie wanted to laugh and cry at the same time. Laugh because she was so happy and excited and then weep because she had this stupid date and wouldn't be able to see him until the end of the evening.

"Where are you?"

He named a local hotel about two blocks from her condo. "I know it's crazy, my being here. I didn't want you to be alone over Thanksgiving."

"I don't care if it's crazy or not; I'm too happy to care." Carrie just hoped she didn't embarrass herself when she first saw him by launching into his arms and bursting into tears. She'd dreamed about seeing him again. He hadn't said a word that he was planning this. Not a single solitary word.

"Do you still have to go to the theater?" he asked, and then instantly withdrew the question. "Forget I asked. Of course you do. I'll be here at the hotel waiting, and when you get back to your apartment, let me know."

Her doorbell chimed, announcing Dave's arrival. "I hope you realize this is torture," she told Finn on her way to answer the front door.

"For you or for me?"

"For us both." Carrie had no idea how she was going to get through this evening, knowing Finn was in town.

"Go. It'll be fine," Finn encouraged her.

"Okay, but you're going to suffer for doing this to me."

He chuckled and ended the call.

Carrie took a moment to compose herself before she opened the door. Dave was impeccably dressed for the evening. He really was an attractive man, but she didn't feel even the slightest stirrings for him. Just thinking about Finn waiting for her in his hotel room had her pulse spinning at the rate of a jet engine.

The Christmas musical they went to see, which had gotten rave reviews, didn't hold Carrie's attention, but to be fair, she doubted she would have appreciated anything outside of a five-alarm fire. Somehow she got through the evening, although she felt it was only fair to tell Dave that she'd met someone else. Their relationship had never really gone beyond friendship, and he took her news well.

Straight from the theater, Dave drove her to her home and briefly parked outside the condo complex. The snow had stopped, but traffic was a mess. It went without saying that he didn't need to see her up. She thanked him for the evening, and then before she climbed out of the car she impulsively hugged him. He'd been decent and thoughtful, and she was grateful for his friendship.

"I hope it works with you and the other guy," he said, and didn't seem to have any hard feelings.

"I do, too." Carrie wished that more than anything.

"He's a lucky guy."

"I'll let him know you said so." She smiled as she said it.

Climbing out of the car, she gathered her coat more securely around her and made a dash for the building's entrance. Dave waited until she was inside the foyer, and Carrie waved before he drove off. The instant he was out of sight, she opened her clutch to retrieve her cell phone. Right away, she sent Finn a text.

I'm home.

I know.

She glanced up to find Finn standing on the other side of the building's glass door. For a moment, all she could do was stare at him. She shivered with the cold, but he wore no jacket. All he had on was a yellow-and-black plaid shirt, jeans, and boots. In her entire life she'd never seen a more strongly appealing man. Hurrying to the locked security door, she opened it for him. Even before he was inside, she was wrapped in his embrace.

Carrie looped her arms around his neck, hugging him and laughing with joy. Right away, Finn swept her off her feet. With his arms around her waist, he lifted her so that her shoes dangled several inches off the ground. With her hands framing his bearded face, they kissed as if they couldn't get enough, as if they meant to consume each other right in the center of the lobby.

A man's voice broke through the fog of longing and joy. "Ms. Slayton? Ms. Slayton?"

Reluctantly, Carrie ended the kiss and looked over her shoulder to find Lester, the security guard, closely studying her.

"You know this man?" Lester asked.

She smiled and nodded. "Lester, this is—"

Finn released her and stretched out his hand to the guard. "Paul. Paul Dalton."

"Glad to meet you, Paul. I apologize if I was rude earlier."

"Not a problem."

Carrie was curious to know what that was all about. "Let's go upstairs," she said, and steered Finn toward the elevator. She waited until they were inside and the doors had closed. "I'm glad you were clearheaded enough to tell him your name is Paul."

Finn smiled down at her. "Clearheaded? You're joking, right?"

Carrie laughed and cuddled close to his side. They had their arms around each other. "What's this about Lester being rude?"

"It's nothing. He didn't like the idea of unsavory types hanging around the building and asked what my business was."

"Unsavory types?"

"Shhh, just let me kiss you again."

Carrie wasn't about to argue with him. They were completely consumed with each other when the elevator stopped on the twenty-fifth floor and the door glided open. Finn reluctantly broke off the kiss and thrust out his arm to stop the doors from closing on them.

Using her code, Carrie let them into her apartment, wondering what Finn would think when he stepped inside the ultra-exclusive high-rise. It was a one-bedroom unit that she'd rented because of its close proximity to the newspaper office and the incredible views of the city it offered.

Staring out the picture window, Finn stood with his back to her. "I'm a bit out of my element."

Wrapping her arms around him, she pressed the side of her face against his back. "I think we're both way out of our comfort zones."

He chuckled and folded his rough, muscled hands over hers. "True enough."

"I'm so glad you're here."

"It was either fly to see you or go slowly mad wondering about you and that pretty boy."

"You saw Dave?"

"I saw you hug him. He's darn lucky he didn't try to kiss you; otherwise, I would have been forced to drag him out of that car and send him flying into the closest snowbank."

Carrie laughed at the mental picture. Dave was a pretty boy, but he wouldn't have stood still for Finn's he-man tactics.

"You think I'm joking?"

"Oh, Finn, if only you knew how close you are to my heart."

He turned and nearly crushed her in his arms before he slowly released her. "I've never been the jealous sort, but Carrie, you . . . you make me feel things." Frowning, he rubbed his chest. "One kiss just before Sawyer took you away and you unbalanced my entire life. I hardly know myself any longer."

"Do you like having your life unbalanced?" she asked, noting how dark his face grew with the confession.

"I don't know. It's never happened quite like this."

She kissed him, letting her lips linger over his. When she pulled away, he groaned softly. "Perhaps I could grow used to it," he whispered.

"I'm thinking I could as well," she confessed.

After a while she brewed them each a cup of coffee, and then they sat and talked away half the night. They bounced from one subject to the next as if it'd been months since they'd last spoken. It felt as if they'd known each other their entire lives. Finn talked about the second book he'd written. It was finished, but he wasn't sure it was as good as the first one.

"That's a problem when a first book is such a success," she said thoughtfully.

"How do you mean?"

"Well, there's all this pressure for you to repeat the performance of the first book. That alone is intimidating enough."

Finn agreed. "New York keeps asking me when they can see this second manuscript, and I've been putting them off, although it's been finished for quite some time."

"Would you like me to read it?" she asked.

"Would you?"

"Of course." It was an honor that he trusted her enough to give her this opportunity.

"You'll be honest with me?"

"If that's what you want."

"I do."

With anyone else she would have doubted their sincerity, but not with Finn.

It must have been close to three in the morning before Finn announced it was time for him to go back to his hotel. Carrie resisted the urge to ask him to stay. They both knew that it wouldn't take much encouragement on either of their parts to convince him to spend the night. She had to go to work in the morning but would be off early. Most of the staff would be away from their desks for the Thanksgiving holiday.

Reluctantly, Carrie walked him to the door.

"Can I see you tomorrow?" he asked, his arms around her.

"Please."

"Any more social obligations I need to know about?"

"Nope. The entire holiday is free . . . well, other than church. The choir is singing. You'll come, won't you?"

He frowned and then nodded.

Carrie rewarded him with a lengthy kiss. "Church might actually do you some good, and then next week is the party."

He frowned again. "What party?"

"The Christmas one Sophie and I are throwing right here. You must come, you really must."

He certainly didn't look keen to join in the festivities. "The first week of December? You'll be here, won't you?"

"Ah . . ."

"See if you can change your flight, Finn. I need to prove to everyone that you're real. If you think you're the only one who's not himself, then you're wrong. My friends claim they hardly know me anymore."

"Carrie, I'll never fit in with your life here."

She didn't argue. Instead, she pressed her hand to the side of his jaw, her eyes round and pleading.

Finn snickered softly, and Carrie knew she'd won.

"Could I refuse you anything?" he asked.

"Good to know." She hugged him, fearing if they kissed again they wouldn't be able to stop.

He grumbled but didn't argue.

"I promise the rewards will be worth any discomfort."

"Rewards?" His dark eyes brightened.

"Yes. We can talk about those later."

He left her then, and while she was practically asleep on her feet, Carrie was far too happy and excited to let go of the exquisite sensation of knowing Finn was only a couple of blocks away, and would be with her for several days.

Chapter Eleven

Late Wednesday morning Finn unloaded the last of the groceries into Carrie's refrigerator. Shopping for their Thanksgiving dinner had been an experience he never wanted to repeat. While she was at the office he decided to make good use of his time and get what they needed for their meal. If ever he wanted a lesson in the differences between their lives, this was it. The trip to the grocery store had taken him hours.

Finn knew his way around a kitchen, his father had made sure of that. But the meat he was most familiar with didn't come from a food market. He found the selection of vegetables and fresh fruit mind-boggling. He had to admit he was impressed. It was like walking into the Garden of Eden. In Alaska, especially at this time of year, fresh fruits and vegetables were at a premium. They were available in limited quantities, but the prices were astronomical.

He glanced at his watch. Carrie should arrive

home anytime now. Just thinking about her produced a sense of lightness that he'd rarely experienced. His decision to fly to Chicago had been last-minute. If he'd been smart he would have planned this trip much earlier.

After all Carrie had gone through in order to find him, he was determined she not be alone over Thanksgiving. She was close to her family, which was something Finn had never experienced. His father had been his only relative, though Carrie would be quick to remind him that his mother was living. But she'd been out of his life since he was a kid and he had nothing to say to her. He loved hearing Carrie talk about her family and their traditions. It made him feel good to know how deeply she valued these relationships; it was something he envied. The more he got to know Carrie, the more he cared about her. He tried to ignore the feeling that he was starting to care more for her than he should. More than was wise for either of them.

Finn pushed those thoughts aside for now. He was determined to make this a Thanksgiving they would both remember.

The door opened and Carrie breezed in, breathless and excited. "Finn?" she called out.

"In here." He had the turkey in the sink and the countertops lined with a variety of food.

She rounded the corner and came to an abrupt halt, her beautiful blue eyes widening. "What in heaven's name is this?" Not waiting for his answer, she launched herself into his arms and buried her face in his neck.

Finn wrapped his arms around her and breathed in the fresh scent of her. In all his life, nothing had felt more right than having Carrie in his arms. If he was living in a dream world, then he never wanted to wake up. She smelled of roses and sunshine. Clinging to him, she swallowed tightly but didn't say a word.

"It's our Thanksgiving dinner," he explained, probably unnecessarily. "I plan to cook for you."

Her arms remained tightly clenched around his neck. "Thank you. Oh, thank you," she whispered.

What struck him was the fact that Carrie thanked him when he was the one who should be grateful. For an instant his throat clogged and he found it impossible to speak. He held her close and then they were kissing, so hungry for each other that breathing no longer seemed necessary. The taste, the feel, the need he had for this one woman was all the oxygen he would ever require. In a single moment all the hassles of traveling from Alaska, the crowded grocery store, and every other irritation he'd experienced evaporated. Being with Carrie was worth all of it.

Finn realized this emotional high, this linking of their hearts, was temporary. He'd long ago accepted that their time together was destined to be limited. He tried not to think about it. One day they would both need to face reality, but it wouldn't be this day. He hoped whatever it was they shared would last, and in the same breath he felt he had to accept that it probably wouldn't. People change, and what had seemed right could suddenly go very wrong. One day Carrie was sure to wake up to their differences. Thus far they'd managed to look past the fact that they were polar opposites. As soon as she stopped, and long before he was ready to deal with letting her go, she would end their relationship. Finn had seen it often enough. His own mother had walked out on him and his father. They were a good example of what happened when a man and a woman who didn't belong together ignored what should have been clear from the beginning.

Gradually and with a great deal of reluctance, Finn released her. Carrie tried to hide the tears that shimmered in her eyes. Because he knew they embarrassed her, he pretended not to notice. One thing that did catch his attention, though, was the reddish marks his beard had caused on the tender skin of her face. He rubbed his hand down the sides of his jaw and felt his prickly whiskers. His thick beard offered his face protection against the bitter cold, but for Carrie he would do away with it. Fact was, he hardly remembered what he looked like without it.

"I was thinking this was going to be the worst Thanksgiving of my life," Carrie confessed.

"Not on my watch," Finn countered, and, taking

her hand, he raised it to his lips and kissed the inside of her palm.

Their Thanksgiving meal was everything Finn had hoped it would be. The turkey was cooked to perfection and the stuffing was delicious. In fact, the entire meal was the best he could remember outside of his early childhood. His mother's cornbread stuffing had been his favorite, and he'd taken delight in wolfing it down in large quantities. Along with that long-buried memory came others, reminding him that at one point, his parents had been happy together. And then they weren't. He knew the lessons from their marriage and divorce remained deeply engraved in his psyche, but he hadn't minded that until now. Finn shook his head, needing to dispel the image of his parents and those early Thanksgivings. He wanted to focus on the present, here with Carrie.

The table was covered with partially empty serving dishes, and their plates were practically clean when Carrie leaned back in her chair and groaned. "If I swallow another bite I will explode. Oh, Finn, you're a wonderful chef."

Finn basked in her praise although the meal had been a team effort. She'd done a good deal of the preparation work.

They sat across from each other. "What were your Thanksgivings like as a child?" she asked.

"Funny you should ask. I was just thinking about that myself." The memories wrapped themselves around him, warming him. "Mom got up at the crack of dawn and got the turkey in the oven so I woke to the smell of it roasting. I don't think I'll ever forget that. She'd be busy baking and cooking, and Dad would offer to help."

"He would? I don't picture your dad as someone who would volunteer to help cook."

"He wasn't. To the best of my memory, he only offered at Thanksgiving. I think he was more of a nuisance than anything. I suspect what he wanted was to be close to Mom. Dad's main job was to peel the potatoes."

"What was your job?"

"To eat the potatoes," Finn teased.

Just the way he knew she would, Carrie laughed. "Then, after dinner, Mom would bring out this Nativity set and she'd let me set it up on the fireplace mantel. I still have it."

"Do you put it out for Christmas?" she asked.

If anyone else had asked, he'd deny it, but with Carrie he couldn't. Everything was different with Carrie.

"What about Thanksgiving after your mother left?" she asked.

He shrugged. "It was just Dad and me, and maybe a few of my father's single friends."

"Did you ever leave Alaska?"

"Why would we?"

"Vacations?"

"Alaska has everything I would ever want, but on occasion I did travel. I went to France once, and England. A couple of times I had business meetings in Texas and got a kick out of the lone-star attitude, thinking they're so big. Minnesota brags about its ten thousand lakes. Do you know how many lakes are in Alaska?"

"I don't have a clue."

"Over a million."

"A million!"

Finn knew she was impressed just by the way she said it.

"You were born in Seattle. Do you have any memories of life there?" she asked.

"None. Mom and Dad moved to Fairbanks when I was a baby. They bought a house there and Dad kept it, but he built a cabin on the tundra as well."

"And then you did, too."

"My father built that house with his own two hands, and he taught me everything he knew. I was fortunate to learn I could survive on my own in the wilderness if it was ever necessary. Some of those experiences are included in *Alone,* but I have a lot more stories to tell."

Carrie leaned forward and pushed her plate aside. "I don't see why you refuse to give interviews. It's not like you're truly a recluse, and from what I've seen you would even be good on television."

He sighed and leaned back while he formulated his answer. When the book had first started selling, his publisher had wanted him to do interviews. But Finn hadn't signed up to have his personal life invaded. He wanted nothing to do with that side of the business. From that point forward, his publisher automatically rejected all interviews and invitations for appearances. All the interest and attention embarrassed him. It wasn't until reporters started making trips to Fairbanks that he grew irritated and stubborn.

"The simple answer is that I like my privacy."

She mulled that over, and he half expected her to bring up the article she wanted to write. She didn't, and gradually the tension between his shoulder blades eased. Maybe he could trust her. He certainly wanted to.

Their conversation drifted to other subjects, and Finn was grateful. He didn't often talk about his childhood. Carrie's had been wrapped around happy memories of cousins and family gatherings. Finn hadn't experienced that and didn't realize all he'd missed. He enjoyed listening to her stories. If he ever had a family, this was what he would wish for his own children.

They cleaned the kitchen together, music playing in the background, using any time they were in close proximity to kiss. Hands down, this had been the best Thanksgiving of his life.

Once they finished with the cleanup, Finn brought out the cribbage board.

"What are we playing for?" she asked, as she sat down and reached for the deck.

He shrugged. "Whatever you wish."

Carrie's smile widened. "Oh, how tempting. Okay, if I win, we go shopping in the morning."

"Shopping?" He couldn't believe she would even suggest something so out of his comfort zone. He knew from previous conversations this was something Carrie and her mother did every Black Friday. "This is a joke, right?"

"No joke. I want you to meet my friends, and right now they'll take one look and know you're from Alaska. From there, it'll be easy to make the leap that you're Finn Dalton."

Gauging by the determination in her eyes, Finn realized it didn't matter what cards he was dealt. Within a matter of hours he would be on the Chicago streets, credit card in hand, and he'd do it gladly because Carrie had asked him to.

The deep-dish sausage and pepperoni pizza sat in the middle of the table in front of Carrie and Finn. Try as she might, she couldn't take her eyes off him. He was gorgeous. His beard was gone, and his hair neatly trimmed. His jaw was clearly defined, and his lips were full and enticing.

"Stop looking at me," he said, clearly uncomfortable with her scrutiny.

"Sorry, I can't help myself. You look more scrumptious than that pizza." The woodsman had disappeared, and in his place sat Prince Charming. Finn was handsome—well, in her eyes, anyway—and if the glances she saw coming from other women in the restaurant were anything to go by, she wasn't alone in thinking so. The transformation was total. Finn exuded vigor and strength, and she found it nearly impossible to keep from staring.

"You have to admit this is the best pizza you've ever tasted," she said, in an effort to keep the conversation going. If she was drooling, it wasn't over the food.

"All right, you win. Chicago pizza isn't half bad, but you have to promise to try reindeer-sausage pizza the next time you're in Alaska."

"I wouldn't miss it," she teased.

"I'm serious."

She loved the idea that he assumed she would visit Alaska again, and frankly, she wasn't opposed to the idea, especially if it meant she would be with Finn. It didn't hurt that he loved pizza as much as she did, either.

"You know what's funny?" he said, wiping the grease from his fingers with a paper napkin. "I keep fighting the urge to text you."

Carrie laughed because she'd experienced the

same feeling. It was the usual way they communicated and had become such a habit that it felt odd not to be exchanging texts even when they sat across the table from each other.

"We're done shopping, right?"

"We are unless you have a secret desire to face the maddening crowds yet again."

He scoffed. "Hardly. I've seen about as many people in one day as I can handle. I'm starting to feel claustrophobic. Is it always like this in the city?"

"Always. Sometimes worse, although not often. Black Friday is a special, magical day." Carrie hid a smile. One disgruntled look from Finn told her he could do without the holiday craziness. "But you haven't been to Navy Pier yet."

"Another time," he pleaded. "I don't think I can take much more of these crowds, let alone the noise."

"Okay." Carrie had no complaints, watching as he once again ran his hand over his smooth cheeks as though he felt naked.

He'd arrived at her apartment that morning clean shaven, and for just an instant she hadn't recognized the man standing in front of her. She hadn't asked him to shave and had been both shocked and delighted.

"And you keep staring at me."

"Sorry, I can't stop myself. I had no idea you were such a hunk."

He chuckled as if she'd made a joke, but she wasn't kidding. The minute her friends took one look at him, they'd be all over Finn, especially Sophie. She frowned, disliking the thought.

"What's wrong?" he asked, as he paid their tab and collected their purchases. Finn reached for her hand, gripping it in his own as they started out of the restaurant.

It amazed her how easily he read her mood. "What makes you think anything is wrong?"

"You're frowning."

"I just got an inkling of how you felt with me spending the evening with Dave." They wove their way around busy tables toward the front of the well-known Chicago pizza restaurant.

He paused, frowning, his brow folding into thick ripples. "I doubt that."

"I was imagining my friends meeting you, and I realized they are going to want you for themselves. You're mine, Finn, all mine."

His eyes grew dark and serious. His grip tightened on her hand. "No one is going to turn my head, Carrie. It simply isn't possible."

Carrie and Finn walked back to her condo, bundles in hand. Until that morning Finn mentioned that the only clothes shopping he'd done in years had been through catalogs or online. It'd been a true test of the strength of their relationship when it came to choosing dress slacks and a sweater for him. All in all, he'd been more than patient, but she could appreciate his unease.

Once back at her condo, Finn collapsed onto her sofa, spreading out his arms along the back cushion. Her tree was up but had yet to be decorated, and although it was only four feet tall, it took up one entire corner of her living room. Finn had placed a gift under it first thing that morning. She eyed it now, wrapped in plain brown paper.

"Curious?" he asked.

"Very." She picked it up, held it close to her ear, and shook it.

"Any guesses?"

"I doubt it's a can opener."

He grinned. "You're way off base."

"Do you want to tell me?"

"And ruin the surprise? No way. You have to wait until Christmas."

Carrie reluctantly set it back down. "You're taunting me, and that simply isn't fair."

"I think you'll be pleased" was all Finn was willing to tell her. Over the years she'd received a variety of gifts from the men she'd dated, but Finn's gifts were distinctive in every way. It wasn't likely she would ever forget that toaster.

Carrie went over to her television and removed a DVD from her collection.

"We're watching a movie?" Finn asked.

"Yes. It's tradition."

"What movie?"

"You'll see in a minute."

"Is it a romance? I don't think I could sit through a chick flick—not after the last three hours."

"Shush." She sat down close to him and reached for her remote control, pushing the appropriate button.

Right away he slid his arm around her shoulders and then let it drop. "*The Bishop's Wife?*" he muttered as the title flashed across the screen. "It's in black and white."

"Have you seen it?"

"Yes, years ago . . ."

"It's my favorite Christmas movie."

"Ah . . ."

"Shhh, you'll miss the introduction."

His arm was back, and she pressed her head against his shoulder. "Just relax and enjoy."

He grumbled, but she noticed that he was soon into the movie. Every now and again he would lean forward and kiss her temple. Carrie snuggled into his embrace. She loved that they could cuddle and be this close.

"Listen up. This is one of the best lines of any movie ever." Carrie mouthed the words along with Cary Grant as he spoke to Loretta Young.

Finn sat up slightly. "You've memorized the movie?"

"Parts of it. Like I said, it's one of my favorites." It thrilled her that he was with her and they could view it together. What she loved was how much he seemed to be enjoying it, too.

"Just how many times have you watched this silly movie?"

"It isn't a silly movie," she insisted, knowing that he enjoyed teasing her.

"Have you ever seen *The Replacement Killers*?"

"Yuck, no."

"Yuck? It's a great movie."

"Tell you what," Carrie whispered, tilting her head back and kissing the underside of his clean-shaven jaw. "I'll watch it with you one day, as long as you promise to hold me just like this."

He smiled down on her. "Deal."

The phone rang shortly after the movie ended. It was Sophie. "A group of us are going to Logan's for drinks. Can you meet us?"

"Let me check."

"Check?" Sophie repeated.

"I have company. F— Paul is in town."

"Seattle Paul? The guy who's got you walking around with your head in the clouds Paul?"

"One and the same." Finn eyed her closely. Carrie was sure he was able to hear both sides of the conversation.

"You didn't say anything about him coming to Chicago."

"I didn't know. It was a surprise."

"Well, bring him. I, for one, am dying to meet this guy."

"Hold on." Carrie pressed her cell against her chest. "What do you think? Do you want to go out tonight?"

"Do you?"

She shrugged. "I'd like you to meet my friends."

He hesitated and then nodded. "Okay."

She leaned forward and kissed him soundly on the lips.

"I could grow accustomed to these little rewards you so willingly hand out," he murmured as he gripped her hand.

Carrie smiled and brought the cell back to her ear. "What time?"

"Does eight work for you?"

"Perfect. See you then."

Sophie hesitated. "Does Paul have a friend?"

"No, and, fair warning, hands off. Got it?"

Sophie laughed before the line was disconnected.

"Who's Logan?" Finn asked.

"It's a bar about six blocks from here. A few of us from the newspaper hang out there when we can."

"Noisy?"

"Afraid so. Sorry."

Finn chuckled. "It won't be so bad if there are rewards involved."

Carrie smiled. "I imagine there will be more than a few."

"Then bring on the noise."

For the rest of the afternoon they simply hung

out together while a medley of Christmas songs played in the background. It seemed they never ran out of things to talk about. And as promised, Finn gave her sections of his new book to read and critique. Carrie found it as good as, if not better than, *Alone* and told him so.

They left the condo around seven forty-five and with her arm tucked in Finn's they walked the six blocks to Logan's. The noise was explosive the instant they entered the bar. Sophie and Bruce already had a table. Bruce worked for the newspaper, and he'd been dating Sophie for the last few months, following his divorce. According to Sophie, it wasn't a serious relationship, and after seeing them together a couple of times, Carrie had to agree.

The noise level made it nearly impossible to talk, but they managed by yelling across the table to one another. Finn ordered a beer. Sophie and Carrie had their favorite dirty martinis before another couple joined them. Introductions were made and a second round of drinks was ordered. Finn stayed close to her side and contributed to the conversation, although it was difficult with the bar so crowded. They left an hour later.

"I enjoyed meeting your friends," he commented when they were outside in the relative quiet of the street.

"But the crowds and the noise bothered you."

"Not bothered, exactly," he said, and reached for her hand. "I'm just not accustomed to it to that extent. We get plenty rowdy in Fairbanks ourselves, you know."

"But this is different."

He grinned and nodded. Soon they had their arms around each other as it started to snow again. They took a leisurely stroll down Michigan Avenue on the way back to Carrie's place. On a side street they walked past a bookstore, and *Alone* took up the entire window display. Finn paused and did a double take.

"How does it feel seeing that?" she asked.

He took his time answering. "I've seen it displayed before, but nothing like this. It leaves me feeling a little . . . I don't know, weird, I guess."

"A *good* weird, though, right?" She felt proud for him and for all that he'd accomplished, proud to be with him. Carrie knew the phenomenal sales of his book had shocked Finn. He didn't seem to understand what it was about his book that fascinated readers. When he'd submitted the manuscript, he'd been amazed at how quickly it'd sold. Then to have it shoot straight to the top of the bestseller lists and remain there for months on end was beyond the scope of his imagination.

"I can see your mind working," he said, and, leaning down, he kissed her brow. "I know what you're thinking."

"So you're a mind reader now."

"You'd love to write that article about me, wouldn't you?"

To deny it would be a falsehood, but to confess that she'd composed it a half-dozen times in her mind, even still had a rough draft on her laptop, would give him the wrong impression. "That's a moot point. I would never destroy the trust you have in me. I wouldn't submit a word until you gave me the approval to do so."

He was silent for a long time and then said, "Fair enough."

They held hands as he walked her to her condo and kissed her good night.

"Come upstairs with me?" she asked.

He shook his head. "I think I should go back to the hotel."

Carrie held on to his hand. "Is everything all right? You're not upset about anything, are you?"

Finn brought her back into his arms and hugged her close. "You're far too tempting, Carrie. If I came upstairs with you now, I wouldn't be leaving until morning, and we both know it."

Carrie went into her building with a happy, excited sense of anticipation and relief. She would see Finn tomorrow. He'd met her friends and not a one had even suspected her Seattle Paul was Finnegan Dalton.

Chapter Twelve

❄

"When is Paul leaving?" Sophie asked on Saturday afternoon. Finn was in her kitchen, fixing sandwiches for their lunch. Carrie had been bringing down dishes when her friend had called.

"His flight is scheduled for Monday. I mentioned our Christmas party, and I hope he'll be able to change his plans so he'll be staying for that." He'd used her laptop to see about alternate flights and to check his emails, but it didn't look promising that he'd be able to delay his return to Alaska.

"Do you think he might?"

"I don't know." The thought of him leaving filled her with dismay, but at the same time she appreciated that city life was completely foreign to him.

And she would need to return to work Monday morning and he'd be restless in the city, although there would be plenty for him to see and do.

"How come you left so early last night?" Sophie pressed.

"Too noisy," she explained, as she strolled into

the kitchen. "It was difficult to hold a decent conversation, and Paul and I had been out and about all day."

"I have an idea," Sophie returned cheerfully, as if she was the most brilliant woman in the universe. "I'll have the two of you over for dinner this evening. I'll ask Bruce, and we'll have a small dinner party with just the four of us—nothing fancy."

"Good idea, but I've already got a roast in the Crock-Pot." A good portion of the leftover turkey had gone into the freezer, and she'd made up plates with turkey, stuffing, and the other side dishes to distribute to her neighbors who were widowers.

"Great," Sophie returned enthusiastically. "Then we'll come to your place. Does six work?"

Carrie glanced at Finn, knowing he could hear the conversation, and he shrugged as if to say it was her decision. "Sure. We'll see you then." Carrie would have preferred to spend the night with just her and Finn, but she had more or less been manipulated into agreeing. Setting her phone aside, she wrapped her arms around Finn's waist. "Are you sure you want to do this?" she asked. "I can call Sophie back and tell her we've changed our minds."

"It'll be fine. I liked your friends." He downplayed her concern, kissed her cheek, and brought their turkey-salad sandwiches to the table.

Sophie and Bruce arrived at six, bringing flowers and chocolate-dipped strawberries for dessert. Her friends wore matching Santa hats. The flowers became the centerpiece, and the meal was served. Conversation flowed smoothly throughout dinner. For obvious reasons, the answers to questions directed at Finn were vague. Sophie was the one who asked one question after another, almost as if she were conducting an interview. At one point, Carrie opened her mouth to stop her, an uneasy feeling filling her chest, but Finn pressed his hand over hers, reassuring her that all was fine.

Following the meal, Bruce and Finn went into the living room to watch a college football game while Sophie and Carrie cleared the table.

The instant they were out of earshot, Sophie hissed, "Who do you think you're kidding? That's Finn Dalton."

Just as she'd suspected when Sophie started hitting Finn with a barrage of questions, her friend had seen through their little masquerade.

Carrie started to explain when Sophie quickly cut her off. "Don't even try to deny it."

"All right, all right, yes, it's Finn. Paul is his middle name."

Sophie rolled her eyes. "Who did you think you were fooling, Carrie?"

"Do you remember," Carrie said, grabbing hold of her friend's forearm, "you said that Finn Dalton could be walking down the streets of Chicago and no one would even know it was him? Well, guess what, he is, and you're right, no one knows."

"Carrie, I'm worried about you. Surely you realize this relationship isn't going to work. Long-distance relationships rarely do. The two of you are night and day, oil and water."

"Well, to this point we seem to be coming along rather nicely," Carrie countered, unwilling to let her friend rain on her parade. Not for anything would Carrie give up on her and Finn.

"For the love of heaven, why haven't you written the article?" Sophie demanded. "We both know what that would mean to you and your career. You could have your choice of jobs with any newspaper. You're always talking about moving back to Seattle one day. This is your golden opportunity."

"The article is off the table." Carrie rinsed the dirty dishes and set them inside the dishwasher, not wanting to have this conversation. "I'd rather not discuss this, Sophie."

"Why can't you write it?" Sophie wasn't willing to let this go.

Carrie straightened and faced her friend head-on. "Finn asked me not to."

"What?" Sophie all but exploded.

Carrie hurriedly glanced around the wall that separated the kitchen from the living room to be sure Finn hadn't heard any part of this conversation. Both men appeared caught up in the football game. Sighing with relief, Carrie turned back to her friend.

"Keep your voice down, would you?"

"Sorry, but you need to think this through; give me one good reason why you aren't writing that article. Just one." She held up her finger and threatened to wag it with every word.

The answer should be obvious. "In case you hadn't figured it out, I'm in love with Finn."

"You barely know the guy," Sophie challenged.

"I know him well enough."

"Listen, Carrie, I realize you *think* you're in love, but you aren't. This is a classic case of wild infatuation. Opposites attract, right?" She didn't wait for a response. "You've gone bonkers for him, and it's understandable. He's not bad looking, and he seems to be a nice guy, but tell me, do you honestly see yourself picking berries out in the wilderness in order to survive?"

Sophie was right about one thing; Carrie couldn't see herself living her life in Finn's cabin, raising a family in such a limited environment. Still, she wasn't willing to give up Finn.

"What about your career?" Sophie challenged next.

"I can write anywhere."

"You can," Sophie reluctantly agreed. "You're smart and talented. But you can't seriously be considering giving up this golden opportunity."

Carrie lowered her voice to a whisper. "I won't betray Finn. I'm not that kind of person."

"I can't bear to see you make this sacrifice,"

Sophie insisted. "You'd be a fool not to take advantage of what you know about him."

Carrie refused to listen to this any longer. "Stop, Sophie. I said I'm not doing it, and I mean it. End of story."

Sophie gave a disgusted shake of her head. "Don't you see what he's doing?"

"What are you talking about? He trusts me, and I trust him."

"Aren't you afraid he might be using you?"

"Using me? For what?" The idea was so preposterous that Carrie nearly laughed out loud.

"To keep track of what you're doing so you won't write the article," Sophie explained.

Carrie shook her head, finding this conversation almost comical. "Finn isn't like that."

"Are you sure?" Sophie challenged. "Take my advice and admit that this relationship isn't going anywhere. If you hang on, you'll only be setting yourself up for heartache. I'm your friend, and I have your best interests at heart."

Carrie actually felt sorry for her. "You are getting to be such a cynic, Sophie. How can you say these things?"

"How can you be sure he isn't with you so that you won't write the article?" Sophie asked. "Against all odds, you found him. You know too much."

"Stop," Carrie insisted. "I don't want to hear it." She was finished with this conversation. She tossed the dish towel down on the counter, jerked the

Christmas apron loose from her waist, and stuffed it in a drawer. "I'm done listening to you," she said.

Abruptly, she turned away from her friend, and to her shock she found Finn standing in the doorway.

Sophie cast her an apologetic glance, murmured, "Oops," and then scooted past Finn. "Hey, Bruce, time for us to leave."

"But the game . . ."

"You can watch it from my place."

Carrie waited until she heard the front door click closed. "How much of that did you hear?" she asked.

Finn had his arms crossed over his muscular chest. His frown compressed his forehead. "I heard enough."

"Don't be offended by Sophie. She doesn't know what she's talking about. She certainly doesn't know my heart."

"Don't be so sure."

"Finn . . ."

"You mean to say you never guessed what caused my change in attitude while we were in the cabin?"

"I . . ." She frowned. "No . . ."

"When you first arrived I was determined not to give you a single bit of information, and then you riled me to the point where I said far more than I ever intended. Very clever of you, by the way."

"I didn't mean . . . That wasn't my intention." He couldn't honestly believe that the argument about his mother had been prompted by anything other than exactly what it was. She hadn't been looking for a way to unearth his motivations so she could share them with the rest of the world. He couldn't actually believe that, could he?

"Despite my best efforts to keep you in the dark, it was clear you had enough on me to write ten articles if that was what you wanted," he continued.

Unwilling to trust his words, Carrie shook her head. "I don't believe you any more than I do Sophie. Are you telling me this has all been a game . . . you don't have any feelings for me?" She shook her head.

"Okay, sure. You're attractive and fun, and for a while I actually thought there might be something between us, but these last few days have shown me nothing permanent will ever come of this relationship." He looked almost apologetic. "I was perfectly content until you came into my life; I will be again, and so will you. We had a good run, but it's time we were realistic enough to accept that this relationship isn't good for either of us. It was always about the article."

He couldn't possibly mean what he was telling her. "Finn, please. You're overreacting. Sophie's like that. She makes assumptions she shouldn't. I would never betray your trust. Never."

He stared at her long and hard. "You're dying to

write the article, aren't you? You as much as admitted it. An article on me would make your career."

"I don't care about that stupid article; what matters to me is you."

"Then you're lying." He wiped his hand across his face.

"I am not lying."

He exhaled slowly. "Carrie, I saw it on your laptop."

"What?" She slowly shook her head. "But that was before—" Abruptly, she stopped and sucked in her breath. She'd never deleted the rough draft of the article she'd written while in Alaska. It remained on her computer, nearly forgotten. Finn had used her laptop to check availability with the airlines and his emails. He must have seen it then. "Okay, yes, there's an article there, but did you look at the date? I wrote that while I was at the cabin before . . . before you asked me not to publish it."

Finn shook his head. "We're in over our heads. This isn't going to work. Sophie's comments should be a wake-up call to us both. She knows it, your mother knows it, and for that matter my mother, too. It's time for us to be honest, Carrie. This relationship is doomed. It always has been."

"Stop saying that. I'm not willing to give up on us. I love you, Finn." She threw her heart out to him and waited breathlessly for him to respond.

For the longest time all he did was stare at her. His shoulders sagged, and he released his breath in a long, slow exhale. "I'm sorry, Carrie. I don't love you."

"Now who's lying?" she asked, hiccupping on a half-sob. It felt as if the floor had started to pitch beneath her feet as though she were on board a ship, tossed about in a vicious storm at sea.

"Believe what you want."

His words hit her with a nearly physical impact. It felt as though he'd reached out and shoved her backward. Despite herself, she stumbled back several steps.

Although she recognized that it would do little good to argue with him, she made the effort. "What about the toaster?" she whispered, hardly able to speak because of the tightness in her throat. She might be able to believe him if she didn't know about the significance of the toaster. It meant far more to him than an antique. It'd been his way of telling her she was important to him. As important to him as his mother had been to his father.

"Ah, yes, the toaster. That was a rather brilliant move on my part. I didn't know yet if you'd take my request seriously. I needed to do something that would have an effect on you, and I figured you'd ask my mother about it."

Her knees suddenly felt like they were about to collapse on her. She needed to sit down, and quickly.

Finn started for the door, briefly hesitated, and turned the knob.

"Take the Christmas present with you," she called after him, anger coming to rescue her pride in those final seconds.

"Keep it," he said on his way out the door, as if it meant nothing.

As if she meant nothing.

Chapter Thirteen

Carrie didn't even bother to go to bed that night or the next, sleeping in fits and starts, a few minutes at a time. She sat up on her sofa with a quilt her mother had lovingly crafted for her while she was in college. With its thick warmth wrapped around her shoulders, she tried to digest what had happened between her and Finn, and what would happen next—if anything. Try as she might, she couldn't make herself believe that the things he said had even the smallest semblance of truth.

At seven Monday morning she tossed aside the quilt, and although she was bone tired, she readied for work. Staring at her reflection, Carrie did her best to disguise the dark circles beneath her eyes, but with little success.

Sophie, who usually rushed into the office five minutes late, was already at her cubicle when Carrie arrived at her normal time. Her friend had left several messages, but Carrie hadn't answered her phone or responded to text messages.

Sophie didn't wait for Carrie to remove her hat and coat before she pounced on her, seeking information.

"What happened Saturday night after Bruce and I left?" she demanded. "Why didn't you answer any of my phone messages or texts?"

Carrie stared back blankly.

Sophie lowered her voice. "I feel terrible that Finn heard the things I said."

Fearing that if she said one word she would give in to the emotion that threatened to overwhelm her, Carrie simply shook her head.

"You have to tell me," Sophie pleaded. "Me and my big mouth. I'll never forgive myself. How could I be so stupid?"

Carrie swallowed against the tightening knot in her throat and gave an offhand shrug. "Apparently, you were right."

"Right?" Sophie's jaw dropped several inches. "Right about what?"

Bending over to turn on her computer, Carrie did her best to sound nonchalant and disengaged. "You might as well say 'I told you so.' Finn and I are over."

Sophie's look of disbelief slowly evolved into a frown. "You're kidding, right?"

How Carrie wished she was. In answer, she shook her head. "Finn wanted to end it; he basically said the same thing you did, that we could never make it work, blah, blah, blah."

"Finn said that and you believed him? Listen, Carrie, I was wrong. Before I left I saw the way he looked at you. If a man ever looked at me like that, I'd be willing to give up chocolate and bear his children."

With all her heart, Carrie wanted to believe that was true, but she wasn't sure it even mattered. Finn was gone. Nevertheless, she was hanging on to that slender thread called hope, only in her case it was ragged hope.

Sophie pulled out a chair and sat down. "Anyone with two functioning brain cells could see he's nuts over you."

"I'd like to believe you, I really would, but he left shortly after you did, and I haven't heard from him since. Frankly I doubt that I will."

Sophie stiffened. "Fine, then write that article. He can't treat you like that."

Why was it everything went back to that stupid article?

"You're going to do it, aren't you? You'd be a fool not to."

Carrie didn't need to think about it. Undoubtedly, it was what Finn expected of her. "I don't want to talk about it." Instead, she reached for her mouse and clicked on an email.

"You've got to write it," Sophie insisted.

"No, I don't."

"Are you off your rocker?" Sophie stood and did

a complete three-hundred-and-sixty-degree turn. "Someone call a medic; Carrie's losing her mind."

Carrie stopped her friend from making fools of them both. "Don't you understand that's exactly what Finn expects me to do?"

"Then give him what he wants," Sophie suggested. "That way you can both have what you want. Don't be an idiot, Carrie. This opportunity is one that comes along once or maybe twice in a career. This is your chance to prove yourself to Nash."

"I can't."

"Why not?"

"Because Finn loves me." It was the only scenario that made sense to Carrie. He had vehemently denied it, but Carrie refused to accept that. For two nights she'd mulled over his words, and ultimately she chose not to believe them. She couldn't feel the things she did if it'd all been a lie.

"Where is Finn now?" Sophie asked. "Let me talk some sense into him."

"Sophie—" Carrie really didn't feel like discussing this now.

"Is he still in Chicago?" Sophie asked, cutting her off.

Carrie shook her head. "He's gone."

"Back to Alaska?"

Carrie didn't know, and so she shrugged. It didn't matter. She was confident that no matter where he was, Alaska or Timbuktu, he was as miserable as she.

"What happens now?" Sophie asked, showing signs of sympathy. "This is dreadful, just dreadful. I don't think I can bear it."

Again, Carrie answered with a lift of her shoulders. "I've spent the better part of the last two days and nights going over a variety of scenarios. I have to believe Finn will have a change of heart."

"You mean he'll come back for you?"

"No . . . he won't do that." That wouldn't be his way.

"I don't understand," Sophie said, speaking softly now.

"He's going to regret the lie that he doesn't care, doesn't love me, and so he'll make it up to me the only way he can."

"And how's that?"

"He'll ask me to be the one to break the story on him."

"Of course." Sophie vaulted to her feet and clapped her hands. "Of course. It's brilliant. And you'll do it, and then . . ."

"No."

Sophie froze. "No?"

"No," Carrie repeated. "I'm going to refuse."

"Stop." Sophie planted her hands on top of her head. "This is like a chess game, and I'm losing track of the moves. If he wants you to write the piece, then why won't you do it?"

"Because if I refuse it will force his hand."

Sophie scratched the side of her head as though puzzled. "I don't follow."

"Finn wants me to publish something about him because it will salve his conscience. It's the one way he has of apologizing, of letting me know he loves me. But I won't do it, because it's the only way I can think to let him know I love him. It's the one thing I can do to tell him my feelings haven't changed."

Sophie sat back in the chair. "You're losing me, girlfriend."

It was a gamble for sure, Carrie realized. And until she got word from Finn, she would need to keep silent. There was a chance, of course, that she was completely wrong and she would never hear from him again. For now, it was a waiting game.

The first week of December passed. Long, torturous days in which there was complete silence from Finn. Somehow Carrie got through her and Sophie's little Christmas gathering. She managed to smile and even laugh now and again. It was a great party, everyone said, and Carrie was grateful she was able to pull it off. The only person who seemed to notice that Carrie's spirits were low was Sophie.

"I'm having a hard time dealing with this guilt," her friend confessed. "I feel like I'm to blame. I look at you and I want to cry. You're so miserable, and it's all my fault."

Carrie did her best to reassure her friend. "Don't worry. These matters have a way of working out how they're meant to be." While she might have sounded confident, Carrie was anything but.

Another week of silence followed. Carrie lost weight. Sleep felt like a luxury.

On Friday a few days before Christmas, just before quitting time, the office threw a small party. Carrie was scheduled to fly back to Seattle in the morning, to be with her family, and she was getting ready to head home to pack when she got word that Nash wanted to speak to her in his office.

She knocked against his door and stepped inside. Without looking away from his computer screen, he motioned for her to take a seat.

Carrie complied.

"I just got off the phone with some New York publicity woman," he said, frowning at her as if seeing her for the first time. "How is it that you know Finn Dalton?"

"Who says I know Finn?" she parried with a question of her own.

"You said you were determined to find him, as I recall."

"So I did." She folded her hands in her lap, afraid the trembling would give her away.

"Well, congratulations. It seems you looked

under the right rock, because this PR person called to tell me Finn Dalton is ready to let someone interview him. The surprising part is that he requested you, and he claims you already know everything there is to know. He's requested you write the piece."

Carrie's eyes drifted shut. This was exactly the news she'd been waiting to hear. She'd been right. Finn had offered her the assignment. A sense of release and joy rushed through her. He was as much as telling her that he loved her. She pressed her hand to her mouth, fearing she was about to break into sobs.

"I can see you're pleased. I'd be crying with joy, too. I don't know what you did, but congratulations. This is one of the biggest coups this newspaper has had in a long time. How soon can you write the piece? If possible, I'd like to have it for the weekend edition."

"Sorry, Nash, Mr. Dalton's publisher is going to need to find someone else."

"What?" Nash nearly came out of his chair. "Is this a joke? If so, I'm not laughing."

Now wasn't the time to back down. Carrie had to remain strong. As badly as she ached to give in, she couldn't do it. "I hate to disappoint you, but you'll need to find someone else."

Nash shook his head. "The publisher insists you have to be the one. No one else."

It was exactly as she'd calculated. "Sorry." She blinked back tears.

The hard-core newsman glared at her. "Your job is on the line, Ms. Slayton. This newspaper can't afford to let this opportunity slip by. I'm giving you twenty-four hours to change your mind."

Losing her job was an aspect of this decision that she hadn't considered. Carrie swallowed hard and bit into her lower lip. "It won't matter if it's twenty-four hours or twenty-four days. I'm not going to change my mind."

Disgusted, Nash shook his head.

"I'm leaving in the morning for Seattle to see my family." It seemed her Christmas break would now be spent seeking another job. It was a steep price to pay to prove her love to Finn, but she wouldn't back down.

"Go have Christmas with your family," Nash said, motioning for her to leave his office. "But take this time to think about what I said. I'm serious, Carrie. Write the article and keep your job. Otherwise, you can clear out your desk when you return."

"And if I write the article, what about your promise to me?"

"What promise?"

"Any assignment I want, any department." He hadn't said it quite like that; still, it wouldn't do any harm to press her point.

Nash hesitated and then sighed. "It's negotiable."

Sophie was waiting for her at Carrie's desk when she returned. Her friend had glittery silver tinsel wrapped around her neck like a Hawaiian lei. "So, what did Nash want?"

When she told her about the call from the New York publicist, Sophie leaped up and gave a loud cheer. "This is exactly what you said would happen."

"This is the way I *hoped* it would play out."

"So?" Sophie said eagerly, shifting her arms back and forth, "what's the next move?"

"I don't know."

"What do you mean you don't know? I thought you had this all planned out."

How Carrie wished that were true. She knew what she had to do, but the rest was up to Finn.

The next day Carrie sat at the O'Hare Airport gate, waiting to board her flight to Seattle, when her cell chirped. She didn't recognize the number but saw that it was an Alaska prefix.

"Hello," she answered hesitatingly.

"Carrie, this is Sawyer O'Halloran."

"Sawyer?" She couldn't imagine why he would be calling her, unless something had happened to Finn. She gripped hold of the phone with both hands, instantly alarmed. "Is everything all right? Has Finn been hurt?"

"Yes . . . He isn't in the hospital or anything, if

that's what you're wondering. What happened between the two of you, anyway?"

Carrie relaxed a bit. "You'll need to ask him about that."

"You're joking, right? He hasn't been himself since he returned from Chicago. I've never seen him like this. He disappeared for a couple of days, showed up drunk as a coyote, which is surprising, because he isn't much of a drinker. He isn't talking to anyone—well, other than me, but it's difficult to understand what he's saying. Furthermore, he isn't eating or sleeping."

Carrie exhaled and whispered into the small receiver. "Frankly, I'm not doing much better myself."

"You two had a falling out?"

"You could say that."

"Listen, before we go any further, Finn doesn't know I'm contacting you. If he finds out about this, he'll have my head."

"How'd you get my personal phone number?"

"Easy. I waited until he passed out and then checked his cell."

"He was that drunk?" This didn't sound anything like Finn. It didn't make her feel any better knowing that he was miserable. All Carrie wanted was for this foolishness to be over.

"No, he wasn't drunk, but practically dead on his feet. I don't know the last time he slept. He kept mumbling something about giving you a shot at what you wanted, and you rejecting that. Don't know what that's about, but I figure you must."

Carrie simply shook her head. "If he wants to talk to me, all he needs to do is call."

"I'm not telling him that."

At this point, Carrie suspected Finn wasn't listening to advice from anyone.

"I have a feeling this all goes back to that article you wanted to publish. The one Finn asked you not to write."

"I'm afraid so. At first he was adamant I not write the piece, and now it seems he's had a change of heart. He's giving me what he thinks I want, but it isn't. What I want is him."

The line went silent. "I'm confused. He's giving you this opportunity because he loves you and you're turning it down because you love him? Have I got that right?"

"You do." Her flight was announced, and the boarding process had already started. "Listen, Sawyer, I need to get off the phone, but I want you to tell Finn something for me, if you would."

"I'm not letting him know we had this conversation. I value my head, which he'd bite off if he got so much as an inkling that I've contacted you."

"Fine, I understand, but if the opportunity comes up and he finds out we chatted, tell him that before I will agree to write a single word, he will need to sit down with me face-to-face; otherwise, it's no deal."

"That's your final answer?" Sawyer wanted to know.

"Yes."

Carrie disconnected the call and felt better than she had in almost three weeks.

Chapter Fourteen

Carrie's flight from Chicago landed at Sea-Tac Airport on time. It would be good to be with family over the Christmas holiday. She needed the comfort of their acceptance and love. Not a moment passed when Finn wasn't in the forefront of her mind.

She exited the plane and automatically reached for her cell, turning it on. Either her mother or father would be waiting in the cell-phone waiting area for her text message. As soon as it powered up, she typed in the information that she'd landed safely, and then headed toward the exit signs. She would go directly to baggage claim and meet them at the curb for pickup.

Dragging her carry-on behind her, she was following her fellow passengers onto the escalator when her phone beeped, indicating she had a text message. Assuming it was one of her parents, she didn't immediately check. About halfway up, she glanced at her phone and saw that the text was from Finn. It shook her up so badly that she dropped the phone. Carrie watched in horror as it went tumbling down the escalator steps. "Please, someone grab that for me!" she cried out in a panic.

"Got it," a woman at the bottom shouted back to her.

As soon as Carrie reached the top, she hurriedly circled around and leaped onto the opposite escalator, racing down the steps, unwilling to stand and wait. The woman remained at the bottom and handed the cell back to her.

"Thank you," Carrie whispered, grabbing hold of it. "Thank you so much."

Her heart raced at a frantic speed as she opened Finn's text.

Why won't you write the article?

Her fingers moved in a blur as she typed her response. I would be happy to.

Good.

Once you give me a face-to-face interview.

His response was immediate. Not going to happen.

Then get someone else. She didn't expect Finn to be thrilled with her stipulation. Seeing her again was the last thing he wanted, because it was sure to be difficult to answer her questions, and, even more so, to send her away.

She waited for a response, but none came.

Having collected her bag, Carrie was standing in the cold outside the airport, waiting to be picked up by her mother, when she heard the ping indicating Finn had responded. *Why are you so stubborn?*

An involuntary smile came over her as she rushed to answer. *Because you lied. You love me.*

Finn didn't deny or confirm her text, not that she'd expected he would. After a couple of moments, Carrie placed her phone inside her purse. The ache in her heart was back, stronger than ever. This could quite possibly be the last communication she might ever have with Finn. The thought sent her Christmas spirits spiraling downward.

Her mother pulled up to the airport curb, and after sticking her bags in the backseat, Carrie climbed inside the vehicle.

"I'm so glad you're home," her mother said, and they briefly hugged.

"I am, too," Carrie assured her. They drove off, heading to the family home, where her brother, his wife, and his children would be waiting. Soon they'd all be gathered around the table, and there would be laughter and conversation. Finn had never known this, and Carrie hungered to share her family with him.

"You okay, honey?" her mother asked, as they merged into the heavy freeway traffic. "You don't look so well. It's Finn, isn't it?"

Carrie nodded.

"How much weight have you lost?"

Carrie shrugged. "A few pounds is all."

Reaching over, her mother gave Carrie's hand a

gentle squeeze. "Mark my words, it will all work out."

Carrie desperately wanted that to be true. Everything seemed so hopeless at the moment.

"Time is the great healer," her mother assured her.

She'd spent an hour on the phone with her mother shortly after her breakup with Finn, pouring out all her hurt and fears. Patty Slayton hadn't offered empty reassurances or reminded Carrie of her own concerns over this relationship; instead, she'd simply listened. At the end she'd said, "You really do love him, don't you?"

"Oh, yes." There was no doubt in Carrie's mind. Finn Dalton owned her heart. He carried it with him, and now the question, the real question, was what he intended to do with it.

"We're just glad you're home for the holidays," her mother said, pulling her back into the present.

"So am I." Carrie didn't mention that she might be returning to Seattle on a more permanent basis. For the first time since she'd spoken to Nash, she actually considered caving in. That was what Finn wanted her to do in an effort to ease his conscience. He could break her heart and then walk away without guilt because he'd done her a good turn. Writing that blasted article was what everyone hoped she'd do.

"I need to run an errand in the morning," Carrie casually mentioned once she was home and had emptied her suitcase. Dinner was over and her brother and family had returned to their home. "Do you mind if I borrow the car?" she asked her parents.

"You going to run off to Alaska?" her father asked.

"Nick Slayton," her mother hissed in a low, warning breath.

"Well, if Carrie is going to break up with Finn Dalton, why can't she do it after we have a chance to meet him?"

Both her mother and Carrie ignored the comment.

"I doubt very much that I'll be going to Alaska," Carrie said.

"Of course you can take the car." Her mother cast her a questioning glance. "I don't have any plans for the morning."

"I shouldn't be gone more than an hour or two," Carrie assured her.

First thing the next morning, Carrie contacted Finn's mother and they set a time to meet. Joan had the front door open before Carrie had reached the end of the short walkway.

The older woman held open the screen door. They briefly hugged before Joan brought Carrie into the house. Her tree was up and decorated with festive ornaments, and her fireplace mantel displayed a wooden Nativity scene. Joan indicated that Carrie should take a seat on the sofa. Finn's mother had a teapot and two cups out, along with a plate of decorated sugar cookies.

"Finn used to help me decorate the cookies every Christmas," she said as they sat next to each other on the sofa. "He enjoyed it, although his father feared I was turning him into a sissy. My goodness, the boy was only four years old."

Joan handed her a cup of freshly poured tea, which Carrie accepted, holding on to the tiny saucer with one hand and the teacup with the other.

"Have you heard from my son?" Joan asked.

"Just briefly." There'd been nothing since their quick text exchanges late yesterday afternoon.

"It sounds like Finn is as stubborn as his father."

Carrie was afraid that was the case.

Joan exhaled as though emotionally bracing herself for what was coming. "You brought Paul's wedding band back to me?"

"Yes, I'm so sorry. I tried."

"I know, dear. I should never have put you in such an awkward position."

Carrie disagreed. "I doubt I could have convinced anyone to fly me to Finn's cabin without it, so the ring served a purpose." She dug it out of her purse, and with regret returned it to Finn's mother, feeling like she'd failed her.

Joan's eyes revealed her disappointment. "I so hoped . . ."

"I know; I did, too."

"I'm confident Paul went to his grave loving me. Unfortunately, pride prevented him from letting me know he wanted me back. He was unwilling to compromise. It could only be his way."

Carrie feared Joan might be right and Finn was like his father. He, too, would be willing to walk away from her and not look back.

They sipped their tea in silence for several moments while Carrie gathered her thoughts. "I'd appreciate your help with something."

"Of course."

Carrie reached into the bag she'd brought along with her. "I need you to tell me what this is." She brought out the Christmas gift Finn had left under her Christmas tree. Unable to wait any longer, Carrie had unwrapped his gift before she left Chicago, but she didn't have a clue as to what it might be. It was a narrow stick of what appeared to be fossilized ivory and was about twenty inches in length.

The night before, Carrie's father had taken a look at it and shook his head. He didn't have an answer for her.

Joan reached for the object and released a soft "Oh, my."

"What is it?" Carrie asked.

Joan reverently ran her hand down the piece, and then raised her eyes to Carrie's. "My son gave you this for Christmas?"

"Yes. What can you tell me about it?"

Joan nodded. "It's an oosik."

"Which is?" This wasn't helping.

"It's a walrus penis bone."

Carrie gasped. "A what?"

Joan laughed at the look that came over Carrie. "Leave it to my son."

"He gave me a toaster and a walrus penis bone?"

"This one is rather rare, though, if it's the same one Paul got all those years ago from an elderly Alaskan native."

"An oosik?" Carrie repeated, the word unfamiliar on her tongue.

"This one is a fossilized baculum and comes from an extinct walrus. They're highly collectible for Alaskan art. It was one of Paul's most prized possessions. At the time, and remember, this was many years ago, it was valued at around twenty thousand dollars."

"Why would Finn give it to me?" She wanted to clasp it to her breast, but that wouldn't bring Finn back.

"Isn't it obvious, my dear? He loves you."

It was too valuable, and it clearly held sentimental value to Joan. "I can't keep this," she said sadly, her mind made up. "I'd rather you take it."

Automatically, Joan shook her head. "Finn wanted you to have it."

"Please," Carrie whispered. "It should stay with you. And if by chance Finn and I . . ." Her voice caught, and she had to stop talking for fear her emotions might overwhelm her. "If Finn and I," she repeated, "manage to get back together, then you can save it to give to one of your grandchildren."

Joan's eyes filled with unshed tears, and she slowly nodded.

Deep down, Carrie believed she wouldn't hear from Finn again. She'd played her hand, laid down her cards, and her ploy had failed. Finn was unwilling to meet her face-to-face for an interview or anything else. He couldn't look her in the eye and say the things he had to her while in her kitchen, and they both knew it.

Christmas Eve day Carrie helped her mother get everything ready for their annual Christmas buffet. Instead of the big traditional dinner, complete with turkey and stuffing plus all the fixings, her mother served a multitude of longtime family favorites: several salads, casseroles, fried chicken, deviled eggs, and a ham, plus a wide variety of desserts.

On Christmas Day, friends and family would stop by to partake. Carrie always enjoyed this special time working in the kitchen with her mother. It seemed the most important discussions of her life had taken place in front of the stove or the refrigerator.

Carrie sliced the cooked potatoes for the potato

salad, her father's favorite, when her mother unexpectedly came to her and hugged her. "I know how hard this year has been for you, honey. Your heart is aching."

"I love him, Mom."

"Talking about him might help. Do you want to tell me what it is that you find so compelling about Finn Dalton?"

Discussing her feelings was exactly what Carrie needed. Everyone else seemed to tiptoe around anything having to do with Finn, afraid to bring up any reference to him. Carrie realized they were simply looking to protect her, but Finn had become the subject everyone had chosen to ignore.

"He's not like any man I've ever known," she told her mother. "He's resourceful and resilient, quick-witted and generous. He has the most wonderful subtle sense of humor. I can laugh with him more than I have with anyone else I've ever met. And he's incredibly intelligent. Everyone looks at us and all they see are the differences, but beneath it all we share the same values, the same sense of what's important. He told me over Thanksgiving how much he envies me my family, and if he ever had one of his own he'd make sure he would be the kind of husband and father my own dad has been." She paused, remembering the night they'd stood out and gazed at the heavens. "And while he'd never openly admit it, he loves Christmas. He helped me put up decorations without a word of complaint. He has a Nativity set from when he was a kid and admitted he sets it up every year. I don't think anyone else knows he does that." She smiled, remembering how she'd amused herself while he was gone from the cabin. "When I was with him in Alaska, I hung paper snowflakes from the ceiling of his cabin."

Her mother laughed. "I can only imagine what he thought of that."

"The truth is, Mom, I don't think he minded. For all I know, they are still up. They should have been stars, though, instead of snowflakes."

"Oh?"

"After the snowstorm had died down, we stood outside under the stars. Oh, Mom, you can't imagine how beautiful the night sky is in Alaska. All those stars—I've never seen anything that could compare to it. They were like fairy dust sprinkled across the heavens. I think it was on that starry night that I realized I was falling in love with Finn."

He'd felt it, too, Carrie knew. Everything had changed between them from that moment on. It'd been magical, wondrous, with his arms around her. He would never admit it, but those few minutes under the stars had shaken Finn. They'd deeply affected her as well.

"What about his family?" her mother asked.

"His mother is wonderful, and she loves her son and wants to be reunited with him. Finn is struggling with that." He'd never come out and say as much, but Carrie could sense it from little things that had happened, things he'd said and done. He wanted to ignore the fact that he had a mother, but try as he might, he still cared.

"He seems to be struggling with a great deal at the moment," her mother said.

"He is," Carrie agreed, and like her, he was hurting. She wondered if he thought about the things they'd discussed when he'd been with her over Thanksgiving. He'd told her his dreams and she'd shared her own, and while they lived in different worlds, they'd found common ground and a deep connection.

Perhaps she was being unreasonable about all this, Carrie mused. If Finn wanted to clear his conscience and be done with the relationship all in one fell swoop, she shouldn't stand in his way. This was what he wanted. No one could write about him the way she could. Carrie suspected that outside of Sawyer, few knew Finn better than she did.

"I'm afraid, Mom—afraid I will never love anyone as deeply as I do Finn."

"Oh, honey, you can't see it now, but in time you'll be able to remember him without pain. Love doesn't die."

"Loving someone shouldn't hurt like this."

"True," her mother whispered, and placed her arm around Carrie's shoulders. "And in the future, when you're able to look back, I promise you it won't hurt as intensely as it does now. You'll feel sad for what might have been, but the pain will be gone."

Later, after all the salads had been made and the dishes washed and put away, Carrie retreated to her childhood bedroom. She sat on her bed, rehashing the conversation with her mother. It'd been a good talk, and while she didn't hold out much hope, she couldn't help reaching for her phone, longing for a text or call from Finn.

There wasn't one.

In a couple of hours, Carrie would be joining her family for Christmas Eve services at their church. She wasn't much in the mood, but she wouldn't disappoint her family by staying home. Church was exactly where she needed to be. This was Christmas, with or without Finn.

Before she could change her mind, she reached for her phone and sent a brief message to him.

Merry Christmas. Look at the stars tonight and remember me.

Chapter Fifteen

❄

Christmas morning, Carrie woke and waited for the dark cloud that seemed to hang over her head to return. It didn't. She sat up in bed with a deep sense of peace. She'd followed her heart, and while she would always love Finn, she was ready to move forward. Today was Christmas, and she wasn't going to allow her current sorrows to mar the day.

Hearing movement in the kitchen, she knew her parents were up. They enjoyed their morning ritual of having coffee together. How fortunate she was to have parents who continued to love and care for each other. Carrie didn't want to disturb their special time, and so she gathered her clothes together and headed into her tiny bathroom for a shower.

Her mother noticed the change in Carrie's attitude right away. "I feel better," she said, hugging both her parents. "I'm going to be okay now."

"I know you will be," her mother said, hugging her back.

"I'd like to give that young man a piece of my

mind," her father insisted. "If I had my way, I'd string Finn Dalton up by his thumbs for hurting my little girl."

"Oh, Daddy," Carrie chided, loving him for wanting to make things right for his daughter.

By noon her brother and his family had stopped by for breakfast on their way to his in-laws'. All the gifts had been opened, and Carrie was busy in the kitchen, helping her mother get everything set up for their buffet, when the doorbell chimed.

"That'll be Charlie," her father called out from the other room.

"Uncle" Charlie Hines was a longtime family friend who'd remained a bachelor. He made sure he was one of the first to stop by for the feast, claiming he never ate better than Christmas Day at Nick and Patty's.

Carrie and her mother had barely gotten the food displayed on the table.

"That Charlie," her mother said under her breath, setting down a pitcher of water. "He comes earlier every year."

"It's probably the only decent dinner he eats," Carrie added, as she followed her mother out to greet him.

Only it wasn't Charlie who stood in the middle of the living room. Instead, it was Joan and Finn. Mother and son. Together.

Thankfully, Carrie had set down the last of the salads from the kitchen; otherwise, there would be lettuce and heaven knew what else tossed all across the carpet.

"Merry Christmas," Joan said. "I hate to intrude, but I brought someone with me I thought you might like to see."

Carrie's mouth had gone completely dry. She couldn't utter a word—not a single, solitary word.

"You're not intruding," Carrie's mother assured her, as she stepped forward to clasp the other woman's hand. "I'm Patty Slayton, Carrie's mother."

"Joan Dalton Reese, Finn's mother."

The two women hugged, and the introductions continued as Nick came in.

Finn's intense gaze settled on Carrie. Everyone seemed to be watching them. Carrie wanted to welcome them both, but couldn't because she found it impossible to speak. Never, in all her life, had she seen a more welcome sight than Finnegan Dalton standing in the middle of her parents' living room early Christmas afternoon. He seemed to fill up the space, his eyes boring into hers, waiting, questioning.

Not knowing what else to do, Carrie did what seemed to be the only sensible thing—she rushed across the room and launched herself into Finn's arms.

He caught her around the waist, lifting her off the floor. And then they were kissing. It felt as if the last few weeks boiled down to this one hungry, passionate kiss. It was as if they were starved for each other.

Carrie's hands framed his face, his beautiful bearded face. The beard wasn't as thick as before, but his whiskers were back. His beautiful, dark whiskers. It didn't matter that they had an audience or that Joan was chatting animatedly with her parents. The only important thing was Finn, the man she loved.

"Come into the family room," her mother was saying to Joan. "I have the feeling these two might appreciate a few minutes alone."

"Before he leaves I want to talk to that young man," her father objected.

"Not to worry," Joan assured him. "I believe Finn wants to talk to you, too."

And then it was just the two of them, as her parents and Joan left the room.

Finn lowered her until her feet were on the floor. Carrie kept her hands on his face, unable to stop looking at him. "You're here," she whispered. "You're actually here."

She led him to the sofa and then sat on his lap. His eyes were eating her up as if he'd been without water for far too long and she was a freshwater spring. "What have you done to me, Carrie Slayton?"

"Loved you," she returned.

"I gave you the career opportunity of a lifetime, and you turned it down." He shook his head as if

even now he couldn't believe that she'd refused.
Carrie found it hard to believe herself, only it had
been necessary.

"My career isn't nearly as important as you are."

"This is crazy, Carrie. We have everything going
against us. You live in Chicago, and I'm in
Alaska . . ."

"I'll move," she said, cutting him off, and then
pulled his mouth to hers and kissed him in a way
that left them both weak and breathless. "We'll
make it work," she insisted, her eyes still closed.
She reveled in the taste and feel of him holding her.
It'd been far too long since she'd been in his arms.
She hadn't realized how badly she'd missed his
touch.

"When you kiss me like that you make me believe."

"Good." She couldn't keep from touching him.
Her hands roamed over his neck and shoulders, sa-
voring the feel of him. "You've reconciled with
your mother?"

He rubbed his hand over his eyes. "I'd pushed
you out of my life. I'd been alone before, but not
like this, and then I remembered something you'd
said."

"Me?"

"Yes, you." He leaned down and kissed the tip of
her nose. "I asked if my mother needed anything,
and you said the only thing she really needed was
her son."

"I was with her yesterday morning." Carrie couldn't believe Joan would hold back the news that she'd heard from Finn.

"I didn't call her before I came. I wasn't sure I had the courage to go through with it until I pulled up to her house late last night. I told myself I was coming to Seattle to make amends with her, but the real reason was I couldn't stay away from you. Not for another minute."

"Oh, Finn, this is the best Christmas of my life."

He couldn't seem to stop staring at her. "You gave my mother the oosik," he commented.

Carrie lowered her gaze. "I couldn't keep anything that valuable, Finn. It was more important that she have it than me."

"But what you said to her," he returned, frowning.

Carrie couldn't remember anything specific. "What do you mean?"

"That if the two of us were to get back together, she should save it for one of her grandchildren."

Carrie relaxed and smiled. The warm, happy feeling that had come over her that morning intensified. Had her heart known Finn was close? she wondered. She hardly knew how else to explain this sensation.

"You want it all, don't you? Marriage, children, a career."

"Of course. It's what you want, too, Finn."

He closed his eyes and nodded. "Yes," he whispered, "more than I ever knew, although I didn't realize it until I met you."

Carrie braced her forehead against his. "It doesn't matter to me where we settle—Alaska, Washington, Illinois—because my home is wherever you are."

He hugged her even closer. "I thought I could walk away from you, but I couldn't. I've never needed anyone the way I need you. I felt alone, truly alone, for the first time. Then you sent me that text, reminding me about the night we viewed the stars. You asked me to remember you. Did you honestly believe forgetting you was even possible? I fell in love with you that starry night."

"That was the night when I realized I was falling in love with you, too," she confessed. It had been that special moment, gazing up at the heavens, when she'd felt that connection with Finn, unaware that from that moment forward their futures would be forever linked. It seemed as though the heavens had smiled down on them both and offered them a blessing.

"I can't believe you're here," Carrie whispered, worshipping him with her eyes, loving him so much it felt as though her heart were about to crack wide open.

"Oh, yes, I'm here and I'm not going away. I doubt Sawyer is talking to me any longer, and even Hennessey looks at me with disgust." He studied her, his gaze delving into hers. "I hardly know myself any longer."

"Oh, Finn, I love you so much."

He brushed the hair from her forehead. "Answer me truthfully, Carrie. Would you seriously consider resigning from your job with the newspaper?"

This wasn't a difficult question. Carrie nodded. Her ultimate goal had always been to eventually return to Seattle. "I don't have to work for a newspaper to be a writer. I'd even be happy freelancing from home."

He hugged her close. "My home is wherever you are. I think to be fair to us both, we can divide our time between Seattle and Alaska."

"You'd be willing to do that?"

Finn smiled down on her and kissed her again. "I want the opportunity to get to know my mother, and this will give you a chance to be close to your own family. We'll make it work, Carrie."

"My home is with you and with Hennessey, and then later, of course, we'll be adding to the family."

His head came back up. "You want another dog?"

Carrie slapped his chest. "No, silly. Children."

"Oh, yes," he said with a chuckle.

Carrie nestled her head beneath his chin. "Things are right between you and your mother?" Although she hadn't been able to take her eyes off Finn, Carrie had noticed the happiness that seemed to radiate off Joan. It seemed both Carrie and Joan were having the best Christmases of their lives.

"You were right about her. She's never stopped loving me."

"You seem to have that effect on women."

He brought her mouth close to his. "Certain women, at any rate."

"This woman."

Finn spread nibbling kisses down the side of her neck. "This man loves this woman."

"Good, because this is just the beginning for us. And this time it's for keeps."

"For keeps," Finn repeated. He was willing to admit he'd been a fool. He'd assumed he'd be able to walk away from Carrie and not look back. At the time, it'd seemed the prudent choice. He knew when he found the article on her laptop that Carrie had never intended to submit it. Finding it gave him all the excuse he needed to break it off. Only she'd called his bluff. She'd forced him to lie. He wasn't proud of the things he'd said to Carrie. At the time, it had seemed necessary. Finn had believed that it would be tough the first couple of days but within a short amount of time he'd be over her.

Wrong.

Miserable didn't even begin to describe his feelings. He felt lost, cast adrift with nothing to anchor him. Before Carrie had entered his life, everything seemed perfectly fine. He'd been content. Happy, even—and perhaps he was.

Then she was dumped into his well-ordered existence—no thanks to Sawyer O'Halloran—and everything changed. All at once he became aware of the dark shadows in what had once been light, the isolation he'd accepted rather than deal with the past and his parents' divorce. At first he assumed he could let her go, and he later realized he was making the same mistake as his father with his unwillingness to compromise. His father had been determined to stand his ground. If Joan loved him, she would accept his terms, and as a result he'd ended up lonely and bitter. Finn refused to repeat history. He loved Carrie, and if loving her meant spending part of the year in Seattle, then that was a small sacrifice in order to make her his wife. In order to make her happy.

His thoughts returned to his ridiculous efforts to sever the relationship. Carrie knew him far too well, had refused to believe he didn't love her. How easily she saw through his ploy. She'd read him perfectly. If that wasn't bad enough, she'd been unwilling to settle for his token apology by giving her the opportunity to write the article about him that everyone seemed to want.

This woman could be stubborn. It didn't help matters that she held his heart in the palm of her hand. Still, he fought it; still, he assumed he could go on without her. What a laugh that turned out to be.

It wasn't only Carrie, either. In all the years since his mother had walked out, not once had Finn felt the need to connect with her again. She'd left him and his father. Pride demanded that he have nothing more to do with her, despite her repeated efforts to reach out to him.

Feeling alone and lost, Finn had to accept that as difficult as it was to admit, he needed his mother. His children would need their grandmother.

Carrie wanted children. The thought both thrilled and terrified him.

"You've got a funny look," she said, gazing up at him, frowning slightly.

Finn kissed her again, and a sense of happiness and joy filled him until it felt as if he could soar. "We're going to be just fine."

"Yes, I know," Carrie agreed.

Her parents and his mother came back into the room, and Carrie scooted off his lap. They stood and he slipped his arm around her waist.

Her mother's eyes were moist with tears, and she held her fingers against her lips, watching the two of them.

"Are you going to love our Carrie?" Nick Slayton asked.

"Dad!" she protested, clearly embarrassed.

"With all my heart," Finn promised, keeping her close against his side.

"That's good enough for me." Nick thrust out his hand for Finn to shake. "Welcome to the family."

The two men clasped hands, and their gazes held for an extra-long moment as understanding passed between the two of them.

Oh, yes, this was definitely going to be the best Christmas of Finn Dalton's life.

Epilogue

❄

From: girlygirl@seattle.com
Sent: October 22, 2014
To: Sophiepeterson@chicago.com
Subject: The Real Article

Dear Sophie,
The only reason I'm doing this is because you're
my dearest friend and I can trust you not to leak
out my notes from the original interview with
Finn. And yes, I'm still a little overwhelmed with
the response it's received. My new job with *The
Seattle Times* is everything I could have imagined
or hoped to have. No more society-page writing
for this girl.

   You can only imagine how difficult it was to get
Finn to be serious. These are my notes from the
initial interview. After reading this you'll have a
better understanding of why it took as long as it
did to write the piece. Finn made it nearly
impossible and answered my questions far too

literally. Even then the news piece required a lot of editing on my end before I was comfortable enough to give it to Nash.

Here is the from-tape-recorder-to-typed-interview exactly as it happened. I think you'll get a kick out of it, but please don't share this with anyone else.

> **Carrie:** *Thank you, Finn, for giving me this interview.*
> **Finn:** *You're welcome. I wouldn't do this for anyone else, you know.*
> **Carrie:** *I do and I appreciate it.*
> **Finn:** *Will I be rewarded?*
> **Carrie:** *Rewarded? What do you mean?*
> **Finn:** *Use your imagination.*

His grin was huge when he said this, and I knew that I had best distract him before I completely lost control of the interview.

> **Carrie:** *Why did you decide to write* Alone?
> **Finn:** *I don't really consider myself a writer although I've always enjoyed putting my thoughts down on paper. It was the winter of 2008. Maybe 2009, I don't quite remember now. The cold was ruthless and it was impossible to spend more than a few minutes outside without the fear of frostbite. I read one of Jack London's stories about*

*life in Alaska and figured the protagonist in
the story could have survived if he'd known
a bit more about surviving in the wilderness.
Then, too, I'd heard about kids being
addicted to computer games and not
enjoying the great outdoors. To me that's
just plain wrong. Kids need to get outside
and breathe in fresh air. When we start our
family, I can promise you that our children
will be as comfortable living in the tundra as
they are in the big city.*

Carrie: *So, basically, in* Alone *your goal was
to inspire others to see Alaska through your
eyes and inspire the reader to explore the
great outdoors?*

Finn: *Basically. I think it's time we talk
about our family.*

Carrie: *This is an interview, Finn. We need
to stay on topic.*

Finn: *You want children, don't you?*

Carrie: *You know I do.*

Finn: *Good. I'd like to start off with a
couple of girls. They should look like their
mother and then follow with two or three
boys because by then I'll have this parenting
thing down pat. . . . Why are you smiling?*

Carrie: *Because you're being completely
nonsensical. When it comes to our children
we don't really have the option; we have to
accept whatever God decides to give us.*

Finn: *I suppose you're right.*

Carrie: *Can we get back to the interview now?*

Finn: *Okay, but it's tempting to shut off that silly recorder you have. When did they start making them so tiny, anyway?*

Carrie: *That's my phone. Now focus.*

Finn: *I am focused. Anyone ever tell you how kissable your mouth is?*

Carrie: *Finn, I'm serious. I need to finish this interview.*

Finn: *Okay, sorry. How much longer before we're married?*

Carrie: *It's next month, as you well know.*

Finn: *Why are we waiting so long?*

Carrie: *We both decided we should wait a year.*

Finn: *You decided, you mean.*

Carrie: *Can we get back to the interview? Please?*

Finn: *How many more questions do you have?*

Carrie: *We just started. I haven't even gotten to the meat of the piece yet.*

Finn: *Will it take much longer?*

Carrie: *At this rate we could be here for days. Wipe that smile off your face, Finn Dalton.*

Finn: *Okay, ask away.*

Carrie: *Moving right along, can you tell me why you titled the book* Alone?

Finn: *Sure. I didn't. It was the publishing company that came up with the idea. My original title was* Surviving the Alaska Wilderness *but my editor thought it sounded too much like a survival guide.*

Carrie: *It's much more than that.*

Finn: *She thought so too and came up with the title* Alone.

Carrie: *I understand you're writing another book. What can you tell us about that?*

Finn: *Nothing.*

Carrie: *Come on, Finn, I'm serious.*

Finn: *So am I.*

Carrie: *I could torture it out of you.*

Finn: *Promises, promises.*

On a side note, I can tell you his second book is about summers in Alaska and it's an absolutely amazing read. Finn let me read the page proofs before it went into print, and I was riveted from the very first page. I predict it will outsell his first book.

Carrie: *Okay, fine, I won't get into the subject of your next book.*

Finn: *Don't give up so quickly. I can be bought, you know.*

Carrie: *Didn't you ever get lonely living on the tundra by yourself?*

Finn: *Not until recently.*

Carrie: *Recently?*

Finn: *It never bothered me before until I met this girly girl who came traipsing into my life and knocked me off my feet. When I fell, I fell hard. I'd never thought of myself as lonely; the fact is, I've always enjoyed my own company, and then I got zapped.*

Carrie: *Zapped?*

Finn: *After I met you, my entire world got thrown off kilter. Nothing was the same. I couldn't stop thinking about you. I couldn't sleep much either because every time I closed my eyes you were there pestering me.*

Carrie: *I pestered you?*

Finn: *Yes, and I didn't like it much, either. I started growling at friends; even Hennessey didn't want to be around me. It's bad when a man's own dog wants nothing more to do with him.*

How is it, Sophie, that a man can say the most lovable, romantic things, and they come in the form of what seems like an insult? Finn isn't much for romance. Remember the toaster he mailed me? What man mails a woman a toaster? And yet when I discovered the story behind it, I swear it was the most romantic gift I've ever received. Not to mention the oosik he gave me for Christmas last year. And yet I will treasure both the toaster and the oosik more than I would Tahitian pearls.

> **Finn:** *Aren't you going to ask me why I agreed to give this interview?*
> **Carrie:** *Okay, why did you agree to give an interview after insisting on staying out of the public eye? Surely you realize how curious the world is about you?*
> **Finn:** *Let them be curious. I like my privacy.*
> **Carrie:** *I know and I appreciate that you're talking to me, but that doesn't answer the question of why you agreed to this interview.*
> **Finn:** *You should know the answer. I fell in love with the interviewer.*
> **Carrie:** *I fell in love with you, too, with or without the interview.*
> **Finn:** *I know. I realized that when you refused to interview me unless we did it face to face. My goodness, woman, you're stubborn. I still don't understand why you'd do that.*
> **Carrie:** *Stubborn? Me?*

As far as I'm concerned, the man defines the word stubborn. As you can see the interview was quickly going off in a completely irrational direction.

Finn: *I was offering you the opportunity of your career and you refused.*

Carrie: *We're getting off subject again.*

Finn: *Answer the question, Carrie.*

Carrie: *I'm the one who is supposed to be asking the questions here!*

Finn: *Answer this one and we'll go back to your interview.*

Carrie: *Okay, okay. I refused to do the interview because it was the only way I could think to let you know I was in love with you. I refused to use you to advance my career. If you wanted nothing more to do with me, I would deal with that, but I wasn't about to let you buy me off.*

Finn: *I wasn't buying you off. I was giving you a gift, silly girl.*

Carrie: *And why were you gifting me?*

Finn: *Because I was in love with you.*

Carrie: *Exactly my point.*

Finn: *Thankfully you came to your senses.*

Carrie: *Finn Dalton, that is grossly unfair. You're the one who came to me, remember? You were the very best Christmas gift of my life.*

The interview completely dissolved after that. Finn grabbed my phone and turned off the recording, and then before I realized what he intended, I was in his arms. It didn't take long for me to forget about the interview entirely.

This will give you a fairly good idea of why writing this piece was probably the most difficult of my career. Although, I have to admit that it was by far the most amazingly fun one I've ever conducted. I mean, really, how often am I going to interview anyone who keeps side-stepping the questions by kissing me senseless. As it is I should be nominated for a Pulitzer for getting this much down on paper.

I'll close for now, Soph, but will be in touch again soon.

Keep me updated with everyone in Chicago. Miss you all.

Carrie

A Conversation
with Debbie Macomber

❄

How did you come up with the idea for *Starry Night*?

The idea came from an interview I did with a former New York publicist who met her husband, a fishing and hunting expert, while she escorted him on a book tour. I was immediately drawn to the juxtaposition of this classy New Yorker and the rough fishing and hunting guide. Some of my best ideas (nearly all) come from real-life situations.

How is *Starry Night* different from some of your other Christmas books?

I believe that *Starry Night* is probably one of the most romantic books I have written. Many of my Christmas novels contain a lot of comedy. But this particular novel has far more strong romantic elements than what I generally include. And, of course, it has the premise of opposites attracting.

Sort of an interesting side note, I had a hard time choosing a title. Then a friend came up with it while we attended a knitting conference. The minute she suggested it, I felt it was perfect. So many of the holiday books have Christmas in the title or some aspect of the season. Seeing that this story was slightly different from the others, I wanted it to have a distinctive title.

What is it about an "opposites attract" premise, do you think, that is so appealing to readers?

I believe the fascination is that it is so real. So many readers can identify with the powerful way that people seem to be attracted to their opposites. They've seen it happen with their friends and in their own lives.

My husband, Wayne, and I are a good example. Wayne is a shy introvert. I am an outgoing people person. And we are a perfect balance for each other, just as Carrie and Finn are a perfect balance for each other, too.

Finn is such a great romantic hero. Why do you think readers have responded so strongly to him?

I believe that Finn represents Alaska in many readers' eyes. Finn is that rugged, strong individual who could face those hard elements and survive. But all strong men are in need of some of the gentleness that comes with falling in love. And Finn found that in Carrie.

You've written about Alaska before. Why is it such a special setting for you?

Wayne fell in love with Alaska first, back in the 1980s when he worked on the north slope of Prudhoe Bay. He instilled that enthusiasm in me, and we later traveled up past the Arctic Circle while I researched my 1990s Alaska series. Like my husband, I was struck by the rugged beauty of this untamed land. I know that there is a strong romantic element in Alaska that appeals to readers the same way it did to me. So it seemed a natural setting for Finn Dalton.

You're particularly well-known and beloved for your Christmas novels. What do you enjoy most about writing them?

Because I love Christmas so much, these stories are a natural extension of how I celebrate the holidays. I know many people get stressed by doing so much extra this time of year. I wanted to give my readers a big hug, and I knew a fun read would help them relax and smile. Many readers tell me that their first exposure to me came through one of my Christmas books, and I have been fortunate enough to have had four of them made into Hallmark movies. The fifth one, *Mr. Miracle*, will air shortly on the Hallmark channel.

You mention at the beginning of this book that some of your fans launch each holiday season by

reading one of your Christmas novels. What are some of your favorite Christmas stories?

Truth be known, some of the most loved Christmas books that I have read in the past had sad endings. I do not want to be sad at Christmas. Instead, I want to spread joy, and that was one of the reasons I started writing romantic comedies at this season. I don't mean to sound negative or discount some of the favorite and beloved books over the years. But for me, I found few that were uplifting, and that is what I prefer to write.

The Hallmark movies of some of your Christmas books, like *Mrs. Miracle* and *Trading Christmas,* have also become favorites and traditions of the season among your fans. Do you have Christmas movies that you watch every year?

I love the original *Bishop's Wife*, with the magical element of Christmas so evident. Then there was also the heavenly element and, of course, there was Cary Grant. The skating scene is one of my favorites. The frozen pond, the almost lyrical relationship growing between them, and the touching dialogue are so moving.

Another Christmas movie I really enjoy is *A Christmas Story*. One year for Christmas our grandson, Cameron, purchased a lamp with a mesh stocking leg as the base. This gift was for my husband, who cherishes it beyond any reasonable comprehension. I only allow him to bring it out at

Christmas. And he has to keep it well away from the living room, where anyone can see it.

It's a Wonderful Life is another classic. My goodness, I had not realized so many of my favorite Christmas movies involve angelic intervention! One of the most stirring elements of the movie is how we often don't realize the impact our lives have with one simple act of generosity or goodwill toward men.

Home Alone is a great movie, too. Who hasn't laughed their way through that one?

Years ago, as the neighborhood mom, I took eight kids to the lake. Halfway home our daughter, Jody, let out a scream. "Ted isn't in the car," she cried. I had left my five-year-old son alone at the lake. I did a U-turn that Jeff Gordon couldn't have made and sped back. Ted had been found and turned over to a local policeman and was riding around in the cruiser looking for his mom. When he found me, he had one immediate question: "Did you miss me as much as I missed you?" Ted has used this memory as a reminder that I would never be nominated for mother of the year.

One of the best parts of Christmas is beloved traditions. Can you talk about a few of your favorite things about celebrating this time of year?

I am very involved with family traditions at Christmastime. We have several. One of my very favorites is taking the grandchildren to a giving tree and letting them pick the name of a child close to their own age. I then give them each money to go shop for that child themselves. Depending on where we get the name, we either take the gift home, wrap it, and return it or we just leave the unwrapped gift beneath the tree.

In another tradition, on the first weekend of December, the families all get together and make homemade goodies. But not the usual cookies and candies. Instead, we save up mason jars and make soup mixes and cookie mixes, along with flavor packets and drink packets. We decorate and divide them all up to use as gifts for friends.

We do a family Christmas progressive dinner each year as well and visit one another's houses, finishing at my house with a rousing game of . . . *bingo*. Whoever wins the game is allowed to open gifts for the family under the tree that night. (Each child has a tree at my house.)

I should also mention that my daughters and I are partially responsible for Black Friday. We tip the scales from red to black in many stores! It isn't so much the gift buying but the time we spend together shopping, laughing, and reminiscing. This is a tradition that started with my mother and me, and we will pass it on to my granddaughters.

I still remember my mother's amazing Christmas gifts of baked goods and homemade candies that she made for family and friends, always thinking of others less fortunate. It is that caring and joy of the season that I hope to pass along to my children and grandchildren.

Creating new traditions is just as important as honoring more established ones. Are there any new traditions that your family has started in more recent years?

As the children have grown and started families of their own, I felt it was important for them to establish their own traditions with their own families. I didn't want to put anyone in the position of choosing between in-laws and us. So we schedule the progressive dinner the weekend before Christmas, and that way the kids have the option of a Christmas dinner at our home for those who can attend. And there is no obligation or pressure. This has carried over with other holidays as well. Easter is always celebrated in our home the Saturday before with our annual, amazing Easter egg hunt, which is *highly* anticipated.

We have one Thanksgiving dinner the night before, and another traditional dinner the next day.

I have to say, I am fortunate that all of our children live within half an hour away.

One of Debbie's Christmas traditions is writing her family's annual letter, keeping friends and family current on the ups and downs, challenges and triumphs of the past year. Here are some memorable ones, starting in 1981, before Debbie had her first novel published, up through her early years in Port Orchard, the seaside town that serves as the basis for the now-famous Cedar Cove that features in her stories. She even talks about her own Alaskan adventures that inspired many of her books!

Enjoy this glimpse into Debbie's life and her special holiday magic!

Christmas 1981

❄

Season's Greetings and God's blessings to Our
Beloved Family and Friends,
The thundering din of four bustling children on
their way out the door to school has settled down
to a quiet hush as I pause, coffee cup in hand, to
scribble down the memories of yet another year.

This has been an incredible year for us, aptly
described in the words of Dickens as the worst
of times and the best of times. Our boys are
developing into fine young men while the girls
have Wayne and I wondering if we will survive
pre-adolescence let alone their teen years.

Jody Rose is a warm, gentle sixth grader. This
has been a monumental year for her as she has
advanced into bras, braces, and Benatar.* Wayne
and I have come to realize the absolute
importance of the proper style of shoelaces in the
development of our daughter. Only those with

---

*Benatar—Pat Benatar, a female rock vocalist.

little red hearts will maintain a level of
sophistication among her peers. Unfortunately
dress codes don't stop with shoelaces. I never
thought I would see the day my daughters were
into designer jeans while I was wearing K-Mart
underwear. Jody continues to play on the Pink
Panther soccer team and placed first in their
division and won the John Campbell
Championship. Our hearts swelled with pride as
Jody was awarded the most improved player
trophy for the year. But Jody twisted her foot
during practice early this year and damaged the
ligaments. A flaring problem has persisted
through most of this year's season and after two
casts and several weeks of physical therapy it
looks like she will be out for the remainder of
the year.

Jenny Adele is a bubbly, enthusiastic fifth
grader whose interests include boys, chess, boys,
the clarinet, and boys. She has a statement posted
on her bedroom door which reads: "The ten
most important men in my life listed in order."
Poor Wayne has yet to recover . . . he isn't
mentioned once. (He lost out to Scott Baio.)
Jenny had the privilege of participating in several
chess tournaments this year and in statewide
competition at the state tournament. A rook
trophy decorating our mantel credits her skill.

I'm not exactly sure how to describe our free-
spirited, vivacious eight-year-old, Ted. Not to be

outdone by Jenny, Ted's bedroom door also boasts a sign which reads threateningly: GIRLS KEEP OUT. As the years pass I have gleaned a bit of wisdom I wish to share with my friends: It takes two to fight and three to start a war. Our Teddy-boy is a unique conglomeration of Tarzan, Luke Skywalker, and the little baby Jesus. After a recent trip to Disneyland, Ted was mightily impressed with the cunning skill of Indians. Putting into practice all he had learned, he deviously stalked his sister who was innocently watching television. With a rubber knife gripped brittlely in his teeth and a wooden tomahawk clenched in his fist, he slithered across the floor to make his ambush. With all the skill of a raiding war party he pounced before Jody, crying a wild, heathen song. Calmly, Jody glanced my way and sighed in exasperation. "Mother, do something with Ted." I wish to revise my former statement: It takes two to fight and *Ted* to instigate a war. Besides ambushes and wars Ted vents his excess energy in sports and plays on the Rockets soccer team. He also plays baseball, Cub Scouts, Heralds, and would gladly forsake his roller skates if Mom would relent and buy him a set of drums. (It'll be a cold day on the equator before I do!)

Our independent six-year-old remains fiercely his own person. Like his older brother, Dale loves sports and between the two of them our backyard holds more sporting events than the Kingdome. However, Dale, as he is with most everything, can be very intense. During one of his first baseball games of the season, he was inadvertently hit with the ball while up to bat. Immediately he threw down his slugger and stormed to the sidelines where I was standing. With tears streaming down his face, he glared at me accusingly. "Mother," he shouted with squinted angry eyes, "you didn't tell me I could get hurt!" Dale is big on wars too, in fact, I haven't taken a bath in six months without little green army men camped along the edge of the tub for company. Besides soccer, baseball, and Heralds, Dale also has a private tutor. It was discovered last summer that Dale has dyslexia, a brain disorder which will always make learning difficult for him. Nonetheless, he is adjusting well to first grade and tries very hard.

This has been an exceptionally difficult year for Wayne. It began last February with a painful and complicated oral surgery followed in March with knee surgery as the result of an innocent game of volleyball. In June while playing a father-daughter baseball game with Jody, he collided with the first baseman and tore the ligaments in his shoulder. Now this is all in addition to his periodic back problems. Wishing to see the year out with a bang, Wayne has currently injured his *other* shoulder and after several weeks of physical therapy and medication there hasn't been much improvement. Besides supporting several medical facilities, my deteriorating husband has met with several small successes by serious contest entering and has won five minor prizes. Our wine cellar has several batches fermenting (in some cases spoiling). He also teaches electrical apprenticeship classes and is a constant encouragement to me as a writer.

I was not exempt from this scourge of ill-health this past year and was laid low with a *ten*-week virus which had me wishing to live only slightly more than I wanted to die. Ted later contracted the same virus and missed a month of school with viral pneumonia. But as soon as I was back on my feet I resumed my regular schedule and was busy enough to drive a normal person straight into the doors of a convent. My teen Sunday School class continues to be a blessing to me, and I also enjoy teaching our church Wednesday night class of Cadets. I continue to sing with the Dayspring Singers and take periodic calligraphy classes. My desire for Ted as he entered Scouting was that he would have a good Christian leader . . . God gave him one. ME! (Actually I share the duties with another brave mother, Betty George.) My writing efforts have met with some success, after several published pieces on the local level I have currently sold two articles which will appear in national publications. But my main objective remains in novel writing and with Wayne's support and enheartenment I continue to trudge the road to fame, fortune, and a live-in housekeeper.

In closing we wish you all a very blessed and peace-filled Christmas. Our verse for you this year is from Colossians 1:16: For in Him all things were created both in the heavens and on earth, visible and invisible whether thrones or dominions or ruler, through Him and for Him. Merry Christmas everyone, we love you all, and remember . . . keep your eyes upon Jesus.

The Macombers

Christmas 1982

God's Blessings to Everyone:
As always the Lord has been exceedingly good to us and 1982 has been an exceptional year. But a year of contrasts. Wayne went from a big, overtime job to months of unemployment. From weeks of puttering around the house this summer to adventures in Alaska and points unknown job hunting. A year in which we spent one week traveling in luxury down the Oregon coast and the next taking baths with little green army men camped along the edge of the tub. It's the year our Jody went from grade school and paper dolls to cosmetics and boys who phone at dinnertime. It was the year I was convinced I was fooling myself with fanciful dreams of being a writer. It was also the year I sold my first novel.

The good and the bad began last January when several doctors assured me I was in perfect health. I felt rotten, but I was healthy. I had surgery a week later. It was my OB who discovered thirty-three gallstones. Wayne came to think of the man as a medical marvel until he got the bill. Suddenly my OB became an SOB. A week after my surgery Wayne broke his arm. He'd prefer it if I told you he narrowly escaped serious injury in a death-defying heroic act. But if the truth be known he tripped over his own two feet. Other than staying on his feet Wayne's had a good year and continues to win several minor prizes with committed contest entering.

My big news for the year is the sale of my novel *Heartsong* to Silhouette Books (a division of Simon & Schuster). A debut date hasn't been set for its release so I can't tell you when to check your favorite bookstore. I have three other novels, awaiting acceptance, including *Heartlight* and *Heartpromise*. (Wayne suggested I title my next book Heartburn—such wit I can live without.) The real success of my writing career can be credited to my agent: God. A marvelous manager, I recommend Him highly. I also have several magazine articles which are scheduled for publication next year. Watch for them!

Our family continues to thrive. Jody is our sweet, sensitive Junior Higher. There's been quite a transformation in our eldest daughter this year. Somewhere along the way she went from the flighty, giggling sixth grader to that half-woman, half-child who surprises us with her insight and budding maturity. Jody attends

Seattle Christian School and is an honor student. She's active in sports: basketball, baseball, and soccer and takes piano lessons.

Jenny is our vivacious, enthusiastic sixth grader. A Valley girl to the mega. Unfortunately, her parents were raised in the mountains. Boys are definitely IN with Jenny and can be categorized as either grody or awesome to the max. As to my feelings regarding my Valley daughter, all I can say is: gag me with a spoon. Other than Valley talk our Jenny is involved! She's active in Camp Fire Girls, participates in baseball and basketball and our church Cadet group. She also plays second chair clarinet in the school band.

Ted, our fourth grader, is interested in music too. He shocked Wayne and me by expressing interest in the violin. The violin? I guess it's an improvement over the whistle but somehow Ted and the violin don't gel. He's more the tuba-type child. We're giving him a year to think on it. As always Ted is a sports enthusiast. He plays soccer for the Rockets and heart and soul baseball. He's also a Cub Scout and church Cadet. Ted experienced a spiritual awakening this spring, after which he decided to become a missionary for Jesus. It's not unusual to find him singing Bible songs and preaching to the neighborhood children. Our sidewalk bears evidence of his faith with arrows pointing to our house and the message: Jesus loves you, ask Ted.

Our first grader, Dale, is no longer a baby. He told me so himself the morning he relinquished his blankey. Dale is seven and ready to forsake his trusted friend. I'm thirty-four and can't bear to part with it. High on the list of Dale's accomplishments this year have been sports. He, too, is involved in baseball and soccer. He's blossomed into a terrific little soccer player this year and scores the majority of his team's goals. No one need ever speculate who his mother is when Dale scores. Wayne's had to restrain me several times from running onto the field and kissing him.

I will close by expressing our heartfelt love for each of you. It's been a difficult year in many ways, but as Paul said to the Corinthians: "We are knocked down but not knocked out. We are at our wit's end but not our hope's end." Wayne and I have come to realize how easy it is to say we trust God when we're sitting on a fat bank account and he's employed. Now we can say that with God's help there isn't anything we can't face.

December 1983

Merry Christmas Everyone:
It seems impossible that 1983 is drawing to a
close and a new year is banking on the horizon.
And what a year it has been. Who would have
believed that when Wayne was laid off the
summer of 1982 that he would be out of work for
ten months? And at the same time, who could
have dreamed my writing career would have
taken off the way it has? But by far we must
claim this to be the year of the guinea pig.

Last Christmas in a moment of weakness I
succumbed and allowed the boys to bring home
two MALE guinea pigs. Hoping to liven things
up, Wayne purchased one FEMALE guinea pig.
By summer our backyard was dominated by
seventeen little critters. Wishing to find good
homes while we still had a yard, Wayne traded
ONE guinea pig for TWO DUCKS. (I believe
this is the same policy often employed by the
Federal government.) Soon Heathcliff and

Gertrude staked their own claim to a portion of our yard, and we have since been granted a continual supply of duck eggs. Ugly Arnie, a wounded crow, arrived next and has since healed and sought a better life. (For a time I was tempted to join him.)

Other than an occasional snake, seventeen guinea pigs, two ducks, two dogs, and our kitty, we live a fairly normal life. The children are growing and our once serene life is filled with loud music and continuous ringing of the phone.

Jody is a tender-hearted, sweet eighth grader. She attends Seattle Christian and is an honor student. The monumental event in her young life was having her ears pierced on her thirteenth birthday. Jody continues to bang away on the piano, plays soccer and baseball, and can recite the Top 40 in one breath. This summer she risked perfectly shaped nails picking strawberries and raspberries to earn enough money to pay for one-half of a leather jacket. Mom and Dad sprang for part two. In case you aren't up on the latest, no decent kid is seen alive without a leather jacket.

Jenny is an outgoing, friendly seventh grader and also an honor student. She plays the clarinet, soccer, and baseball. After a recent school soccer game she rushed home with good news and bad news. The good news was she'd scored a goal, the bad news was it was for the other team. This has been a big year for Jenny. Not only did she work this summer picking raspberries, she has since taken on a paper route, delivering the local news three mornings a week.

The girls continue to enrich our lives with Valley talk. It seems the whole world fits into two categories: "gross" or "awesome." I worried about their lack in vocabulary until I found a verse in Psalms that stated, "The Lord is awesome." I looked at the verse for several minutes, shrugged my shoulders, and thought, "Fer shur."

Ted Gair at ten astounds us with his enthusiasm for life. He plays intense soccer for the Rockets and loves baseball. This summer Ted was hit in the face full force with a baseball bat. Wayne and I rushed him to the hospital where the doctor assured us Ted would be fine. Unconvinced, I promptly fainted. After nineteen stitches for Ted and a sedative for me, we returned home. In addition to keeping life full of surprises, Ted plays the saxophone in the school band and is a top-notch sailor with his father.

Dale Wayne, a fiercely independent eight-year-old, is in second grade and a sports fanatic. Any sport! He loves to watch televised football, basketball, hockey, or any other game he can find. He is counting the days until he's old enough to stay up for all of *Monday Night Football*. In a burst of patriotic fervor, Dale has decided to defend our country and the world. If his unreasonable mother would let him, Dale would wear army fatigues every day. The neighborhood children affectionately call him "The Bush" as he stalks the area looking for wars and rumor of wars. He plays soccer, baseball, and swims like a fish.

For all its ups and downs this has been a good year for Wayne and me. We celebrated our fifteenth wedding anniversary with a trip to Mexico. While doing research for a plot we had a marvelous time going places most tourists wouldn't. Wayne shares in my success as a writer. In addition to giving me the needed moral support, he is my technical adviser and works several hours a week running the different programs on my computer and printing the final copy for the publisher. Our family recently joined a sailing club and Wayne enjoys shouting orders to his mostly willing crew.

As for me, I have several books coming out from Silhouette next year and recently signed a six-book contract. Beginning with *Heartsong* in February, *Undercover Dreamer* in May, *A Girl Like Janet* in August, *That Wintery Feeling* in September, *Tundra Promise* in October or November, and *The Greatest Gift* in December. Also my Harlequin book will be out next year under my maiden name (Adler). In addition to writing, I teach the Junior High Sunday School class, drive in four car pools, and participate in several writing workshops. The highlights of my year include being a panelist at the Pacific Northwest Writers Conference, dinner with Karen Solem, editor in chief of Silhouette Books, and participating in "A Touch of Romance," a seminar in Portland.

In closing, we would like to wish you all a blessed Christmas. My verse this year is a promise from Psalm 69:32. "All who seek for God shall live in joy."

December 1984

Merry Christmas:

It's astonishing that 1984 has come and is almost gone. But what a good year it's been. This is the year I taught the girls to cook dinner and heard Dale plead with God that his mother resume the task. 1984 was the year I warned Jody against the evils of gambling and watched her win $50.00 playing bingo with her Grandma Marie. In 1984 Jenny received the top award on Nerd Day at her school, wearing MY clothes. 1984 saw Ted and Dale venture into the world of high finance by supplying guinea pigs to local pet stores. With his paper route, Ted has learned the value of a dollar by spending his money on candy, gum, and baseball cards.

It's difficult to believe our Jody is a high school freshman. She's a gentle, sweet fourteen-year-old who carries Oil of Olay in her purse. Her love of sports continues and she made the varsity basketball team and JV volleyball team. Jody and

I recently played in a mother-daughter basketball game. This was a brave venture for me since the only slam dunk I've ever made was with a doughnut. In addition to her fifty dollar bingo money, Jody won the door prize on a television show on which I was appearing as a guest. Her prize was to be served breakfast in bed by a gorgeous "hunk." We fought for weeks over who should collect the prize, creating the first serious rift in our relationship. In a gesture of noble worth I acquiesced to her demands.

Jenny, at thirteen, has walked out of the Valley and straight into New Wave. In addition to yard-long earrings and clothes that glow in the dark, she's sprouted a long tail at her neckline. Jenny's an eighth grader at Seattle Christian and, like Jody, an honor student. Also like her older sister, Jenny has decided to "go straight" and has braces. Her interests include journalism, talking on the phone, reading, talking on the phone, checking out the latest guys, and talking on the phone.

The big thing with the girls this year is learning how to sneer like rock star Billy Idol. It seems ironic to me that Wayne and I are spending thousands of dollars to straighten teeth of girls who are planning to never smile.

Our boys are growing and enriching our lives with such wonders as break dancing. Their room looks like a riot scene, but I don't investigate often. Since the snake Ted brought home got loose I tend to steer away from their domain. The only time I pull out their beds is if something smells like it's rotting underneath. In truth, I'd rather not know what treasures they're storing upstairs.

Ted Gair is eleven and astonishes us with his energy and enthusiasm for life. He sings in honor choir at school and plays a bloody game of soccer. Ted's a competitor in whatever he does. Recently, our eldest son decided to finance the local medical center. Within one week he made four visits to the emergency room. He broke two bones in his hand and the same week stepped on a nail, embedding part of his sock in the heel of his foot which had to be painfully dug out.

Our nine-year-old, Dale, continues to be the sports fanatic in the family. He plays soccer, basketball, football, hockey, runs, and wants to take tennis lessons. He's scored all but one of his team's soccer goals and is a fierce competitor. Dale never simply strolls into a room—he somersaults, cartwheels, or moonwalks. For an entire month after seeing the movie *Karate Kid*, Dale faced everyone with his feet braced and hands in the attack position.

Wayne continues to be my technical adviser for my books and spends nearly as much time as I do on a manuscript, running the various computer programs. He flew with me to New

York and Toronto this summer and is the main source of moral (and immoral) support. Besides building the fish pond with the boys, Wayne's done several minor projects around the house. Even more amazing is the fact he's completed them. The fence still isn't painted, but after five years why shock the neighbors. Now that he's forty, Wayne tends to take life far more seriously. He flosses his teeth daily and wears his underwear right-side out.

As for me I doubt that I could ever have another year as exciting as this one. I was reviewed in *Publishers Weekly*, photographed in *Newsweek*, interviewed by several major magazines. I made a television appearance and did a half-hour radio interview. I've been invited as a speaker for writing conferences as far away as Texas and as close as Tacoma. Recently I was elected to be vice president of Romance Writers of America. My books are coming out almost monthly. I don't think anyone need worry that success has gone to my head. Wayne and the kids have innumerable ways of keeping me humble. Perhaps the biggest change in our lives is a housekeeper. Keeping the living room spotless was something I thought I'd do when the kids left home. But recently Wayne discovered tulip bulbs in the refrigerator that I've been meaning to plant since fall of 1983. That was when he decided that maybe I could do with some help.

Our verse for you this year comes from Ephesians 3:17. "I pray that Christ will be more and more at home in your hearts, living within you as you trust in Him. May your roots go down deep into the soil of God's marvelous love."

December 1985

Merry Christmas from THE MACOMBERS:
Wayne, Debbie, Jody, Jenny, Ted, and Dale
   The sun is slashing through my workroom
window and a pile of stubborn snow that refuses
to melt is glistening across the way. It's difficult
to believe that Christmas is around the corner.
Another year has slipped past with hardly a
notice and it's time to write again. 1985 has been
a year of joys and sorrows. We said good-bye to
Princess, our loving, faithful collie, and lost
Gertrude, our duck, to a marauding raccoon.
And yet our joys increase as Wayne and I watch
our children mature. With three adolescents in
the house Wayne and I have come to a deeper
understanding of why there isn't a single word in
all of scripture about Christ's teenage years.
   Our sweet, sensitive Jody is a high school
sophomore and continues to do exceptionally
well in all her endeavors. This was a particularly
monumental year for Jody. This summer she

took Driver's Education classes and brought spiritual renewal to both her parents. All these years I've faithfully attended Woman's Retreat with the express purpose of getting closer to God. I needn't have left home. One driving experience with Jody and I have never felt closer to the Lord. Even now, weeks after she's graduated from class, I climb into the car and instantly the chorus from "Closer My God to Thee" plays through my mind. In addition to keeping her parents spiritually fit, Jody is actively involved in school sports. She played on the JV softball team this spring and recently completed her first year of varsity soccer as goalie. The team went to state for the first time in four years. Not only was Jody awarded her letter, but she was chosen as second team goalie for her league. She was elected the sophomore class secretary and had her braces removed after nearly four years.

Jenny, our high school freshman, is a bundle of magnetic energy. Her interest in journalism continues and she's on the yearbook staff for the second year. She writes marvelous stories and has a wonderfully creative imagination. Appearance is important to Jenny, and she uses hair spray, gel, and mousse to style her hair so that it looks amazingly like mine when I first get up in the morning. After a recent trip to the mall, Wayne claimed that every teenage girl he saw were all clones of Jenny. Although Jenny frowns upon team sports, she's a natural-born runner. She might have considered track this spring if it hadn't cut into her phone time.

The big news for Ted this year is that he didn't break any bones. He did manage to hobble around on crutches twice, but for the most part, Ted has been healthy. This is the year our son discovered the importance of being "cool." As a seventh grader at Seattle Christian, Ted has been told repeatedly by his two older sisters that he has a rep to protect. They're "cool" so he has to give up his disgusting ways and continue the tradition. Hence, Ted washes his hair daily, uses lightly scented male hair spray, gel, and mousse in a ritual that takes no less than fifteen minutes. The way he walks, talks, and acts is also under scrutiny. His friends and clothes are inspected and approved by the girls. For his part, Ted is learning, but he told me recently he never thought junior high would be so difficult. Ted continues to play soccer and was upgraded to play on the team that won the state championship last year. He's a fierce competitor in all that he does.

Ten-year-old Dale also loves soccer or any sport and seems to be a natural. He enjoys playing the striker position on his team and laps up the glory of scoring the majority of this team's goals. Dale's most recent love is "horses." At camp this summer he had the opportunity to go riding and has relived that glorious moment a thousand times. He reads about horses, talks about horses, dreams about horses, drives everyone insane with his fascination with them. He's even gone so far as to write the federal government and request a free horse be delivered to us.

Wayne is settling nicely into middle age. He watches television with an afghan covering his legs and mentions smoking a pipe now and again. Now that he's forty-one he feels it's his duty to give comment on the political issues of our time. For example, Wayne claims the French government reacted hastily to the sinking of the Greenpeace ship in New Zealand. After all, that was their first naval victory in this century. He says that he also understands why so many communist dissidents have returned to Russia. It's the new Coke. He's been a wonderful help to me with my books and works long, tedious hours running the various computer programs. I couldn't do it without him.

My writing career continues to prosper and I have eight and possibly nine books coming out in 1986. Last month I was awarded Waldenbooks Romance Writing Award for my 1984 Christmas book. For the second year, I'm the vice president of Romance Writers of America and busily involved in that organization. In addition to writing, my energy is devoted to the children. I'm the art docent for the second year at the grade school and attend more soccer games than I care to count. It astonishes me that I could have mothered such athletic children. I have problems walking and chewing gum at the same time. In an effort to get physically fit, I got a rowing machine. Believe me, it's not as easy as it looks. The last time I breathed that deeply, I was in labor.

    Our verse this Christmas is Zephaniah 3:17: "He will take great delight in you, He will rejoice over you with singing."

2396 SE Lund Avenue
Port Orchard, WA 98366-5550

Merry Christmas Everyone!
Another year has slipped through our fingers and
out of our grasp. And what a year 1986 has been
for us Macombers. I always suspected that it
would take an atom bomb planted under Wayne
to convince him to move into another house.
This year proved me right. Last year we learned
that our home in Kent sat on a huge vein of
migrating methane gas. The city of Seattle
bought us out and we're enjoying our new home
in Port Orchard. This is the year we spit in the
eye of fate and handed the car keys to Jody. We
challenged the muses by presenting Ted with his
own skill saw. Yes, he retained all ten fingers—it
was his arm he almost cut off. But Wayne's and
my one major accomplishment this year is the
fact we've managed to survive an entire twelve

months of living with three adolescents and one preteen.

Our athletic, industrious sixteen-year-old, Jody lettered in varsity softball this spring, held down her first full-time job, and in-between time discovered men. Before I knew what had happened, she'd thrown out her Cabbage Patch Doll and reached for my Giorgio perfume. She pumps her own gas, can figure the quadratic formula, and recite the Lord's Prayer in German. In addition, she's an honor roll student, her room is always neat, her closet is organized, and she can't tolerate a mess. The girl is an absolute marvel.

Fifteen-year-old Jenny Adele's year was eventful. She took up jogging and runs twenty miles a week. This summer Jenny was hired as a housekeeper for a Christian camp. Only those of you who have seen her bedroom will understand the irony of this. Although we were told she did a marvelous job, Wayne and I have trouble comprehending it. She's adjusted well to her new school, is an honor student, and marched with the Color Guard at the football games. Currently, our Jenny is suffering the heartache of first period swimming. She's looking forward to applying for her driver's permit. This could be equated to spiritual aerobics for her parents.

Ted Gair is thirteen now and hit his teen years with a loud wallop. Cool is still vital. He wears designer clothes, tries to sneak out of the house without socks, and uses enough hair spray to hold up the Berlin Wall. His soccer team won the state championship last spring and Ted lapped up the glory like a true Macomber. This summer while horsing around, he fell through his bedroom window and severely cut his arm. No one was home at the time, but Ted kept his wits about him and contacted 911. Wayne and I were reached in time to give verbal permission for surgery. As the result he has an "awesome" scar to add to his growing collection. His most recent interest is skateboarding. Given our son's penchant for disaster, Wayne and I view this venture with humble hearts and paid-up insurance premiums.

Of all the kids, eleven-year-old Dale Wayne has adjusted best to the move. We weren't in Port Orchard two weeks before he had the entire neighborhood reorganized. Girls have discovered my suave son and on any given night, he receives calls from no less than five adoring females. Dale had a spiritual experience this year in which he claimed God had spoken to him. The message was an interesting one: Dale wasn't supposed to have to eat green beans again.

Ted and Dale continue to share a room although I only go in there with a guide. I recently told them Indiana Jones wouldn't risk a journey into that vast wasteland. The girls,

however, were quick to assure me, Indiana was
welcome into their bedrooms any time.

This year will long be remembered by Wayne.
In 1986 he gave up cigarettes. After nearly
twenty-five years of the habit, it was no easy
task. As just reward, he bought himself a twenty-
two-foot sailboat and banished me from it after
one day of choppy sailing. He claims he'll give
me another chance if I promise not to fall to my
knees and pray aloud at the first sign of a brisk
wind. He's already showing signs of twofootitis
and planning adventures for us this coming
summer.

As for me, this has been an equally
adventuresome year. For the second time I made
the finals on the Romance Writers of America
contest for the best romance of the year. I was on
Waldenbooks bestseller list in August for *White
Lace and Promises* and recently signed a five-book
contract with Silhouette. I have books coming
out in March, May, June, July, August, and
November of 1987 and look forward to writing
many, many more.

Our verse for you comes from Psalm 91. The
words have come to mean a great deal to us over
these last twelve months. This hasn't been an
easy year for us. With all the problems
surrounding the Kent Landfill, the trauma of
moving, the hassles surrounding the new house
have given a deeper meaning to God's promises.

We can tell you from experience that God is merciful and just. We have been firsthand recipients to his day-by-day faithfulness. "This we declare, that God alone is our refuge and our place of safety. He is our God, and we trust in Him. For He rescues us from every trap and protects us. He shields us with His wings. He will shelter us. His faithful promises are our armor." Psalm 91:2–4, Macomber paraphrase.

December 1987

2365 SE Lund Avenue
Port Orchard, WA 98366-5550

Merry Christmas!
It's happened once again. The last time I looked
up from my computer it was early June and here
it is the middle of December and I can't
remember what happened to all those months in
between. The same thing is going on with the
children. Jody is a high school senior and I
vividly recall sending her off for her first day of
school. Jenny is an editor for her high school
yearbook, which astonishes me since she spelled
her name ynnej for years. Sometime this summer
Ted shot up four inches and is now nearly as tall
as his father and I can still remember the
troubles we had potty training him. Dale is
running in races, breaking school records, and I
didn't think that child would ever walk, let alone
give up his blankey. The years have slipped past

with hardly a notice and before Wayne and I knew it, two of our children are perched on the edge of the nest, ready to test their wings.

Jody is seventeen and looking forward to college next fall—but not nearly as much as Ted who will inherit her bedroom. She's witty and warm and our joy. Last year she was nominated by her teachers as Outstanding Junior of the Year. She holds down a part-time job with Godfather's Pizza, religiously saves her money, and charges loan shark fees when her younger siblings borrow from her. Her head is filled with sugarplums this winter, dreaming of traveling to Europe after graduation, finding the perfect boyfriend, preferably someone rich and handsome, and a college that doesn't require chemistry.

Jenny, at sixteen, has a schedule that keeps Wayne and I shaking our heads in wonder. In order to fit all her required classes into her school day, she had to take zero period this fall and left for her first class before 6 A.M. In addition to being on the yearbook staff, she performs with the state's top-ranked drill team, and until recently worked part-time at Saucy's Pizza. She continues to be a high honor roll student, goes through money like water, and dresses like a fashion consultant. The highlight of Jenny's year was homecoming when her boyfriend, Tom, rented a limousine and took her to the Space

Needle for dinner. Thirty-some books and I'VE never ridden in a limo!

This was the year Ted discovered not all girls are like his sisters. Some even have redeeming qualities. He spends anywhere from one to three hours a night on the phone and claims he's only talking to a "friend." Our enterprising fourteen-year-old recently started his own business and raises guinea pigs to sell to the local pet stores. This spring he wrestled for his school and enjoyed that so much he decided to take up boxing, using Dale as his victim. Dale, however, is quick on his feet, and Ted suffered a boxer's fracture in his right hand and spent the first six weeks of the school year with his arm in a cast. The need to be "cool" continues, and he spends more money for shampoo and hair spray then some countries do on national defense.

Unlike his brother, Dale discovered girls in first grade and his popularity with the opposite sex continues. If Ted isn't using the phone, Dale is. His teacher recently reported that she was forced to give Dale detention for misbehaving in class, and immediately four girls ran up to her desk, demanding that they get detention too. Other than females, the big love of Dale's life is horses. We sent both boys to horsemanship camp this summer and of the four top ribbons awarded for skill and knowledge, Dale received two. After camp, our son was convinced his life would be incomplete unless he, too, owned a horse. He's nearly got Wayne and me convinced. In addition to women and horses, Dale remains interested in sports. He plays center striker for his soccer team and runs cross-country. In his first race, he ran a 5:41 minute mile and broke a forty-three-year-old school record!

Both Wayne and I have adjusted to the slower pace of life here in Port Orchard. Wayne enjoys puttering around the house, and recently completed a brick patio behind the pool and built a series of shelves in the garage. We had an acre of trees cut down and are now in the process of clearing that land. Once again, Wayne's been having problems with his lower back, and after weeks of physical therapy it looks like he'll be able to postpone having surgery, and for that we're grateful.

I'm still busy as ever, dividing my time between family and career. In October, I started oil painting classes and am enjoying those. Another writer, Linda Lael Miller, and I walk twenty miles a week at the high school track. In wind, rain, or snow, we're out there plotting our books, working out our frustrations, and getting gorgeous in the process. The first book of my Legenday Lovers trilogy, *Cindy and the Prince*, will be out in January, followed by books in March, May, September, October, and possibly December.

Our verse for you this year comes from the first chapter of John. "And the Word became Flesh, and dwelt among us, and we beheld His glory, glory as of the only begotten from the Father, full of grace and truth." John 1:14. Merry Christmas—we love you all.

The Macombers

*Available in print for this edition,
Debbie Macomber's short story*

"Lost and Found in Cedar Cove"

*Jo Marie prepares for the grand opening of
the Rose Harbor Inn, including the planning
involved for her notorious rose garden, while
squabbling with everyone's favorite
handyman, Mark Taylor, and embarking on
a series of adventures led by her adorable
rescue dog, Rover, which leads to an unlikely
surprise for two very special people.*

Chapter One

Jo Marie Rose had an advantage over most widows. Seeing that she'd lived a good portion of her adult life as a single woman, she was accustomed to taking care of herself. Still, there were times when she would have welcomed a man's help. Welcomed a man. She missed Paul dreadfully, but she'd married him knowing he was a soldier and the risk that involved. Even now, knowing what she did, she would always be grateful to have been loved by Paul Rose.

Rose Harbor Inn had become her sanctuary, a safe harbor for her and for Rover, the stray dog she'd adopted. Although she'd owned the inn for only a few months, she had already compiled a long list of upgrades and changes she wished to make. Unfortunately, many of these improvements were above and beyond her limited capabilities.

That was where Mark Taylor came into the picture. He was a local handyman, and if she were to describe him, the first thing that readily came to mind was *prickly*. To say he was a man of few words was to say a mime talked too much. Usually he answered with one or two words, as if any question she were to ask irritated him. Mr. Personality he was not.

Jo Marie was willing to put up with his gruff ways because he did a good job, and at an acceptable price. The problem was that Mark had a habit of taking three times longer than necessary to finish a project. As he was keen to remind her, others had hired him, too. She wasn't his only customer, and he'd finish in a reasonable amount of time. To be fair, he generally did. What Jo Marie needed, he often reminded her, was a bit more patience.

Recently, however, Jo Marie had discovered a secret that had Mark stopping by to work on her project a bit more routinely.

Cookies.

Mark loved cookies, and she baked a batch every other day or so for her guests. It'd taken her only a short while to recognize that Mark tended to show up for work on baking days.

This morning it was peanut-butter cookies, one of his favorites. Right on cue, her doorbell chimed. Ever at the ready, Rover immediately barked and raced to the door.

Sure enough, it was Mark. "I got your message," he said, sounding none too pleased. He made it seem as if the voice mail she'd left him had upset his all-important schedule.

"Good."

"What do you need this time?" he asked.

Rover stood on his hind legs and placed his front paws on Mark's thigh, looking to be acknowledged. Mark grudgingly patted the mutt's head and then, scowling, added, "Down."

Rover immediately obeyed.

"I'd like to remove part of the lawn for a rose garden." She wanted a gazebo built as well but didn't want to overwhelm him with too much at once. "I mentioned the project earlier," she reminded him.

Mark frowned. "I've got other projects right now."

"I know," she said, doing her best to remain patient and calm. She was forced to bite down on her tongue to keep from asking about the cradle he'd been working on for weeks. When she'd said how lovely it was—and it truly was—he said he'd gotten it in his head to build it, although it wasn't a commissioned piece and he didn't know anyone in need of a cradle. Far be it from her to tear him away for a *paying* job.

Mark must have smelled the cookies, because he moved into the kitchen without waiting for an invitation.

"Coffee?" she asked.

He shrugged. "I wouldn't mind a couple of those cookies."

Before she handed over the goods, she wanted it

understood she had a stipulation to go along with this project. "I have a deadline for the garden."

Mark shifted uncomfortably. "I'm not good with deadlines."

She ignored that, poured his coffee, and brought down a plate but didn't hand over the cookies. "Peggy Beldon suggested I have an open house, and I was thinking it would be nice to have it in late spring."

"How late?"

"I don't know yet. End of May or so. Can you do it?"

Mark's gaze focused on the peanut-butter cookies cooling on wire racks along the countertop. "It shouldn't be a problem."

"You're sure about that?" He might not find planting a rose garden particularly significant, but she did. This garden would be a tribute to her husband, to Paul. While it might not mean anything more than a job to Mark, it was important to her, and his cooperation in this would be greatly appreciated.

Mark scowled and shrugged.

Jo Marie set two cookies on the plate and brought it over to the table, where he'd plopped himself down. He'd eaten both by the time she returned with her own coffee and sat across from him. Rover curled up at her feet.

"When can you get started?" she asked, unwilling to be put off.

"That depends."

"On what?"

"Where do you want the rose garden?" he asked.

"I'd like to have my guests view it as soon as they pull into the driveway." That made sense to Jo Marie.

"You'd better show me."

"Okay, fine." Reaching for a sweater, she led the way outside. The morning was dark and gloomy, the skies overcast with thick slate-gray clouds that threatened more than the customary March drizzle.

Standing on the top porch step, she pointed in the direction that seemed the best choice to her. The chill got to her, and she wrapped the sweater more tightly around herself.

"The drainage there might be a problem."

Jo Marie hadn't thought about that. She'd assumed roses would bloom wherever they were planted.

"Where else would work?"

Alongside the shed, she guessed, but she'd hoped to have the gazebo close by, and she'd rather it not be close to any of the outbuildings. "Around the other side of the inn, I suppose." She wasn't keen on that idea, although it was an option.

"Let me check it out."

"Okay." She followed Mark as he led the way down the steps and along the pathway that meandered around the inn. Rover dutifully followed.

With his hands braced against his hips, Mark surveyed the area. "I'm going to need to do a bit of research first."

"For what?" This sounded like a delay tactic to her.

"I want to read up on roses, learn what I can about planting and growing them before I start tearing up the yard. Then you and I can decide where would be the best spot for your rose garden."

He came across as practical, and she didn't have an argument. "Okay, but I want to remind you I'd like this done fairly quickly."

"If you want to hire someone else, that's fine by me. I'll do my best, but I'm not making any promises."

"Okay, okay," she muttered and shook her head. Oh my, he was in a rare mood this morning. She led the way back into the house. "How much do you figure this will cost?" she asked, reveling in the welcome warmth of the house.

"That depends," Mark said.

To show good faith, she replenished his plate with two additional cookies. "Just a rough estimate is enough."

"I'll be fair."

"I know you will," she said, sitting down across from him. She was half tempted to offer to pay him in cookies, but he might take her seriously, in which case she'd be baking for him for the next several years.

"What do you want me to do first? Put together a bid or research where best to plant the garden?"

It wasn't an easy choice. "Do whatever will get my rose garden in by Memorial Day," she suggested.

"Fair enough." He quickly ate the two additional cookies and emptied his coffee mug. "I'd better get started, then."

"Perfect."

"I'll head down to the library and get a few gardening books and get back to you by the end of the week."

"Sounds good."

Standing, he carried his mug to the sink. "Those are some of your best cookies yet."

A compliment? From Mark? This was worthy of a reward. "Why don't I give you a few to take with you?"

He almost smiled. "I won't turn them down."

Unable to hide her amusement, she looked down at Rover, but her faithful companion wasn't under the table. Nor was he curled up in front of the refrigerator.

"Did Rover come in with us?" He followed Jo Marie everywhere. It wasn't like him to stay outside, especially when it threatened rain.

"I didn't notice."

Jo Marie hadn't, either. She opened the door off the kitchen and called for him.

"Rover."

Nothing.

"Rover," she tried again.

Nothing.

"He can't have gotten far," Mark said. He shouted out her pet's name himself and didn't get a response.

"I'm sure he must be around here," Jo Marie insisted. The inn was his home. They were good for each other, kept each other company. With this inn they'd both found a safe harbor, a place of healing. She'd come to rely on Rover, on his presence, his protection. It would sound half crazy to explain to anyone, in particular to Mark, that she genuinely felt Paul had sent Rover to her as a friend and constant companion.

For a long time, Jo Marie had toyed with changing his name. Rover was the name the animal shelter had given him. It was clear when he was brought in that he'd been on his own, roving for a good long while. It was such an ordinary name, though, so bland. Over the last few months she'd scoured pet-name books and come up with several unique and funny names, like Soldier (Paul would have loved that), or Wilson, after one of her favorite Seahawks players. Any number of good, solid dog names came to her, but none suited him better than just plain Rover.

Together with Mark, she searched the entire property, and Rover was nowhere to be found.

"Has he done this before?" Mark asked.

"Never."

"He'll be back. He knows where his dog dish is."

If Mark thought he was helping, he wasn't. "I want to find my dog," she said, in danger of losing her composure. She hurried to the end of the driveway and looked both ways up and down the street.

Rover was nowhere in sight.

Mark waited for her on the porch steps. It had started to rain in thick sheets, but Jo Marie was oblivious to the hammering downfall.

"Don't look so worried, he'll be back," Mark said again.

Jo Marie ignored that and raced inside the house for something warmer and her umbrella. "You don't understand. It isn't like him to disappear like this."

"There's no need for you to panic."

"Yes, there is," she snapped.

"I've had pets," he challenged. "They like to explore. You're overreacting."

"I'm not!" she insisted. "Rover doesn't leave the property. This is his home now, and he knows that, and furthermore, he's more than a pet to me."

She quickly jerked her arms into the sleeves of her rain jacket. Generally she avoided an umbrella, but the rain was coming down too heavily now.

"You aren't seriously considering going out in this weather?"

"I told you I need to find my dog." She wouldn't explain why she was so strongly attached to him because Mark would find her fanciful ideas amusing. Too many factors about Rover convinced her that this was no ordinary pet.

First and foremost, Rover had chosen her and revealed an uncanny ability to comfort her. It was almost as if he could read her mind. From the moment she'd brought him home from the shelter he'd been by her side. He sensed her moods, and when she was especially sad, he would place his chin on her knee and look up at her with dark, soulful eyes as if to assure her she would laugh again, love again. Which was why she was convinced that he was a special gift from Paul.

"I'll drive around the neighborhood and see what I find," Mark offered.

Jo Marie appreciated the effort. "Thank you."

"I'll meet you back here in twenty minutes."

Jo Marie checked her watch. "Okay."

Despite the rain, she took off, her steps filled with purpose. Rover had never done anything like this before, and she couldn't imagine what had possessed him to leave. If the sun was shining and he'd been chasing butterflies, she might have understood it. But in the middle of a wretched March rainstorm? It didn't make the least bit of sense.

Twenty minutes later, Jo Marie returned to the

house with her feet drenched. She should have changed her shoes, but, filled with a sense of urgency, she hadn't wanted to take the time.

Mark stood alone on the porch, his hands buried deep inside his jean pockets.

"Did you see him?" Jo Marie called out as she hurried toward the inn. Despite the evidence, she had to ask.

Mark shook his head. "No sign of him anywhere. You?"

Jo Marie shook her head. The knot in the pit of her stomach tightened.

Mark frowned at her and then growled, "You're soaked to the skin."

"I'm fine."

"Get inside. Rover's been a stray. He's used to being free to go where he pleases. He's smart enough to know what to do to stay safe and dry. Eventually he'll find his way back. Like I said, he knows where his food bowl is filled."

"I'm not giving up until I find Rover." If this was Mark's idea of reassurance, then she'd rather he left right now.

"Rover knows his way around town."

"He knows the route I walk him and little else. He's probably lost and confused." Part of her realized that the way she connected Rover with Paul made losing him feel as if she were losing Paul all over again. It sounded crazy, something a psychologist would want to analyze in great depth, but she couldn't help it. Despite her best efforts, her voice trembled.

"You need to get warm." Mark practically dragged her inside the inn and went directly into the kitchen and poured her some coffee.

Trembling now with cold and dread, she willingly accepted the mug. He didn't take one for himself. Instead, he paced her kitchen as if unsure what to do next.

Neither of them spoke.

Jo Marie sniffled in an effort to hold back the emotion that threatened to spill over at any moment. She started to shake, but not from any chill.

"I can't lose Rover," she whispered, utterly miserable. "I simply can't."

"Give it time," Mark insisted. "It's only been less than an hour."

"I told you before, Rover is more than a pet." Her voice wobbled like a drunk attempting to walk a straight line. "He's gone, I feel it in my gut . . ." She refused to accept that, refused to believe she would lose him, too.

"Maybe his time with you is over and he's ready to move on," Mark offered. "I've found it's better not to get too attached."

At any other time his words would have struck her as tremendously revealing, but all she could think about was Rover lost in the storm.

"Don't say anything more, please; you're not helping."

Mark shuffled his feet a couple of times, and then, as if he didn't have anything more to add, he walked out the door.

Not knowing what else to do, Jo Marie went to the front window and watched Mark drive away. She shouldn't have expected anything more of him. The moment she fell apart emotionally, he was at a complete loss. His sole thought was to escape.

To expect Mark to be her friend was asking too much of him. All at once she was angry with him . . . angry with the world. She'd lost so much already, and to lose Rover was more than she could take.

Never one to give in easily to bouts of weeping, Jo Marie no longer had the internal fortitude to hold them back. With tears raining down her cheeks, she went into her bedroom, stripped out of her wet clothes, turned on the shower, and stepped inside. Once under the hot spray, she let the sobs come, choking on what she was convinced was another hit, another loss she would be forced to face and absorb. She wasn't going to stop looking. She couldn't and wouldn't until she found him.

Chapter Two

Unable to sit still and do nothing, Jo Marie dressed and drove into town, parking at the library. Grace Harding, the head librarian, glanced up from where she stood at the front desk.

She must have immediately sensed something was drastically wrong because she asked, "Jo Marie, what's happened? You look like you've lost your best friend."

"I have," Jo Marie choked out. "It's Rover. He's missing." She extended her hands to her friend, needing advice and comfort and something to hold on to, someone to hold her together.

Gripping both of Jo Marie's hands, Grace asked, "When did you last see him?"

"The thing is, I don't know. Rover followed Mark and me outside. We went out to select an area to plant the rose garden. You know how he barely leaves my side. Rover was with me then, but a few minutes after we were inside, talking details, I noticed he wasn't in the house. I've looked everywhere I can think of to look and he's . . . gone. Vanished. I can't imagine where he went or why." Again, her voice did that wobbling thing as if she were on the verge of having an emotional breakdown. Which, as a matter of fact, she was.

Grace was instantly all business. "You had the microchip put in, right?"

Jo Maric nodded.

"Then any shelter that finds him will have your contact information."

Jo Marie had forgotten about that, but it did little to assuage her fears.

"I'll call Olivia, too."

The family court judge? "What can she do?" Jo Marie asked.

"Well, for one thing, she knows Hank Hampton over at Animal Control personally. I do, too, but she has more sway with him than I do. If he finds Rover, she'll have him get in touch with you directly and sidestep the shelter."

"She'd be able to do that?"

"Olivia can ask. She knows how attached you are to Rover."

"Would you mind asking?" The thought of Rover being chased by a dogcatcher wasn't a comforting one.

"I wouldn't mind in the least. Anything else I can do, other than talk to Olivia and the animal shelter?"

"I . . . I don't know." Jo Marie's brain felt as if it

was about to explode. She couldn't sit idly by and do nothing, though; that was driving her nuts. She pressed her fingertips against her lips. "Mark says I'm overreacting."

"You aren't. You and I both know Rover is a special dog and that the two of you are meant to be together," Grace assured her. "We all love our pets; they're like family."

That was the bottom line, she realized. To Jo Marie, Rover was family. Her family. "Thank you," she whispered, tears filling her eyes.

"We'll find him, Jo Marie, don't worry. Rover will be back before you know it."

Because she so desperately wanted to believe that, Jo Marie didn't argue, although it felt as if Rover was completely gone from her life. What Mark said echoed in her mind . . . maybe she was supposed to have him for only these few months while she grieved for Paul. Perhaps it was time for him to move on to someone else who was badly in need of comfort. She didn't want to think that was the case, but she couldn't come up with another logical explanation.

Rover had left of his own accord.

He'd gone outside with her and Mark, and he hadn't returned. Nothing had prevented him from following her back into the house. Maybe he'd moved on to someone else. Another hurting soul in need.

* * *

Amanda Palmer found Travis Kilroy sitting at the farthest, darkest corner table in Java Joint. He'd slouched down in the chair so far he was in danger of sliding onto the floor. His neck rested on the back of the chair and he held his cell phone and was either texting or playing games. Either way, his fingers moved over the keys with practiced ease.

"Hello, Travis," she said, doing her best to sound like she was eager to be his math tutor.

He glanced up and reluctantly straightened. "Hi." The greeting was flat and devoid of any welcome or appreciation.

Amanda pulled out the chair next to him and set her backpack on the floor. One point in his favor, Travis was on time, although he looked as if he'd rather be just about anyplace else than with her.

"Mr. Wilcox asked if I'd be willing to meet with you and—"

He stopped her. "Okay, I get it. I'm not good with numbers."

"Which is the reason Mr. Wilcox asked me to tutor you. He wants to see you graduate and asked if I'd be willing to work with you."

"I don't need your help."

"Mr. Wilcox says you're failing."

"Like I said, I'm no good with numbers."

"And like I said, that's the reason I'm here."

Travis snorted. "Why did Wilcox ask you?"

"Because I love math."

"Why'd you agree?"

That was the same question Amanda had been asking herself from the moment she'd walked in the door. "Would you rather someone else tutor you?" That was fine by her.

"Wilcox would probably just send some other brainy geek, so do what you want."

If he wanted to dish out insults, she had a few of her own. "A brainy geek is ten times better than an empty-headed jock who isn't smart enough to get into a lifeboat when a ship is ready to sink."

"Very funny."

Amanda stood and held up her hand. She didn't need this, no matter how popular Travis was. All she'd been looking to do was offer a helping hand. If graduating from high school and playing college football wasn't incentive enough, then nothing she said or did was going to change his mind.

"Children, children." Connor Leesburg came toward them with his hands on his hips and shaking his head. "There's no need to trade insults, is there?"

Staring at Travis, Amanda defensively crossed her arms.

Travis held her look with the same dark intensity.

"Lighten up, Travis," Connor said. "Otherwise, you'll end up like me, working in a coffeehouse for a pittance while you're saving up enough cash for a few college classes or trade school."

"So?"

"So you've got the talent to make it playing college football. If nothing else, think of all the chicks who'll want to be with you."

Amanda snickered.

"As for you," Connor said, turning his attention to her, "chuck the attitude."

"He started it." She wasn't sure what she'd expected from Travis, but it wasn't this.

"Let the guy have some pride," Connor interjected. "It isn't easy admitting he needs help. I heard you're going to be named valedictorian, right?"

She nodded.

"Congratulations, but loosen up a bit, will you?"

"What is that supposed to mean?" she demanded.

"It means exactly what I said. Travis doesn't want anyone to know he needs a math tutor. It's bad for his image. Why do you think he asked to meet you here rather than at school or the library?"

As much as Amanda didn't want to admit it, what Connor said made sense.

"Travis has athletic ability in spades. If you were on the football field and he was on the line protecting you, trust me, you'd feel differently. And if he had to teach you to throw a perfect spiral, think how you'd be feeling! It's nice of you to help him, but let go of the attitude."

"Do I have an attitude?" She directed the question to Travis.

He shrugged. "A little."

She wasn't the cheerleader type, nor had she been a member of the drill team. But no one could attend Cedar Cove High School and not know who Travis Kilroy was, and to be fair, she wasn't immune. Travis was popular and easy on the eyes. It went without saying that she'd never have a chance with him, and frankly, she wasn't sure she'd want one. No use fretting about it; Travis saw her as a geek. From the moment she walked into Java Joint, he'd made it plain that he viewed her as nothing more than a brain.

"This is much better," Connor said as he rubbed his palms together. "How about a latte on the house?"

"Sure," Travis agreed.

"Sure," Amanda echoed.

"Coming right up."

Before Connor even got back behind the counter, a tall, lanky man in a wet coat and jeans walked into Java Joint. "You kids happen to see a dog recently?" he asked.

"I've seen lots of dogs," Travis said.

"What kind of dog?" Amanda asked.

The man described Rover.

"Doesn't sound familiar, but I'll keep an eye out," Connor said.

"Take my name and phone number, and call me if you do," the man said. He walked over to Connor and handed him a card. "This is an important dog. He belongs to a friend of mine."

Connor looked down at the card. "I'll call if one shows up."

"I'd appreciate it."

And then he was gone. With that distraction over, Amanda turned back to Travis. "You ready to crack the code to the quadratic formula?" she asked, pulling out a chair and taking a seat.

Travis sighed. "I guess, but it's a waste of time as far as I'm concerned."

"Really?"

"Think about it, Amanda. How am I going to use the quadratic formula in my life?"

"That's an easy question. You're going to use it to pass algebra, graduate from high school, and get a scholarship to college. Is that answer enough?" she asked.

He smiled at her. He actually smiled. For a moment, it was all Amanda could do to look away. Thankfully, she caught herself in time and was instantly all business. "In that case, let's get started."

Connor delivered their lattes, and before long Amanda and Travis were sitting side by side with the algebra text open in front of them. She reviewed the formula and showed him a couple of tricks she'd used to remember how best to work it out. Soon their heads were close together.

"I don't get it," Travis murmured, clearly frustrated.

"You forgot a step," she said, doing her best to remain patient. She reviewed the formula again.

It took four tries before Travis figured it out. He looked to her when he finished. "Right?"

"Right. You got it." She offered him a congratulatory smile.

"How did you get so good at this stuff?"

"It comes naturally; it's just the way I think."

"In other words, you're the brains, I'm just the dumb jock."

"I didn't say that. Why are you so defensive? And what's with all this negative self-talk?"

He chose to ignore her questions and returned his attention to the textbook, refiguring the quadratic formula. Once again he came up with the correct answer.

The door to Java Joint opened, and in walked Hailey, another high school senior. She apparently didn't notice them, which was a good thing, and headed directly to the counter, where Connor waited to take her order. Amanda watched as Travis closed the text and slipped it back inside his backpack.

Hailey had her Almond Joy latte in hand before she saw the two of them. Right away her eyes widened. "Hey, Amanda, Travis. I didn't see you." She tried to hide her surprise but wasn't nearly good enough an actor to carry it off. She carried her drink over to their table.

"How's it going?" Amanda returned weakly.

"What are you doing?" Hailey asked, and seemed unable to hide her curiosity.

"We're just hangin'," Travis explained, his gaze shifting nervously between Amanda and Hailey.

It didn't escape Amanda's notice that being seen with her wasn't good for his image. Someone just might guess that he needed tutoring, and that definitely wouldn't be cool. What was that saying she'd heard—no good deed goes unpunished?

"Really. I didn't figure the two of you . . . you know." Hailey left the rest unsaid, as if she was afraid she might have wandered into uncomfortable territory.

An unsettling silence followed that Amanda felt no obligation to fill. She'd let Hailey make all the assumptions she wanted.

Their classmate continued to study them, as if she wasn't sure what to think.

Coming out from behind the counter, Connor approached just as the silence was getting more than a little awkward. His gaze went from Amanda to Hailey. "Did you hear Hailey recently got hired at Rose Harbor Inn?" he asked in a blatant effort to change the subject.

"That's great, Hailey. Congratulations." Amanda needed a summer job herself, but prospects were few.

"It's just until I head off to college in the fall," Hailey clarified. "The lady from the library introduced us."

"Grace Harding?"

"Naturally, you'd know the librarian," Travis whispered under his breath to Amanda.

"Naturally," she repeated, unwilling to let him think he'd scored a point.

"As soon as Grace heard I was interested in majoring in hotel management, she contacted Jo Marie and arranged for an interview. It's not every day, but I'm learning a lot."

"Cool," Connor said.

"Speaking of which, I was headed up to Rose Harbor Inn now. See ya."

Amanda raised her hand. "See ya."

Travis waved farewell.

As soon as Hailey was out the door, she heard Travis heave a deep sigh. "You know what's going to happen, don't you?" The words were more accusation than question.

Amanda did know.

"By tomorrow morning, it will be all over school that you and I were sitting in a corner, cozying up with each other."

He made it sound like a disaster in the making.

"And that bothers you?" she asked, and then, before he could reply, she added, "You don't owe anyone an explanation, and for that matter, neither do I. Besides, you can make up an excuse—we just happened to run into each other or something."

His frown deepened. "You mean to say having

gossip spread around the school about us won't bother you?"

"Should it?" she asked flippantly. "What about you? Will this ruin your chances with the nominees for prom queen?"

"What about you and Chad?"

Chad Mullin had been her date for the Valentine dance. The fact that Travis knew anything about the two of them surprised her. "What about Chad?" she asked, needing to know.

"I thought the two of you—"

"You thought wrong," she said, cutting him off.

Travis shook his head as if it was of little concern to him one way or the other. "Are we done here?" He was halfway out of his seat, eager to escape.

Unwilling now to drop the matter, Amanda asked, "Is gossip a problem on your end?"

He took a moment to answer. "I guess not. What you said about making up an excuse should work."

Amanda had no idea if he was dating anyone or not, and he had taken a risk letting Hailey make an assumption.

She'd barely touched her latte, so when she stood to leave, she reached for her backpack, slinging it over her shoulder, and grabbed hold of her drink. Travis seemed more than eager to leave. "When's the test?" she asked as they walked toward the door.

"Friday."

Travis hesitated and then nodded toward her as if to show his appreciation before stepping outside.

It was better than nothing, Amanda supposed, as she followed him.

Thankfully, it had stopped raining, and the sun was out. Large drops dripped off the roof and bounced against the pavement, causing a prism effect.

She was a couple steps behind Travis as she headed toward the parking area behind Java Joint.

"Are you following me?" Travis asked as he glanced over his shoulder.

"That's a pretty egotistical question. Why would I be following you?"

"Maybe to add to the gossip." Unsure how to answer, he apparently threw out the first thing that came to mind, which was ridiculous.

"Oh please." If she wasn't so irritated, she might have laughed. All in all, this tutoring session hadn't gone well. Amanda wasn't sure what she'd expected from Travis. Gratitude, perhaps. Or at least a little appreciation. Wrong again. She wasn't getting anything out of this other than the satisfaction of being able to help. Deep down, she'd expected more. Unfortunately, they were too far apart in the social ranks to connect, even as friends, and that disappointed her.

She was only a few feet away from her car when

all at once a dog appeared and started barking, first at her and then at Travis. The animal wouldn't allow her to get near her car. Every time she stepped in that direction, the dog barked. It wasn't a threatening bark but more a warning bark.

"What's he trying to tell you?" Travis asked.

"I don't have a clue. Do you?"

"No."

Amanda tried again, and the dog's barking grew more frantic.

"You might as well give it up," Travis said.

"You think I should leave my car here and walk home?" As far as she was concerned, that was a ridiculous idea.

"No, give it time." He hesitated and then suggested, "Do you wanna hang out at the waterfront park? We could finish our lattes there."

"Aren't you worried about your reputation?" she asked, enjoying egging him on.

"I can live with it, if you can."

Amanda shrugged as if it wasn't a big deal. "I suppose I can, too."

As soon as they started toward the gazebo, the dog trotted off in the opposite direction. The sky had turned a South Sea shade of blue. This was actually turning out to be a great day, after all.

Chapter Three

Jo Marie's cell buzzed, and she grabbed it out of her purse, praying with all her heart that it was someone with news about Rover. She'd been out searching for hours and had lost heart that she would ever find him.

"Yes?" she said eagerly.

"Jo Marie, it's Olivia. Is everything all right? You don't sound like yourself."

"I'm not myself," she admitted, struggling to hold herself together. "Rover is missing."

"So I heard. Grace called and asked if I'd check with Hank Hampton over at Animal Control."

"Did you?" She hated to sound this anxious, but any word was better than the agony of not knowing. This limbo should be familiar. It brought back a far-too-familiar ache. Paul's body had yet to be recovered from the side of a mountain in Afghanistan. At the time his helicopter went down she'd been told the crash site was in an inaccessible area. Translated into civilian speak, that meant it was deep inside enemy-held territory. She'd been assured there were no survivors. Still, she couldn't help wondering if it was possible, if there was any way Paul might have come out of the horrific crash alive.

"I was able to talk to Hank," Olivia continued, breaking into Jo Marie's thoughts. "He's got the word out. If Rover is out and about, then I'm sure he'll be located soon."

"Thank you so much. I can't tell you what this means to me." Jo Marie knew she sounded pitifully appreciative, but she couldn't help it. She wasn't ready for this emotional roller coaster.

"Keep me updated, and don't worry, Rover will be found."

"Yes, of course," Jo Marie assured her. "And Olivia, thank you. If there's anything I can do for you in return, please don't hesitate to ask."

"This isn't about returning favors, Jo Marie," Olivia said. "It's about friendship and community."

Jo Marie was a woman who prided herself on keeping tight control of her emotions, but Olivia's kindness nearly choked her up.

"I'll let you know the moment I hear anything," Olivia promised.

"As will I," Jo Marie said.

"Everything will work out," Olivia reassured her. "Rover will find his way home."

"I pray you're right."

They ended the conversation, and although Rover was still missing, Jo Marie felt considerably better. Since moving to the small Puget Sound community of Cedar Cove, Jo Marie had been blessed beyond measure by the friends she'd made.

Peggy Beldon, another B&B owner, had been one of the first to extend a helping hand. Later, she'd met Grace, and through Grace, Olivia and of course Mark.

Her mind circled back to Mark. It hadn't escaped her notice that he couldn't seem to get away from her fast enough. As soon as he'd realized how upset and emotional she'd become, he'd hightailed it out of the inn. His reaction had been completely different from that of Grace and Olivia. He was probably sanding the cradle he was building. Sometimes Jo Marie was left to wonder if she would ever figure him out.

Getting to know Mark Taylor was like becoming friends with a porcupine, which went along with his prickly personality. She almost smiled at the analogy, realizing she didn't know enough about porcupines to realize what their redeeming quality was once you got past the bristles. Nor had she figured out why she found Mark compelling despite everything he did to make himself otherwise.

Thankfully, the rain had stopped, and after spending the last several hours wandering aimlessly around town in a fruitless search, Jo Marie reluctantly returned to the inn. As she walked up the steep hill leading to the inn she hoped and prayed she would find Rover curled up on the front porch, patiently awaiting her return.

When she arrived, her heart plummeted. Rover was nowhere to be seen.

After a dreary day, late that afternoon the rain tapered off and the sun broke out over Puget Sound as Travis and Amanda walked side by side down the boardwalk that edged the waterfront.

"Our marine biology class was here last week, and we saw a starfish that I swear was about the size of a basketball," Travis commented, looking over the railing and into the water that gently lapped against the rocks below. "It had wrapped itself around a big rock. I could barely believe my eyes."

"Was it pink?"

"Pink? No, it was white."

Amanda had to be careful—she didn't want to intimidate him by rattling off a bunch of facts about local sea life, although she knew quite a bit. It was on the tip of her tongue to tell him starfish weren't the only species that grew to inordinately large sizes in Puget Sound. Octopuses did as well.

Travis leaned against the railing, focusing his attention across the water to the lighthouse in the far distance. "I didn't thank you for helping. I appreciate it, Amanda."

He was actually thanking her.

"You're welcome."

"The truth is, Hailey stopping by rattled me, and I might have given you the wrong impression with what I said. I didn't mean to do that."

He still hadn't looked at her. "What do you mean?"

He exhaled as if to say she wasn't making this any easier by asking all these questions. "Mainly that it wouldn't be that big a deal to me, for the two of us, you know . . ." He let the rest fade.

"The two of us . . ." she pried.

"You know, to be seen together."

Amanda moved closer to the railing and rested her arms across the top rung. "The truth is, I wouldn't mind it, either."

He glanced her way and smiled.

She smiled back.

"I knew who you were long before you were named valedictorian."

"Oh?" She wasn't sure how else to respond. Earlier, he'd mentioned her date for the Valentine dance, and that had surprised her.

"You play the flute, right?"

"Yeah."

"You were in band?"

"When I was a sophomore and junior. You weren't, though."

"No, but I play the guitar and was in the music room just before the band came in for practice."

Amanda searched her memory for any clue she remembered. It came back blank. She didn't recall ever seeing Travis in the music room. "Were we ever in any classes together?" she asked, but she doubted it.

"Junior high."

"No way." Amanda didn't believe it. She'd gone through twelve years of school in the Cedar Cove system, and she would have remembered Travis if he'd been in any of her classes.

"The end of seventh grade," he clarified. "My mom and I moved to Cedar Cove the last week of school after she got a job with the shipyard."

"You remember me from seventh grade?" Unbelievable.

Travis hesitated and then spoke so low she had to strain to hear him, and even then she wasn't sure she'd heard correctly.

"I'm sorry, I didn't hear that."

His gaze remained focused in the distance. "You were the first girl I ever noticed in Cedar Cove."

His admission stunned her to the point she was left speechless. It took a couple of seconds before she was able to find her voice. They passed in the halls, but he ran with a completely different crowd than she did. Furthermore, his lunch period didn't mesh with hers. Still, she was fairly certain that until that very afternoon Travis hadn't spoken a single word to her. "You've basically ignored me," she challenged.

"Well, duh, you're the class brain. I'm a jock."

"So?"

"Be honest. If I'd asked you out, would you have seriously considered going?"

Good question. "I . . . I don't know."

He snorted softly. "At least you're honest."

She didn't want to give him the impression that she considered herself better than him. The only reason she might have hesitated was because she didn't know what to expect and could be a bit shy sometimes.

"I might now, though, after today."

His gaze bounced against hers and then returned to look out over the cove. His look had been so quick she didn't have a chance to read his expression.

She thought she detected a hint of a smile. "See what happens once you conquer the quadratic formula?"

He looked at her, and a frown created thick folds across his forehead. "What does that have to do with anything?"

"You're going to ask me out, right?"

"Maybe," he hedged.

"Figuring out that formula gave you a boost of confidence. Would you have even considered it if you hadn't cracked the code for the math equation?" Amanda was fairly certain she knew the answer.

"Probably not."

"I rest my case."

Travis chuckled. "So now you're a lawyer?"

"Maybe someday," she said, "but I'm leaving my options open."

"You sound like an attorney. One thing is sure, you can certainly argue a point."

"What about you?" she asked. "What are your plans for the future?"

"College football."

"What about after football?"

He shrugged. "I don't know yet."

"What are your interests, your passions?"

Travis looked away and laughed.

"Come on, I'm serious."

He took his time answering. "I play acoustic guitar. And I like graphic design."

A surprise. "If you could have any job in the world, what would it be?"

He turned around, leaning his elbows against the railing with his back to the cove. "You promise not to laugh?"

"Cross my heart."

"I'd like to attend the California Institute of the Arts."

Travis was such a completely different person than what she'd thought. It shocked her that she had been so blind to him, and probably to countless others as well. She skimmed over the surface, making assumptions about what she saw at first glance. If they hadn't been thrown together like this, she might never have known the hopes and dreams lying just below the surface.

He seemed to be waiting for her to comment.

"I think that's wonderful, Travis. I really do."

He responded with a shy smile, as if her words had pleased him.

"Now I have another question for you," she said.

"Okay." He seemed far more relaxed now.

Leaning against the railing, she watched as the Bremerton ferry sluggishly made its way toward the dock on the far side of the cove. "How come you were such a jerk when I first arrived?"

"Me? A jerk?" He slapped his hand across his chest as though shocked by the question.

"Yes, a jerk," she challenged.

He kicked at a pebble that skittered across the boardwalk. "I guess I should apologize for that."

"I don't want an apology, just an explanation."

He looked down as though he expected something to crawl out from beneath the walkway. "I hated the thought of you tutoring me."

"No kidding!" Still, that didn't explain why he'd greeted her as if she had the bubonic plague.

"I didn't want you to think I was stupid."

That made no sense. "So you'd rather I thought you were rude and arrogant?"

He exhaled with what seemed like regret. "Put that way, it makes me a first-class idiot, doesn't it?"

"Sort of," she murmured, "but I wasn't exactly the picture of graciousness, either."

"The thing is," Travis said a bit defensively, "you could have any guy you wanted."

Amanda couldn't keep from laughing. "This is a joke, right?"

He shook his head. "No, it's true."

"Despite what you might think, being smart doesn't exactly endear me to the boys in our class, or any other class, for that matter."

Travis frowned again. "Are you saying it's lonely at the top?"

"I'm not sure, but I can definitely tell you no one has shown any great interest in me."

"Say you could date any guy in history," Travis insisted.

"But I just told you—"

"Hypothetically," he insisted. "If you had your choice of anyone in the entire world, who would you want to go out with?"

Now he was really putting her on the spot, and it wasn't a comfortable place to be. "Anyone in the world?" she asked, pressing for time.

"Sure, why not, and no fair saying Abraham Lincoln or Channing Tatum."

"Okay, okay." At just that moment, her cell rang. Grateful for the interruption, Amanda reached inside her purse and retrieved it. Glancing at caller ID, she looked up at Travis. "It's my mom," she said, and answered. "Hi, Mom." She looked over at Travis and smiled.

"How'd the tutoring session go?" her mother asked.

"Great. I'm with Travis now. Mom, would you hold on a minute?" She needed to ask her mother something, and she didn't necessarily want Travis to hear what it was. "Give me a couple of minutes, okay?" she asked Travis.

"Sure, no problem."

Amanda walked over toward the gazebo and sat on a bottom seat of the bleachers just outside the structure. She spoke to her mother for a few minutes, and when she'd finished, she placed the cell back inside her purse.

Travis joined her, sitting on the bench beside her. "You get along with your mother?"

"Both my parents are great. What about you?"

Travis shrugged. "It's just Mom and me. She's tough, but in a good way. We've had our share of differences the last couple of years, but for the most part we're cool."

"That's good."

"You were about to answer my question," Travis reminded her. "Anyone you wanted to date—who would it be?"

"Hypothetically, right?"

"Right."

"This is one of those party-game questions, isn't it? Like if you could have dinner with someone from the past or present, who would you choose?"

"I guess. You can tell a lot about a person from how they answer."

"No doubt," she agreed. "Well, in thinking it over, I believe I've made my decision."

He leaned a bit closer.

"I think it would be you, Travis. I feel like I've gotten to know you this afternoon, and I'd like to know you better."

He shook his head. "I didn't ask because I was fishing for compliments."

"Yes, you did," she countered, "but that's all right, because I like you. I like your honesty and your vulnerability."

He frowned as if he wasn't sure he should believe her. "You're serious?"

Travis didn't say anything for a long time, and then he nodded. "I'd like it if we went out, too."

"Great."

Frowning, he looked across the gazebo. "Amanda?"

"Yeah."

"Isn't that the dog that was barking at us earlier?"

"Where?"

"There." He pointed to the gazebo, where a small dog rested on his haunches and looked across the area, pinning his gaze on Amanda and Travis.

Chapter Four

As soon as Amanda saw the dog, his eyes seemed to lock on to her. While it might sound a bit theatrical, he seemed to stare straight through her. Amanda wasn't sure what made her come to her feet. Before she knew it, she was off the bleachers and had bent down on one knee.

Right away the dog trotted over to her. Much friendlier now, he looked up at her and held her gaze for the longest moment. He seemed to be telling her something, but she had no idea what it might be. It was silly to think a dog was trying to give her a message. Silly and nonsensical, but she couldn't shake the feeling that he'd come to her with a purpose.

"Are you lost?" she asked as she ran her hand down his back. His short hair was thick and groomed, and he looked to be well fed. Clearly he had a good home.

"He isn't a stray," Travis said, kneeling down next to her. "My guess is that he belongs to someone at the marina."

That made sense. The Cedar Cove marina was just down the waterfront, close to the library and Java Joint, where they'd first seen him. Somehow the dog must have gotten locked out. Maybe his owner was on his boat and unaware.

Perhaps the dog was looking to her to take him home. "We should check around to be sure someone isn't looking for him," Amanda suggested.

"Good idea."

Walking side by side, Travis and Amanda headed in that direction. Sure enough, the dog followed, trotting along beside them as if he understood their plan. As they neared the library, Travis gradually slowed his steps.

Amanda looked over at him quizzically.

"Remember that guy?" he asked.

"What guy?"

"The one who came into Java Joint and spoke to us about a lost dog?"

Until that moment, the incident had completely slipped her mind. She'd been irritated with Travis and caught up in her own world and hadn't paid that close attention. The man had mentioned a lost dog. "Oh my goodness, you're right."

"And he said the dog was small, with short brown hair."

"Mixed breed, probably part terrier," she added.

"This could be that dog."

Travis was right. "Did you know the guy?"

Travis shook his head. "I've never seen him before. I don't remember him mentioning his name."

"He didn't, but he gave Connor a card with his phone number, remember?"

"Right."

By unspoken agreement, they headed back toward Java Joint, checking to make sure the dog followed. Sure enough, he trotted along, directly into the coffeehouse, as if it was his right.

Connor looked up and, seeing them, frowned. "Sorry, guys, no dogs allowed. It's a state law."

"We think this is the lost dog," Travis explained.

"Lost or not, he can't be inside." As he spoke, Connor looked pointedly toward the table by the window where Sheriff Troy Davis sat with the newspaper editor, Jack Griffin.

"Do you still have the name and phone number of the man who was in here earlier, looking for a lost dog?"

"I do." Connor opened the cash register and handed Travis the card. With that in hand, Amanda and Travis stepped outside.

Travis drew his cell phone out of his pocket and used his thumb to punch out the number.

Amanda knelt down on one knee to pet the dog. "I bet you're a good dog," she said, running her hand down the full length of his spine. Again, he stared at her with those dark, soulful eyes as though conveying a message meant solely for her.

"I wish I knew what you're trying to tell me," she whispered.

Travis finished the call. "The man's name is Mark Taylor, and the dog belongs to a friend of his. He's on his way to collect him and take him home to his owner."

"Is he sure this is his friend's dog?"

"No, but it certainly sounds like him."

"What's the dog's name?" Amanda asked.

"Rover."

Right away, the dog twisted his head and looked up at Travis. "He seems to know his name. This is the missing dog, all right."

"He doesn't look lost to me," Amanda commented.

Just a few minutes later, a pickup truck rounded the corner and came to a stop in front of Java Joint, pulling into an angled parking slot. No sooner had the engine been turned off than the driver's-side door opened and the same lanky man they'd met earlier stepped around the front of the vehicle.

Without the least bit of hesitation, Rover trotted over to Mark.

"Worthless mutt," Mark said, glaring down at the dog. "I hope you realize what you've put Jo Marie through."

Rover lifted one foot, offering Mark his paw as if to apologize.

"Jo Marie might forgive you for running off, but I'm not that easy. Now get in the truck." He opened the passenger door, and Rover reluctantly walked toward the vehicle. Mark lifted him inside and closed the door.

"He seems like a special dog," Amanda said.

"Spoiled rotten is what he is," Mark muttered, frowning.

"My mom would say he's much loved," Amanda corrected.

"Whatever. All I can tell you is that I've spent a large portion of my day searching for this mutt when I had better things to do."

"But you're happy he's been found, right?" Travis said.

"Oh yes, sorry, I forgot." Mark reached into his rear pocket and pulled out his wallet. "Here's your reward."

"No need," Travis said, as he held up his hand in a stopping motion.

"It would be more accurate to say Rover found us," Amanda explained.

Mark looked from Travis to Amanda and then back again. "I was sincere about the reward."

Again, Travis held up his hand. "I appreciate the offer, but it isn't necessary."

Mark shrugged. "Your choice. Thank you both."

"You're welcome," Amanda told him.

With that, Mark climbed into his truck and drove off. Amanda watched him go and wondered if she'd have a chance to see Rover again. It was good to know that this special dog had someone who loved him.

"I better get home," Amanda said, sorry that their time together was at an end.

"Yeah, me, too," Travis chimed in. "Thanks for the help. I'm pretty sure I've got the hang of it."

"Do you want to meet tomorrow?" she asked, hoping he'd agree.

"Do we have to study?" Travis asked, holding her look. "I'm done searching for your X. He's gone, and I don't know Y."

Amanda laughed. "Meet for a latte, then? Same time, same place."

"Sounds good to me," he said.

They each took off in separate directions. Amanda had a warm, hopeful feeling that she'd be seeing a lot more of Travis in the coming weeks, and that suited her just fine.

Jo Marie made busywork around the inn. It was either do something to keep her hands and her mind occupied or slowly, surely, go insane fretting about Rover. She tried not to think of where he might be or why he'd left her.

Anytime she left the house without him, he gave her a look that suggested that he was afraid she was about to abandon him. He'd stare at her with those dark eyes of his, and it was all she could do not to apologize. Almost always, she paused to assure him she'd be back.

Rover hadn't afforded her the same courtesy, however. Instead, he'd simply disappeared, and from all evidence, he'd done so voluntarily. Dusting shelves, Jo Marie took time to carefully remove each knickknack and wipe down each shelf.

Someone knocked, but before she could get to the door, it opened. Even before she turned the corner, Jo Marie heard Rover's bark. It was just one bark, as if to announce he was back.

"Rover," she cried, dropping the dust rag.

He raced around the corner, skidding on the hardwood floor in his eagerness to reach her. Jo Marie fell to her knees, and Rover practically launched himself into her arms. He was licking her face and then yelping before he stretched his neck toward the ceiling and released a howl.

It wasn't until she saw Mark's boots that she realized he was the one who'd brought Rover home.

"You found him." Her heart softened with gratitude.

"Not me," he said, hands buried deep in his jeans pockets. "A couple of teenagers. They said he basically found them. They were at Java Joint."

"What in the name of heaven was he doing there?"

"How would I know?" Mark countered with a question of his own.

"I walked all along the waterfront," she said, sitting back on her haunches, Rover in her lap. "I looked all over that area and there was no sign of him anywhere."

"Does it matter? He's home now."

Mark was right. She nodded. "Home, and that's where he belongs. Thank you. Thank you so much."

"No need. It was those kids who found him."

"I'd like to give them a reward."

"I tried. They weren't interested. Nice kids."

Jo Marie looked down at her precious pet. "You won't be running away again," she insisted. "Understood?"

Rover held her look and seemed to be thoroughly chastised.

"I suppose you're going to want me to install one of those invisible fences?" Mark made it sound as if she were about to burden him with yet another project.

"I'd rather you saw to my rose garden first. If Rover takes off again, we can discuss the invisible fence."

"Why wait? Do you want to go through another day like this one?"

"No." That was for sure.

"What makes you think he won't decide to disappear a second time?"

Jo Marie wasn't sure, but she suddenly had a sneaking suspicion that Rover had been on an undertaking of his own. Once he'd completed his mission, he would have returned of his own accord. Naturally, that was only speculation on her part.

"Thank you, Mark."

He shrugged as if bringing Rover back to her was just a little thing. She'd misjudged the handyman. True, he hadn't been able to handle her emotional breakdown, but he'd done what he could. Unable to deal with her feelings, he'd taken action.

"What can I do to thank you?" she asked. With anyone else, that might be a leading question. Not Mark.

He shrugged. "I wouldn't object to a few more of those peanut-butter cookies you baked this morning."

Ah, she should have known. "You can take the entire batch home with you." He deserved every one of those cookies.

His eyes widened appreciatively. "The whole batch? I guess I could take them off your hands."

How like him to make it sound as if he was doing her a favor. "Great." She climbed up from the floor and went into the kitchen and loaded the cookies into sealed bags. As she worked, she heard Mark talking to Rover.

"I hope you know you're nothing but a damn nuisance."

"Mark," she warned

"I was talking to the dog."

"I know. You might consider Rover a nuisance, but I don't."

"Maybe you should."

"Do you want these cookies or not?" she threatened as she joined him in the front parlor.

He went silent as his gaze rested on the filled plastic bags. He seemed to be debating his answer before he finally murmured, "Like I said, I'll take them off your hands."

"That's what I thought."

Mark left as soon as she handed over the cookies, and Rover, who appeared exhausted, curled up and went to sleep on the rug in front of the refrigerator. It was one of his favorite spots for napping.

Jo Marie poured herself a cup of coffee and sat down at her small desk, reaching for the phone to call the library to let Grace know her news. After a few minutes, Grace came on the line, her voice anxious.

"Jo Marie, did you find Rover?"

"Mark Taylor did."

"Oh, thank heaven. I couldn't stop thinking about you all afternoon. I know how I'd feel if Beau turned up missing."

"Rover is home, napping. I can't imagine what made him take off like that. He's never done anything like this before. But I think . . ." She hesitated, wishing now she hadn't said anything.

"Think what?" Grace pressed.

"That Rover had a task in mind, someone he wanted to meet. Does that sound a little crazy?"

"Not at all. Animals have highly developed intuition. Look at the way the two of you bonded, almost from the instant you saw him."

Jo Marie had gone to the shelter at Grace's suggestion and had assumed she wanted a large dog, a protector. Instead she'd come home with Rover, this pint-sized canine who'd chosen *her*.

"I promised to let both you and Olivia know if Rover was located, so I better give her a call."

As soon as she hung up, Jo Marie contacted the family court judge. Olivia answered on the first ring.

"Rover is home."

"That's wonderful," Olivia said, and sounded genuinely pleased.

"I can't thank you enough for all your help."

"No problem, Jo Marie. We all know how important our pets are to each one of us."

Remembering what Olivia had said about friendship, Jo Marie said, "If you have time this afternoon, come over with Grace for a glass of wine to celebrate."

"You're on. I'll give Grace a call, and we'll meet at the inn. I'll bring the wine."

"Perfect. I'll set out a few munchies."

By the time Olivia and Grace arrived, Jo Marie had a platter set up with cheese and crackers and a bowl of nuts. The three gathered in the parlor by the fireplace. A gentle fire flickered from the grate as gray thunderclouds once again darkened the early-evening sky.

Jo Marie raised her glass of wine for a toast. "To those of us who are lost and then found," she said. The Rose Harbor Inn and Cedar Cove had become that for her. After losing Paul, she'd been lost, and she'd found a safe harbor here in this welcoming community.

They each tasted the wine. It was an excellent merlot.

"To friendship," Jo Marie added.

"To friendship," Olivia and Grace echoed.

"We'll have to do this again," Jo Marie suggested. "Perhaps in a few weeks we'll be able to sit on the porch and look out over the rose garden and gazebo."

"It's sure to be beautiful," Olivia added.

"Rose Harbor in bloom," Grace whispered. "I can hardly wait."

Beloved #1 New York Times bestselling
author Debbie Macomber celebrates the
most wonderful time of the year in her next
heartwarming Christmas novel of romance,
hope, and the comforts of home—coming
soon as a Hallmark Channel original movie!

Mr. Miracle

Get into the spirit of the season with
this special sneak peek

Available from Ballantine Books

Chapter One

This wasn't the way it was supposed to happen. Six years out of high school, Addie Folsom had envisioned returning home loaded and driving a fancy car. Instead, she was limping back in a twenty-year-old Honda with close to three hundred thousand miles and her tail between her legs.

So much for the great promise of moving to Montana and walking into a get-rich-quick opportunity. She'd left Washington state with such high hopes . . . and ended up living in a leaky trailer and waiting tables in a run-down diner. It took all six of those years for Addie to admit she'd made a very big mistake. Pride, she'd learned, offered little comfort.

Oh, she'd returned home for visits at least a couple times a year. When asked pointed questions about her work in the silver mine, she'd made sure her answers were vague.

Then, last summer, her chiropractor father had died unexpectedly of a heart attack.

Addie had adored her dad as a child, but the moment she hit her teen years, their relationship had deteriorated. She hadn't really repaired things when he'd passed away so suddenly. In retrospect, she suspected she and her father were too much alike. Both were stubborn and headstrong, unwilling to admit when they were wrong or make the effort to build bridges.

They'd argued far too often, her mother stepping in, seeking to make peace between her husband and her daughter. How sorry Addie was for the strife between them, now that her father was gone.

For now, she was home for good. Addie parked in front of the single-story house where she'd spent the first eighteen years of her life. She loved that it had a front porch, which so many of the more modern homes didn't. Normally, the Christmas lights would already be up. Her father had always seen to that the Friday after Thanksgiving. This year, however, the two arborvitae that bordered each side of the porch seemed stark and bare without the decorative lights.

Her mother must have been watching from the living room window, because the minute Addie climbed out of the car, the front door flew open and Sharon Folsom rushed out with her arms open wide. "Addie, Addie, you're home."

Addie paused halfway up the walkway and hugged her mother close.

Sharon Folsom brought her hands up to Addie's

face and smoothed back her dark brown hair. Her mother's chocolate-brown eyes, a reflection of her own, held her gaze with an intensity of longing.

Addie found she couldn't speak. It felt so good to be home, to really be home.

Her mother hugged her even tighter this time. "You said you were coming back, and I'd hoped . . ." She left the rest unsaid.

"I'm not returning to Montana this time, Mom."

"Oh, Addie, really? I couldn't be happier. So you decided you are definitely back to stay?" She wrapped her arm around Addie's waist and led her up the porch steps. "It's so wonderful to have you home, especially at this time of year . . . it's the first one that's so difficult, you know."

The first Christmas without Dad.

"I talked to your uncle Roy," her mother said.

"Yes?" Addie tried hard not to show how anxious she was to hear what her mother had found out.

"He's pleased to know you're interested in healthcare. Your dad would have been so happy; that was what he always wanted for you. Roy said once you get your high school diploma, he'll do everything within his power to get you the schooling you need. He's even willing to hire you part-time while you're in school and to work around your class schedule."

Addie hardly knew what to say. This was an opportunity she had never expected. More than she could ever hope would happen. Now it was up to her not to blow it.

"Aren't you excited?"

Again, her throat tightened and she answered with a sharp nod. She knew that no matter what she hoped to accomplish, she'd need her high school diploma. One class credit was all she needed. Why she'd dropped out when she was so close to graduation was beyond her. How stupid and shortsighted she'd been. Her one missing credit was in literature, so she'd found a class she could take at the local community college.

B-o-r-i-n-g!

As a high school sophomore, Addie had been assigned to read *Moby-Dick*. Because of her dyslexia, she was a slow, thoughtful reader, often using her finger on the page to help her keep track of the words. Then to be handed that doorstop and work her way through it page by excruciating page had been pure torture. Following *Moby-Dick,* she'd been completely turned off to reading in general . . . although lately, after her television had stopped working, she'd gotten a couple books at the library and enjoyed them immensely. Finding pleasure in reading had given her hope that maybe . . . just maybe she could return to school.

"I already signed up for a literature class. It starts this week, which I understand is a bit unusual; apparently, it was delayed until a teacher could be replaced." Addie had thought she'd need to wait until mid-February when the second semester began. This class was perfectly timed for her.

"You enrolled already?" How pleased her mother sounded, and her face brightened with the news.

They were inside the house now, and after removing her coat, Addie tucked her fingertips in the back pockets of her jeans. Standing in the middle of the kitchen, she looked around and breathed in the welcome she found in the familiar setting. Her mother had placed a few festive things around the house to help celebrate the season. The Advent wreath rested in the center of the kitchen table. The first purple candle had been lit.

When she was growing up, it'd been a big deal to see who got to light the candle every night at dinner. Addie or her brother. Generally, Jerry was given the honor. Oh, how her brother had loved lording it over her. He lived in Oklahoma now, was married and worked as a physical therapist for a center that trained Olympic athletes. He'd always been athletic himself, just like his best friend, Erich Simmons, who lived next door. The two had been inseparable; any mental image of her brother also conjured up his constant sidekick and the way she'd humiliated herself over Erich.

At one time Addie had thought Erich Simmons was the cutest boy in the universe. He was a star athlete, class valedictorian, and the homecoming king. Addie hadn't thought of him in a long time and didn't know why he'd popped into her head now. As a teen, she'd idolized Erich and hadn't bothered to hide the way she felt. He, unfortunately, found her hero worship highly amusing. Oh, there'd been the usual antics when they were kids. Her brother and Erich had wanted nothing to do with her, despite all her efforts to follow them around. It wasn't until she was fourteen and fifteen that she'd viewed Erich in a different light and sent him Valentines and baked him cookies. It embarrassed her to no end to remember what a fool she'd made of herself over him, especially since he treated her like a jerk.

"Addie?" Her mother broke into her thoughts. "You look a million miles away."

"Sorry, Mom."

"Bring in your suitcases. I've got your old room all ready for you."

It felt wonderful to be home.

Addie unloaded her car, which, sadly, took only a few minutes. Everything she'd managed to accumulate in six years was contained in two suitcases and a couple boxes. When she finished unpacking, she headed directly for the garage.

Her mother found her there ten minutes later. "Addie, my goodness, what are you doing here?" she asked. "I've been looking all over the house for you. Are you hungry? Would you like me to fix you something to eat?"

"In a little while."

"What are you doing?"

Addie stood in the middle of the garage, sur-rounded by several clear plastic boxes she'd brought down from the shelves. Her father had been a whiz at organization, a trait she'd inherited. "I'm look-ing for the outdoor Christmas lights."

"But Addie—"

"It won't feel like Christmas without the trees by the porch lit up."

"But Addie—"

"Mom, please, let me put up the lights." Her dad would have wanted her to do this for her mother, Addie was sure. She owed him this, even if things hadn't been so good between them when he died, or maybe because of that.

"Erich offered to put them up for me, but I said no."

"Good." Perfect Erich. She bristled at the mere mention of his name. He'd always been so thought-ful and kind . . . to others. But he tortured her at every opportunity. For one thing, from the time they were in first grade together, he'd insisted on calling her Adeline. Addie had always hated the name. She'd never even known the great-grandmother she'd been named after. Saddling her with that name had been her father's doing, no sur-prise.

Her mother moved a couple steps into the garage. "Um . . . there's a reason I didn't want Erich to put up the lights."

Addie straightened. Her mother's voice revealed

hesitation and a bit of apprehension. "What is it, Mom?"

"I mentioned all those firsts without your father, remember . . ."

"Yes." It was one of the reasons Addie had returned home when she did. She didn't want her mother spending this first Christmas without Dad by herself. Jerry couldn't get away, but Addie could. Actually, she'd been more than ready to leave Montana. Although she'd come to love the state, everything else there had proved to be less perfect than she'd hoped. Her job at the mine had fizzled out after a few months, but pride hadn't allowed her to return home so soon after her grand departure. For a while she drifted from job to job, until finally settling in at the diner. She'd made friends and the tips were good. It was easy enough to coast through the next few years.

"I didn't say anything earlier when you called to say you were coming . . ." her mother said, interrupting her thoughts. Her mother wrung her hands.

"Mom, what is it?" Clearly there was something her mother didn't want to tell her.

"Please don't be upset with me."

This was all very strange. "Mom, please, don't worry. You're not going to upset me."

"You're sure?"

"Positive. Just tell me."

Her mother squeezed her eyes tightly shut. "I'm

going on a two-week Christmas cruise with Julie Simmons."

It took a second for the information to sink in. "A cruise?"

Her mother still hadn't opened her eyes. "Julie's a widow. I'm a widow. We figured that we'd both get away this Christmas with a trip to the Caribbean. We booked a few days in Florida before the cruise as well. The sunshine and all . . . please tell me you're not upset with me."

"Of course not," Addie assured her, although her heart sank. This meant she'd be spending Christmas alone.

"Julie and I talked about it for months, and then right before Halloween we found this great deal from the cruise line and Julie said we should do it. If not now, when? I had no idea you'd be coming home, let alone for good, and . . . and, oh Addie, if you want I'll cancel the trip." Her voice became half plea and half regret.

"No way," Addie insisted, strengthening her resolve. "You're going on that cruise and you're going to enjoy every minute of it while I hold down the fort here."

"Erich offered to look after the house."

Of course he would.

"He's not married, you know, and neither is Karl."

Erich's younger brother.

As if she felt the need to keep talking, her mother

continued. "Karl is dating a wonderful young woman and is spending Christmas with her family someplace back east. Neither Julie nor I have grandchildren yet, and being this has been such a difficult year . . ."

"Mom, please, you don't need to make excuses. I want you to do this, please go."

"But you'll be alone."

"It's fine. I'll connect with a few friends and it won't be a problem. Don't worry about me."

"You're sure . . . ?"

"Absolutely positive."

"It's just that Julie and I have been so looking forward to this, and . . ."

Addie walked over and hugged her mother. "Stop. I wouldn't dream of letting you cancel this trip. It's perfect. You and Julie together on those warm sandy beaches. I'll be fine, I promise."

The relief in her mother's face was nearly palpable. Addie was sincere. She wanted her mother to get away for Christmas. "I still want to put up the outdoor lights," she said, returning to the plastic boxes her father had packed up the Christmas before and stored away.

"Oh, sure, sweetheart, if that's what you want. Do you need me to help you?"

"I can do it." Among all the other valuable life lessons Montana had taught Addie, she'd learned resourcefulness. Though she'd never done it before, she'd figure out a way to string the lights on those two trees. It wouldn't feel like Christmas without them.

"I'll start dinner, then."

"Great. I'm starving."

After her mother left, Addie found the strands of outdoor lights and carted them to the front of the house. She needed a ladder, too. At five-foot-three, she wasn't nearly tall enough to reach the top.

She'd gotten everything set up when she heard the sound of a car door behind her. Standing halfway up the ladder, she glanced over her shoulder to see a bright shiny silver BMW parked at the curb behind her dilapidated, fender-rusting, once-blue Honda.

Erich.

Her heart sank. He was sure to make some derogatory comment about her car, right after he called her Adeline. He might even be so obnoxious as to mention her girlhood crush on him. Even before he spoke, her teeth were clenched.

"Adeline, is that you?"

Unbelievable! "It's Addie," she said coolly.

"Oops, sorry, I forgot," he teased, when clearly he hadn't. Then he had the audacity to laugh.

She brushed a long strand of dark hair away from her face.

"Need any help with that?"

"No thanks," she said, as she continued to wind the strand around the bushy tree. She needed no help, least of all from him. It wasn't only the teasing she'd taken as a kid that contributed to her dislike of him—that was only a small part. Erich, Karl, and her brother had often ganged up on her. Being something of a tomboy, she'd followed them, hungering to join in their fun. Instead, Erich had teased her mercilessly. It'd gotten worse as she grew older and got braces. He'd called her "live wire" and poked fun at her until she'd run and hide in her bedroom. But that was nothing compared to the way he'd stepped all over her tender, young heart.

"You home for Christmas?" he asked.

"Something like that," she answered, without looking at him.

He hesitated, and when he spoke he sounded genuine and sincere. "Like I said when we spoke at the funeral, I'm sorry for your loss. I loved your dad."

"Yeah, me, too." The lump was back and she swallowed hard, determined not to let him see how his words had affected her. Funny thing was, she didn't remember speaking to him at the funeral. She'd been in a fog then, confused and grieving.

"Maybe I'll see you around."

"Maybe," she returned dismissively. At the moment, all she wanted was for him to leave her alone.

By the time she had the lights wound around the first tree it was pitch dark. The only illumination came from the porch light.

A little while later, when Addie was half finished with the twin tree on the other side of the porch, her mother opened the door and called out, "Dinner's ready."

"I'm almost done," Addie promised, unwilling to quit now. She worked quietly, traipsing up and down the ladder as she moved the string of lights around the tree, stretching her arms as high as she could and not lose her balance.

The Simmonses' front door opened. "Let me hand you the lights," Erich offered, crossing the yard and coming up behind her.

Addie's initial reaction was to reject his offer. She was more than capable of finishing this—she'd managed the first tree on her own. She'd rather avoid Erich's company.

"It's the least I can do to make up for calling you Adeline," he said.

"If you had to place lights on trees for every time you called me Adeline, you'd be decorating the entire Olympic National Forest."

"True enough. It's Addie from now on. I promise."

She wasn't sure she should trust him not to be a jerk, but she was tired and hungry. So while it dented her pride to accept his help, at this point, she was willing. "Okay." The second part took more of an effort. "Thank you."

His sigh was audible. "That wasn't so hard, now, was it? Come on, Addie, admit it."

"Harder than you realize."

Erich chuckled.

He continued to feed her the string of lights, and they didn't speak for several seconds. "I talked to Jerry the other day. We stay in touch on Facebook, but . . ."

Addie finished and hurried down from the ladder. "Listen, Erich. You don't need to make small talk with me. We've never really gotten along and there's no need to pretend otherwise." She guessed he felt a little sorry for her—back at home, having failed at her big adventure. In her sad, decrepit car . . .

"Fine." He held up his hands as if she'd pointed a gun at him. "You can't say I didn't try."

"Thanks for the help with the lights," Addie said, before heading into the house.

Harry watched the scene, standing beneath an evergreen tree, from across the street. Celeste stood next to him.

"What is it I'm supposed to do for these two, again?" he asked, unable to hide his dismay. It had seemed like a piece of delicious rum cake earlier, but now that he saw the way Addie bristled around Erich, he was a bit more daunted. She was like a porcupine around him, defensive and unfriendly. And that was only a small part of what he sensed in her. She was full of fear, and trying desperately hard to hide her feelings of inadequacy.

"You'll find out soon enough. God has obviously

crossed their paths for a reason. There must be something they need to learn from each other, don't you think?" she said, turning the question back on him.

"Just how am I supposed to help them find out what it is when they can barely tolerate the sight of each other?" he asked. He was an English teacher and Addie was in his class. There was only so much he could do while teaching her literature.

"As I explained earlier, circumstances have been set in motion."

"Yes, but—"

"Patience, Harry, patience."

"Do you have an idea about what's going to happen?"

"I do."

Harry frowned. "Don't you think you should fill me in, seeing that I'm going to be working with Addie?"

Celeste grinned. "Wait and see."

Harry wasn't pleased. "Is there anything else you want to tell me?"

"Not yet," she said, and tucked her arm around his elbow, shivered, and then glanced toward the sky. "Let's get back, the roads are getting icy."

Harry watched as Erich sped off in his shiny car. He had the distinct feeling Celeste had been trying to tell him something important.